Part of the Spell

Rachel Heath was born in Bristol in 1968. She worked as an editor in publishing, and then as a literary consultant for television and as a reader before writing her first book. Her first novel, *The Finest Type of English Womanhood*, was shortlisted for the Costa First Novel Award 2009 and for the Authors' Club Best First Novel Award 2010. She is also a contributor to the short story anthology, *The Best Little Book Club in Town*. She has three children, and lives in Bath.

ALSO BY RACHEL HEATH

The Finest Type of English Womanhood

Part of
the Spell

Rachel Heath

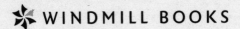
WINDMILL BOOKS

Published by Windmill Books 2013

2 4 6 8 10 9 7 5 3 1

First published in Great Britain in 2012 by Hutchinson

Windmill Books
The Random House Group Limited
20 Vauxhall Bridge Road, London SW1V 2SA

Addresses for companies within The Random House Group Limited can be
found at: www.randomhouse.co.uk/offices.htm

The Random House Group Limited Reg. No. 954009

www.randomhouse.co.uk

A CIP catalogue record for this book
is available from the British Library

ISBN 9780099532750

The Random House Group Limited supports the Forest Stewardship
Council® (FSC®), the leading international forest-certification organisation.
Our books carrying the FSC label are printed on FSC®-certified paper. FSC
is the only forest-certification scheme supported by the leading environmental
organisations, including Greenpeace. Our paper procurement policy can be
found at: www.randomhouse.co.uk/environment

Typeset in Joanna MT by Palimpsest Book Production Limited,
Falkirk, Stirlingshire
Printed and bound by CPI Group (UK) Ltd, Croydon CR0 4YY

for Stewart

People glorify all sorts of bravery except the bravery they might show on behalf of their nearest neighbours.

Middlemarch, George Eliot

Nothing is so difficult as not deceiving oneself.

Culture and Value, Ludwig Wittgenstein

> And the quietness,
> Yes, I like to be quiet
> I am habituated
> To a quiet life,
>
> But always when I think these thoughts
> As I sit in my well
> Another thought comes to me and says:
> It is part of the spell.

from 'The Frog Prince', Stevie Smith

A small, quiet town sits in a slight valley, encircled by barely-hills and surrounded by the ancient fields and trees of Essex, by acreage of barley, wheat and yellow rapeseed, grasses and vegetables. Above is a large blank sky, white as paper. The air is soft, earthy and easy, when not chilled by easterly winds and low-slung mists or cut by the marshy tangs of salt carried in on a breeze from far away.

At first sight, approached from the motorway or from one of the long, winding roads from Suffolk or Cambridge, it appears as serene, snug and self-contained today as it has always been during a long, yet unruffled, history. Nothing has been broken down; everything is preserved. Restored. Looked after.

The streets are lined with a seductive, companionable variety of buildings. It is a town of the big and small. There are those that bend from Tudor age, half-timbered, lathed and plastered, painted yellow, red and pink, with thatched or tiled roofs, and white weatherboarded houses with crumbling chimneystacks, and buildings with old plastered walls adorned with pargeted patterns and swirls. A massive Victorian red-brick bank stands brazenly proud in the market square with large, leaded windows of coloured glass;

opposite is the old corn exchange, now the library, a golden pheasant atop its roof.

Three streets away, ancient medieval houses bend over one another, their roofs tipping apologetically towards the pavement, and a couple of streets further on again are a cluster of grey, modest and sober post-war cottages and bungalows. On the fringes of the town is a stately home with walled gardens, ornate greenhouses and a lake, Palladian bridges and vast sweeps of lawn and wild woodland.

It is a town of windows, some narrow and wonky with age and fitted low on a house, some high and Georgian-grand with painted white mantels, opaque or clouded glass, moulded mullions and splayed sills. There are Gothic Arts and Crafts windows neatly tucked under gabled ends and the welcoming windows of medieval shops: large, sun-streamed openings ready to show their wares. Some are central-glazed with plastic edges and others are discreet, elegant fanlight windows. The town cannot help but refract light; the glass distorts, and the town reflects back endlessly upon itself.

Once the town's trade was in saffron, the fields around ablaze with carpets of crocus bending their delicate pale heads against the easterly winds. Then they built maltings; the sleepy, yeasty smell of fermentation swamped, blanket-like, the curved, toppling cottages and slums of the town. The Quakers took charge, arriving with Victorian visions of civic pride and community responsibility, and are to be thanked for the public gardens laid out below the ruins of the twelfth-century castle to the north of the market square; for some of the clay-bricked merchants' houses and villas; and for the museum built in the grounds of the castle.

It is neither here nor there, neither this nor that. It is both. Historically, it's everywhere. An off-to-the-side kind of place — too far from here, but within touching distance of there. Eerily, emptily preserved, yet real and alive and inhabited. It is a town that seduces with its alluring, rolling, continuing sense of conservation through time. It balances time and contains contradictions; promises ease, patience and nostalgic comfort, but supports the modern world. When the commuters stream towards the railway station each morning, the stage is perfectly set and the town opens up, slips into action; shops open, schools fill and the tiny narrow pavements load with oversized prams jostling to fit through medieval doorways. The light pours down and the performance and business begin.

*

This morning it is very quiet. There are no cars in the market square, the pavements and the roads are empty, grey and slowly warming under the pale autumn early-morning sun.

There is a figure, a little stooped but walking with purpose, with a new sense of purpose, rounded shoulders, walking faster than she has for years. Hastily checking her watch, her hands shaking a little, her skin mottling and loosening. She keeps her head down as she walks up beside the bank, pausing at the cash point. She looks over her shoulder guiltily, and then fumbles for a moment with a large white plastic purse, its catch slippery and stiff in her loose and trembling fingers. It is very quiet. She takes the money quickly and stuffs it into the purse, except that there is too much. She must calm down; she leans for a moment against the wall of the bank, the mess of money still in her hand, papery, warm and, she imagines, incriminatingly excessive. She feels the bank's reassuring brickwork through her thin anorak; closing her eyes, she tells herself not to be such a fool.

She feels the daylight on her face. She breathes deeply. She has known this wall, this bank, this market square for years, for whole long tree-lined avenues of her life. Behind the red-orange of her eyelid she can trace the square, the outlines of the buildings, the places where the pavements dip and where the buildings meet. She can even trace the roads off the square, and knows all too well the one she will shortly take up towards St Mary's Church.

It is six o'clock in the morning, the early sun falling in even slants across the market place. She walks on, in front of the library, across and up Market Hill, a quick look over her shoulder, one hand trailing the bumpy wall of Lydgate Antiques, and then she disappears from view.

After nursery

Stella blinked in the sunlight. She was standing half-in and half-out of her front door, listening to the thin, puling sound of the baby in her pram. It was a small sort of noise, timid and plaintive. She pushed her hair back from her face, waiting to see if the noise would grow and bloom to one of open-throated, face-creasing anguish and alarm. She did not want to look in the pram – if she looked the other way, the noise would stop, and if it didn't, what could she do? She had to go up to the nursery on the industrial estate to collect Jack. This is why she had one foot on her front step and one on the hallway carpet, the pram balanced on either side too. Waiting.

Stella did not want to walk through the streets with her baby screaming; she thought people would find her wanting, when she knew that she was not. Maybe even stop her on the pavement and gather around the pram, putting their fingers on the baby's face, they might cluck or frown as they bent over to inspect further – these imaginary women in dove-grey raincoats with Perspex hoods, smelling of lavender and face-powder – pressing around her and the baby, making Stella feel airless, whilst offering conflicting, helpful advice: 'Ignore her!', 'Poor mite, pick her up!', 'Is he hungry?', 'What a bad baby, giving you the runaround', 'Sssh, is she windy?' And Stella would have to smile at them, and listen to their thoughts, be patient and interested, and she would then have to say quite firmly, 'She needs to sleep. That's all. Let her sleep.'

She looked down at her shoes; she could see her daughter in her mind, could still feel the weight of the baby in her arms. She did not need to look in order to see the black tufts of hair feathering the side of her face, the white around the mouth, those new livid, pimply spots on her cheeks or the streaky red rash under her chin where the milk seemed to gather and curdle, or the heart-breaking reality of those fine, delicate translucent ears. She waited. A veil descended over the baby, and she fell silent.

Reaching behind her, Stella pulled the front door shut, wheeled the pram carefully down the short path and turned left onto the pavement, walked up to the Peaslands Road, alongside the leisure centre and then along the Thaxted Road, which was wide and busy and took her a while to cross. Then she walked up the hill towards the industrial estate. She kept her head down past the garages, along the oil-stained pavement, the air heavy with petrol fumes and the thin, metallic sound of a radio deep inside one of the buildings.

When Stella's father worked up here, at the printer's, her mother had called the estate soulless. She'd told Stella that it made her shiver, and she'd wondered at the council letting them build such a place. Stella understood these days what she meant: there is nobody about, just her and the baby. All the offices, sheds and warehouses, some no bigger than a Portakabin, appear to have no windows and hidden-away front doors, making the buildings look blinded. It is only the large signs on the side of the buildings, and the few cars parked outside, that suggest the buildings have any purpose at all.

Stella's dress felt sticky against her back, her legs damp, her hands were hurting. She stopped for a moment and unclenched her fists, inspected the red welts and patches of white on her palms. She had been gripping the pram handlebar too tightly.

*

Dawn, the health visitor, had erupted through the front door that morning, on her first visit, dressed in blue polyester trousers and a sky-blue shirt with severe collars. Stella had thought she looked like a prison officer or a policewoman, someone official who had come bustling into Stella's house full of outside air and efficiency. Dawn's flaxen hair had been strictly pulled back into a tight, uncomfortable-looking ponytail, so that when Dawn had bent over Mary, Stella had been able to glimpse the lines of Dawn's pink scalp. It had reminded Stella, for some drifting reason, of rabbits: the pink and the peroxide, like the way a rabbit's skin must look under pale fur. Stella had stared too at Dawn's laminated identity tag, attached with a vast silver clip to her waistband, which had bounced playfully against her plump hips as she had unzipped her black bag to produce a pair of scales. When Dawn had caught her looking, Stella had blushed and made a mental note to try and stop staring so much. She thought it was tiredness perhaps, the odd-shaped fuggy reality that a newborn brings, which had encouraged this tendency to stare and dream, to be entranced by the strangest, smallest and most inconsequential of things.

'Let's see how baby is doing,' Dawn had said. 'Where can I wash my hands?'

Stella had silently shown her into the narrow, rather dirty kitchen. 'It all goes to pot when you have a baby, doesn't it?' Dawn said cheerfully, pulling three saucepans full of cold, grimy water out of the sink.

'She isn't my first,' Stella told her, watched Dawn squeeze some washing-up liquid into her hands, the liquid slimy and gloopy between her fingers. 'The other one is at nursery.'

'Right. Let's get baby undressed. Isn't she a big girl? What a lovely baby. Is she being good for you?'

Were they taught this patter at health-visitor school, sitting behind desks in bright sunny rooms, crying out in unison in their cheerful, fulsome, sing-song voices, 'What a big boy!', 'How is baby today?'

Stella dutifully followed Dawn back into the sitting-room, thinking that perhaps it was similar to the script that car salesmen have to learn. She and her husband Zeki had watched a television programme the other night about salesmen on the forecourt and had been surprised to discover that, when they'd looked into buying a car, they had fallen for this rehearsed spiel themselves. Zeki had been cross about it; he'd stood up and walked over to the window, kicked at the wall, his dark hair standing up at the crown, as though electrified. 'Jesus! I didn't know,' he'd said to Stella, shaking his head. 'And I work in sales.'

She'd grinned at him, and shrugged, so he'd sat back down on the couch next to her. 'Who'da thunk it?' he'd said, trying to sound light-hearted.

Are you looking for part-exchange? What car do you drive now? An Astra! Oh, they're great cars those – I used to have one, very reliable. What colour is it? What a lovely baby! Isn't he big? Aren't you doing well! Any problems with baby?

Mary had looked odd in the scales, her mouth open in shock at the cold plastic, one leg hitting out against the side, those purple, mottled thighs chafing against the papery nappy. Stella had thought she looked a bit scrawny in just the nappy, like an underweight chicken, newly plucked, all crinkled skin and bony joints.

'Are you new, Dawn? I don't think I've seen you before?'

Dawn absent-mindedly stroked her ponytail; it was a strange gesture, girlish and nervous, inappropriate for a woman in a blue polyester trouser suit and a laminated badge.

'I've been here for about a year now. Right, get baby's clothes back on, Mum, or she'll catch cold.'

'Do you like it here?'

'Love it.' Dawn filled in forms, barely paying Stella any attention. 'Have you done the Edinburgh test yet? You feeling okay?'

'How do you mean?' Stella asked her question carefully.

'Do you feel like you are coping? Post-natal depression is very common, you know – nothing to be ashamed about.'

'I'm not depressed.'

'Do you have a partner? You're very young to have two children. Do you have any help?'

'I grew up here, my mother lives here, and my auntie; my husband works in town. I've always lived in Saffron Walden.'

Stella had sat down in the armchair by the window, picked up a cushion to rest Mary on. She looked across the room at Dawn, wondering at her asking such questions. Should she say more? Should she tell Dawn that when she felt the soft dome of Mary's head resting against her neck she thought her knees might buckle, that the sight of her blank, deep-black eyes made her exhale, and that just the thought of her toes made her want to weep? That she wanted to lick her daughter's feet? That she felt the same for her son, too. The same, but different. No, she could not say these things to Dawn. She could only feel them in herself, like a pulsing, vibrant force beyond her articulation. They were not up for discussion.

Stella wanted to feed Mary, but was worried about Dawn coming over and pulling up her top and holding her breasts, wanting to see the 'latch'. She found it embarrassing. Stella liked the dark, intensely private and lapsed swimming feeling she got when feeding her baby. She didn't want Dawn to be involved. Three years ago she'd been uncertain about how best to feed Jack and had asked her mother's advice.

'Oh Stella,' her mother had said, lightly. 'I suppose, the general rule of thumb is simply this; do what feels right.'

Stella had frowned. She wanted and needed more than that.

'Breast or bottle?'

'I can't decide for you, darling,' Sheila had said, smiling down at her. And Stella, who wanted her mother's good opinion and involvement, more than anything, had felt slighted and cross, in spite of herself.

Mary was fretful and squirmy in her arms, she would have to feed her.

'Oh, I see, you're a local girl.' Dawn said this with a gossipy edge, coming over towards Stella, her ponytail swinging behind her. 'There are a lot of commuting families here. And a lot of women on antidepressants, too.'

'Why?'

Dawn had shrugged and parked herself companionably on the arm of the chair. Stella had been able to feel Dawn's thigh pressing against her shoulder.

'I don't know – a lot of people move here, don't they, find they're a bit isolated, a long way from family, husband away in London all day. It's a high percentage of mothers. I won't tell you how high, but believe me, it's *high*.'

'Are they depressed because they are lonely?'

'Aren't you good, to still have her on the breast. Well done, you. Right, let's have a look at baby's latch.'

*

Before setting off to collect Jack, Stella had stuffed the depression questionnaire in her bag, because she was going on to her mother's house afterwards. She thought her mum might like to see the questionnaire. Stella worried about her mother being so quiet on the subject of her having Jack when she was nineteen, and Mary only three years later. She'd tried, only a week ago, to provoke a response in her mother.

'You think I'm too young.'

'No, of course not. Who am I to disapprove of anything?' Stella had sensed a whiff of impatience. 'I was twenty-nine when I had Marie, and thirty-six when I had you. It didn't make much difference. I don't suppose there is a right age.'

'All the same, I couldn't do it without you, Mum.'

'Of course you could.' Her mother had laughed. 'You're a natural.'

*

A key-worker at the nursery asked for 'quick word', but Stella didn't want to give her one, feeling too hot and tired by the time she got to the top of the hill for any kind of word, quick or slow. She just wanted to pick Jack up and run, but the key-worker, in her logoed Aertex shirt and tabard, beckoned Stella over towards her.

'Nothing serious, Mrs Robinson, but I had to have a few words with Jack this morning. His key-worker is off sick today,' she said, putting her hair behind her ear and smiling insincerely at Stella. Stella thought she knew this key-worker from somewhere else – not the nursery, but somewhere light and free. Perhaps she knew her from school?

'Oh, right,' Stella nodded. 'He's settled in all right, he only started a few weeks ago.'

'He got into a fight,' the key-worker continued. 'With another child.'

'That's not Jack. He's not like that,' Stella said quickly, feeling stubborn.

Stella could see Jack standing on the other side of the cloakroom waiting for her, while another member of staff was trying to distract him with some old book. But he wasn't looking at the book; he looked at his mother, wanting to leave, wanting to get away from these girls with their bacterially washed hands and cheerful tabards, wanting to get out into the sunshine and up to his granny's house.

'No, I know that, Mrs Robinson,' the key-worker said, slowly. 'But there have been some changes at home, haven't there? With your new little one. There was hitting and punching involved, and I wanted to let you know that we'd had words. We've not got any serious worries about Jack.'

Stella stared at her. How old was she? She still had spots, which

she'd tried to cover up, badly, with a too-dark, too-thick founda-
tion. Chrissie Smith! That was her; she'd been at least two years
above Stella at the High School. She'd played netball, they'd both
played netball – that was how Stella knew her. Stella had been very
good at netball, built for it: tall, naturally athletic, with springy
legs and long arms; she had played above her age – there had been
talk of her trying out at county level.

'You're Chrissie Smith, aren't you?' Stella said. 'I thought
I remembered you. Netball squad. I didn't know you still lived
here.'

Chrissie Smith blushed under her make-up – Stella could just
see the livid tinge of red around the edges of her pancake face. She
felt bad; she hadn't meant to embarrass Chrissie, she didn't think
she had, so why should Chrissie suddenly look so uncomfortable?
Stella felt quite cross with her for blushing.

'Yes, that's right. Home time now then, Jack,' Chrissie Smith said
quickly, nodding at Stella and turning away.

Jack was released and ran over to his mother, hugging her leg.

'I hate nursery,' he said. Stella looked down at the top of his
dark head leaning against her thigh; she cupped her hand
around his tiny chin, forcing him to look at her: his eyes were
smiling, his small perfect mouth thinned out into a look of
pretend misery.

Stella knelt down and gave Jack a kiss, rubbing her nose against
his cheek, feeling the new buzzy sensation of the shaved hair
behind his ears. Zeki had taken Jack to the barber's at the
weekend, after a letter had come home from nursery warning
of a nit outbreak. Jack had walked in the door, with his father,
looking like someone else's child. That was what Stella had
thought: 'That's not my child.' She'd scanned his face for

something familiar – panicked, like the time she'd lost him in the supermarket, had run up and down the aisles, stopping small boys she knew were not Jack, small boys sitting in the shopping trolleys with their mothers; boys so clearly, so obviously not Jack, but she'd stared into their faces, trying to see some semblance of Jack, willing these strange children to be her son. She had always kept his hair long, treasuring that baby hair, and when she'd looked at him striding down the hall towards her, she'd found it impossible to navigate his face. Of course she knew it was Jack, it had to be – logic dictated it must be – so she'd made a joke of her nerves.

'Who is this boy then? Who is this boy you've brought home, Zeki. Where's Jack?'

'It's me, it is Jack, Mummy, look!'

'No, no, you can't be. My Jack's got long hair.'

And then Jack had taken off his shoes and thrown them at her, catching her arm, hurting her. He'd run across the room and lain on the floor and burst into wild, angry tears. Zeki had leant against the fridge and frowned at her.

'You could just say, "Great hair, Jack",' he'd said, with some disbelief. 'It's a cool cut, Jack. Stop crying – she's kidding you.'

Stella had gone over and picked up his hot, cross, writhing body.

'Jack! Stop it! It was a joke, a bad joke. I'm sorry.' And she'd held him until his angry fists, which were raining down on her back, had linked around her neck instead, and his violent sobs had stopped. 'I knew it was you, I knew it was.'

Remembering this scene, Stella stood up and said, 'That haircut really suits you, mate.' Then, kicking the brake off the pram, she added, 'You don't hate nursery', for Chrissie Smith's benefit. And then, 'Right, come on then.'

She backed the pram out of the double-doors covered in stickers and into the heat of the day.

They took the shortcut through the cemetery. Stella went to visit her mother every Thursday afternoon and, since Mary was born, she and Jack had started 'popping in' after his nursery session on Monday too. Sheila had asked that they set definite times in the week, though Stella preferred a more fluid arrangement. She'd asked her mum for her own key, but Sheila hadn't got around to getting one cut yet. There was a faulty part in the fence behind one of the warehouses on the estate, which she had known about since school and made the shortcut possible, though it was difficult to navigate them all down the incline without anyone getting stung by nettles or caught on a bramble, and tricky to hold up the broken bit of mesh and push the pram through the undergrowth too. They walked on the proper path past the unmarked war graves, unscathed.

Stella stopped for a moment and looked across the civic graveyard at the municipal bushes and waste bins, the signs and untended graves. She used to come to the cemetery with a group of friends as a teenager; they'd bunk off school and come and hide amongst the gravestones, lying on the grass, staring up at the sky, getting drunk and reckless on stolen bottles of Poppy vodka.

She screwed up her eyes a little and tried to see herself as she had been: leaning against a tree, her long legs thrown flirtatiously over Rick, wearing a bikini top, running her hands through her hair, lighting a cigarette, pouting and pulling at her earrings. Trying not to look like the good girl who was doing a bad thing – rolling in the grass like a dog to remove her natural scent, her stainless veneer of light, clean hair and perfect teeth, to remove the shine which told the world she was the sort of girl who had prospects in netball at county level.

How funny that Chrissie Smith was back in the town and Stella hadn't even heard about it. Most of Stella's friends had left as soon as they'd finished school. Some had gone to university or college, or to flats and jobs in bigger towns. She'd occasionally bump into them when they came back during the holidays to visit their parents. It seemed extraordinary to Stella that she should be in her own home, pushing a pram, being responsible for children – a mother herself no less – whilst her peers were coming back trailing dirty washing and rumbling stomachs and acting like children themselves. Stella thought of it this way, it was her way of thinking. She'd dropped most of them anyway; she disliked the way they talked to her, looked at her.

'Still in Suffering Boredom, Stella,' they would say, using their old school nickname for Saffron Walden. They were different when they came back too, and each time Stella felt a great yearning gap open on the ground at their feet, deep and dark with jagged edges. They might blink at one another across it, unable or unwilling to leap across. Stella couldn't understand their disloyalty to the town – this was how she thought of it – why they were so scornful, full of themselves, proud of their wider horizons. She knew they pitied her, thought her trapped, suspended in the quiet streets of the market town they had so quickly left, without so much as a backward glance. She didn't recognise this version of herself; she didn't feel pitiable, she felt safe and certain. Known. For Stella, her pleasures were small, simple matters: tending and thinking about her immediate, known-about life, her children, her husband, her friends, the town, her mother. As she saw it, that was all that mattered. She thought herself lucky not having to move away, make her life up somewhere else. Zeki had even been found a job in town at the local estate agent's, which meant that he was now home more often and had got a decent wage. They were lucky.

Some people had stayed — like Denise-in-the-optician's — but most of her friends had left. At school she'd run with a lively, popular crowd who had upped and gone at the first opportunity, with the wild, giddy enthusiasm of dogs being let off their leashes. Her best friend at school, Carly, had come to visit Stella in the maternity hospital. She'd sat on the end of the bed, ignoring the newly born Jack — the obvious, startling evidence of Stella's new life — and said, 'I got my A-level results then.'

Stella had struggled to focus on Carly, sitting beside her wearing a pale vest and shorts. Carly's streaky fake tan, white sunglasses and painted nails had looked stunning under the hospital lights. Stella had wanted to get over the vast misunderstanding that had risen between them, but her whole body had been stinging and hurting, her breasts tight and swollen with milk and shock. She was still frightened by the sounds of her own screams echoing through her head, as well as the midwife's quick slap on her hand, telling her she was overreacting and that she was hardly the first girl to have given birth, was she now?

'So,' Carly had said, blowing her cheeks out and looking bored. 'I guess I'm off to college.'

Carly had visited them on her first holiday home from Portsmouth. Her clothes had been different — Stella considered them a bit dark, a bit dirty — and the way she spoke had changed too. She'd told Stella in long paragraphs of speech, accompanied by new hand gestures and an odd fake laugh (like someone off an American television show, Stella had thought), all about college, and the union bar, and a bloke she'd been seeing; only it wasn't one bloke, it was four or five, and all their names had sounded the same — Jed,

Red, Ded. Stella had looked at Carly's new friends on Facebook and hadn't liked the look of them at all.

Later that evening after Carly had left, promising she'd come back soon (a declaration that sounded like an ordinary excuse), Stella and Zeki had slipped into bed. Zeki had been sleepy and a little drunk, Stella more tightly wound.

'What did you think to Carly then? She wasn't the same, was she? I thought she was a bit up herself.'

'People change, Stella,' Zeki said. 'You have to let them change. College must make you a bit different.'

'A bit arrested, more like. I didn't like how she was with Jack, either, all that pretending not to know what to do and screaming about his nappy.'

'She doesn't know.'

'I don't see that college is all *that* – not if it makes you act a bit special, like her. She doesn't know anything about kids, does she?'

'No.'

Stella had slid down beside Zeki and wrapped her body around his, humming as she swam through the warmth of her careful life until she fell asleep.

The next day she blocked Carly from her Facebook page. Stella had been quite addicted to Facebook for a while, but then she'd found herself going round and round in circles, thinking that every-thing and everyone looked so glamorous, so well designed; in the end she'd decided that it was untruthful and overwhelming.

*

'Why are they dead? You come here if you die, don't you?' Jack said quietly, standing next to her, hands on hips, foreman-like.

'Come on,' Stella nudged Jack, 'not far now.'

They walked out of the formal stone gates of the cemetery onto the Radwinter Road, and then eventually up Elizabeth Way and across to the bungalows behind the private school. Jack was tired and scratchy, refusing to hold the pram when crossing the road; he wanted Stella to pick him up and carry him. He banged the backs of Stella's legs with his Thomas the Tank Engine lunch box in protest.

'Stop it, Jack,' she said, bending down, practising her reasonable calm-under-pressure voice. 'You're hurting me. You have to walk, I can't carry you. It's not far, and you want to see Granny, don't you?'

'No,' he said, looking pink-hot. 'I don't want to, I hate her. I want to go home.'

Stella could see traces of white film across his neck and down his pale arms. She touched him and tried to rub the suncream in. (*'Now the weather is hotter, please supply _named_ sunblock for your child in a _named_ clear plastic bag, together with a note, signed by a parent or guardian, giving permission for members of nursery staff to apply the sunblock as necessary for playtime. However, we are not always able to apply sunblock to every child, so please make sure you have applied suncream _before_ your child's session begins. All children need to have a sunhat — if they do not have a sunhat in nursery, they may be banned from attending the outdoor play sessions. Thank you.'*)

Stella liked the smell of the suncream, it made her feel in control. Jack was wearing his sunhat with a flap down the back, and peered out at her from under the brim, looking hot and uncomfortable. She wanted to take the heavy, dark-blue hat off his head. She couldn't see that it kept him from feeling any hotter. His shorts were too long on his legs, she realised; there wasn't enough space between his knees and socks and trainers. He was too small and too hot for clothes.

'I like *you*,' Jack said matter-of-factly, watching her face carefully for a response.

'I know,' Stella sighed. 'I like you too. Come on, we'll feel better when we get there. Maybe Granny will have her paddling pool out?'

'Paddle,' Jack said.

She tried very hard to stay patient for the rest of the walk, and didn't shout when Jack stopped to forensically inspect blades of grass or to pick up a leaf; talked to him in her high plastic voice, which always sounded fake, even to her. It was hotter than it had been last week, than it had been for the whole of the summer. Stella thought she could see a heat-haze coming off the road.

By the time they arrived at her mother's bungalow Stella was exhausted, dripping sweat, or milk, or sweat and milk. She could smell herself, feel the drips on her stomach. She pushed the pram around the side of the house, giving a warning knock on the kitchen window as she passed. Jack opened the back door first and burst in, throwing his lunch box on the floor.

'Granna, I'm here now,' he shouted with glorious confidence. 'Granna, Jack's here.'

Stella left the pram in the shaded alleyway to the side of the house and followed Jack into the cool of the dark, neat kitchen. The window blind was down, and the kitchen smelt of bleach and cleaning things. The ceiling fan was on. Stella stood underneath, feeling the wisps of cold air lift across her sweaty head. On the draining board was a single plate and her mum's favourite mug – cream with an acorn on the side. Stella wondered at that being all the washing-up her mother had: one plate, one mug.

'Granna,' Jack shouted again, taking off his shorts in one go, but getting in a muddle with his shoes. He sat with a bump on the tiled floor and started to cry, but within a second changed his mind and lay down on the cool floor in his Thunderbird pants and waved his caught-up feet at her, giggling to himself.

'You numpty,' Stella said, laughing along with him.

She felt better being in the well-ordered kitchen, standing under the ceiling fan and taking in the clean, bare unit tops, the mug-tree, the varnish on the oak-unit doors, the gentle hum of her mother's clean fridge, the line of tea towels hanging on their pegs, the bright-yellow pot by the sink housing one washing-up brush, the reassuring sight of a cleaning cloth hung neatly over the central mixer tap, the veiled light and the chairs, with matching cushions, grouped around the small kitchen table. It felt like paradise to Stella.

'Mum,' she shouted out, squatting down to help Jack take off his shoes and his hot little socks. 'Mum, you'll never believe who I just met at the nursery. Go and see if the paddling pool is out, Jack.' She prodded him gently in the tummy.

Obediently, and wondrously free of clothes, Jack got up and padded out of the kitchen door. Stella followed, peered around the corner of the house and saw that the pool was there on the patio, garishly bright and populated by cartoon characters all set for a day at the beach; they smiled and bulged their too-large, expressive eyes at her.

'It's got things in it,' Jack said, peering over the edge, his hands on his knees.

'Oh, just get in and cool down, Jack,' Stella said, looking at a new hanging basket attached to the outside wall, spilling with blue-purple geraniums. She took a quick look inside the abandoned pram, where Mary still slept, her hands thrown up by the side of her head, and then went back to stand under the kitchen fan again.

She gazed at the lunch box on its side, and at Jack's clothes all over the floor. She closed her eyes.

'Mum,' she shouted again from the inside of her black-and-red eyelids. 'We're here.'

Stella wandered over to the sink and turned on the tap, gathering the cool, falling water in her hands and splashing it over her face. Leaning forward, she pulled the blind up to look at Jack, who still wasn't in the pool; he was holding a plastic spade and trying to fish out whatever it was in the paddling pool that he didn't want there. She knocked on the window.

'Get in the pool, Jack.' She motioned to him with her hand. He stared at her, uncomprehending, his face screwed up in the sunshine. He looked unnaturally white, and the sun bounced off his thin, rounded shoulders. She let the blind fall back again. Where was her mum? She never went out on a Thursday, and she never went out without locking the back door first. Jack appeared at the side door, carrying the spade.

'Mum?'

'What?'

'You said.' Jack banged his spade against the step.

'Stop that noise, Jack.'

'At the winnow.'

'Pardon? Get in the paddling pool.'

'Get in?'

'Yeah.'

'I am fishing,' he told her, holding up the plastic spade.

'Oh, right, okay,' she said quietly, her throat feeling narrow and tight. 'I want you to get cool – get in the pool, get in the cool pool.'

'I am fishing,' he repeated, looking at her carefully. 'If you eat too many sweets you die, don't you?'

'Put your hat on, Jack,' she said, surprised to hear her distant and exhausted voice issuing this instruction. Jack ignored her and went back out into the garden. He didn't have any suncream on his back, or his legs. It wouldn't matter if he would get in the bloody paddling pool, like he was meant to; if he'd sit down and find some protection in the water. Life was suncream applied at the correct times to the proper and relevant parts of the child's body to protect them from the terror of burning light. *Thank you.* She'd do it in a minute – a naked minute of Essex afternoon sunshine wasn't going to kill him.

Stella walked out of the kitchen and into the quiet, carpeted hallway. She opened the door to the lounge, but the room was empty. Wondrously empty. Everything was still, quiet and neat and just as it should be: the curtains, the dust-free windowsills, the careful arrangement of family photographs inside the glass-fronted cabinet. Stella stepped back into the hall and banged on the bathroom door, but that opened to her touch. She stepped into the bathroom and leant her head for a moment against the tiled wall, stroking the top of the thick cream bath towel hanging on the rail beside her. Then she went into her mother's bedroom: the door was half-open and she didn't bother to knock this time.

The room was dark, the curtains still closed and the bed unmade. That's unlike Mum, Stella thought. Drifting over towards the window, she pulled the curtains back, looking for, and seeing, her mother's car parked outside on the street. Stella caught sight of herself in the wardrobe mirror on the other side of the bed. She stared at herself, without meaning to, put up a hand to tuck her hair behind her ears, smiled and pulled at her dress. She didn't know the person who was staring back at her in that quiet bedroom, posed behind her mother's crumpled apricot-coloured duvet. Mary was born three and a half weeks ago, and Stella hadn't thought she had left a mark on her – she was especially and particularly proud of this fact, had worn it like a badge, a justification even, for having another baby at twenty-two rather than later, when she'd be old and stale-looking, when she was certain her skin would bag and sag, never pinging back into place. She had seen these women everywhere in town, old – to Stella's eyes – and tired, with drooping stomachs and unwieldy breasts, struggling to fit their outsized, expensive three-wheeler buggies through the narrow shop doorways, running their hands through their expensively cut, streaky grey hair. She was still slim, but her breasts were more swollen than she'd realised and there was still a rise to her stomach, which pushed against the waist of her summer dress. But it was the passive, haunted look on her face that made her a stranger to herself – pale, staring eyes, hollow and glazed, the off-centre set of her mouth, a line of sweat sitting on her collarbone. She stuck her tongue out at her reflection and bent down to straighten the bed. Perhaps it was tiredness that made her look so different. She thought it was this tiredness that made her body soft, her eyes unfocused, her arms ache and her mind fold over and over with fleeing, half-realised, but endlessly repeating thoughts.

Pulling the duvet up and stroking the creases out of the soft, cool cotton made the bed look inviting. She decided to lie down for just one minute, close her eyes for less, to listen to the ticking of the gold carriage clock sitting on the bedside table beside her mother's library book.

When her dad had retired from the printing works, only a year before he'd died, they had presented him with this clock. Everyone in attendance in their best suits and dresses, her mother watery-eyed behind the camera, prompting her sister, Marie, to whisper, 'Couldn't they think of something more original?' To which her mother had, uncharacteristically, snapped, 'I think it's very kind of them. It's a lovely clock, Marie. It'll have a super chime. They've been very good to us, very good to your father.'

The bedroom was as spare and empty as the sitting-room. Gloriously, invitingly empty. An absence filled the room. She felt the nothingness all around her. It enveloped her. Stella wanted to surrender to its spilling nowhereness; to evaporate, dissolve into the promise of its dark, pooling absence. She could almost taste the blankness of the bedroom, unfettered by character-socks, bright packets of nappies, wipes, boxes of breast-pads and Power Rangers. Her mother's bedroom was dangerously desirable. Laying her head in the dent left on the pillow, she smelt her mother on the sheets, her perfume and talc, and that calming, clean chemical smell of her favoured fabric conditioner — what was it: *summer breeze* or *spring fresh*, or something like that? Stella reminded herself to ask her mother; she would like her own sheets to smell this way. Where was her mother?

'I'm not going to sleep,' she murmured out loud. 'I just want to lie down for a minute.'

*

Jack woke her by bouncing on the bed, his plump legs cold and wet, and by banging his wet hands down on her stomach.

'Mummeee, Mummeee,' he shouted, buoyant with news, 'Granny's in the water, Mary is in grass and she's crying.'

Stella heard his words: Granny, water, Mary, crying, grass. She leapt from the bed, knocking Jack back against the pillows and ran from the bedroom, guiltily registering his shout of slighted fury, down the thick carpet in the hallway; ran shoeless and half-asleep through the kitchen and out around the side of the house, across the patio, where she felt the heat of the stone flags under her feet. She saw, as she ran, the tiny wet shadows of Jack's footprints all over the patio, as though he had been dancing or chased by a demonic wasp – perhaps he had. They went in tight concentric circles right up to the creosoted fence, all around the plastic pots of the patio: careful rings of Jack's feet dancing around the drooping Busy Lizzies, the red, yellow and purple pansies. She had fallen asleep. Why had she let herself fall asleep, leaving Jack outside, alone and in water? Finally to the paddling pool, blinking, hardly able to look inside, afraid of what she might see.

Her mother's drowned, dead and possibly mutilated body was not inside the paddling pool. There was water made particularly blue-looking by the pool's bright plastic bottom, and Jack's spade and a few dead flies floating on the surface along with blades of grass. Then she saw, lying in the centre of the pool, her mother's long, gold chain woven like a vine along the spade's handle, and the familiar gold locket nestled neatly alongside.

Stella bent down and carefully removed her mother's necklace and held the locket in her trembling fingers. She closed her eyes. She felt the sun on the backs of her legs, her mouth dry and fluffy with sleep, and cold water dripped down onto her hot swollen feet.

It was only then that she heard, now that her ears were finally open, the sound of Mary crying. Following the noise, she turned to see her lying on her back in a flower bed, under a clump of pale-mauve asters, next to the side of the patio. Mary looked like a fairy, a changeling child, the dry earth stuck to the back of her head, blades of grass and three daisies balanced on her round, protruding stomach, hands thrown up behind her head, back arched, her legs stretching out across the dry earth.

Where was her mother?

Washed Up – One Woman Swearing at Her Kitchen Sink

THURSDAY

Lots of questions continue to be asked in the comments section about where we're living. While debate continues to rage about The Project, I guess I should tell you a bit more. So you can put me, The Marriage and The Project in context. Have I led you all to think it's weird? I'm not sure it is, it might just be that I find it weird. Or that I'm weird. Or any of the above. Here are some key facts:

1 It's a really, really, really lovely place to live. Quiet, historic and sweet, but perhaps, just perhaps, a little bit . . . um . . . dull?
2 It drives me mad (see archive).
3 There are more hairdressers and charity shops here than you can ever imagine needing or wanting.
4 It's the kind of place a person would be VERY surprised to end up living in, by accident.

Also, sometimes, because it's so small, I think everyone here in the town must be reading this blog. I don't know whether that's because I've got delusions of popularity, or it might be just good old-fashioned paranoia. Hey, if you are, PLEASE let me know. Wink at me in the supermarket, nudge me in the Market Place. But just don't tell my husband!

10 comments

The day

It was Auntie Joyce who alerted the police to Sheila Buttle's disappearance in the end, not Stella.

It was not that Stella hadn't thought about her mother's whereabouts during the weekend or at the start of the following week; she had. When she'd got home that Thursday afternoon, having locked her mother's house with her own key, she'd hung the necklace on one of the hooks in her kitchen (the ones she'd asked Zeki to put up because she'd wanted to hang her drying-up cloths there, like her mother did, but never had). It had dangled there like a talisman. Every so often she would catch sight of it, glimmering in the sun, and would go over and hold the silky, cool chain in her hand.

This necklace was her mother's most precious possession, given to her on the day Marie had been born. Stella's mother had told her and Marie the story many times when they were children, usually at Stella's wheedling insistence; she loved to imagine her mother in the hospital, composed and serene, dressed in a starchy white nightdress (she presumed), her long, dark hair falling around her shoulders, her bed neat and the nurses impressed with her, and then her father arriving, proud and perhaps a little bashful, and presenting, with some pomp, a small velvet box containing the gold necklace.

'Why do you get presents when you have a baby?' Marie had wanted to know, sucking on the end of her plait, leaning back in her chair, cocky.

'To say well done, and thank you for the baby,' Stella had said promptly, sitting up straight, pleased to know the answer, drinking her milk. 'What did you get when you had me?'

'Yes,' her mother had said thoughtfully, smiling at them both and fingering the necklace around her neck. 'Yes, I suppose that must be why.'

Stella had tried to get Jack to explain where he had found the necklace that afternoon, but he kept giving her different answers, and she'd ended up getting cross with him, shaking him quite roughly on the pavement. It had been madness. Just thinking about that pointless exchange at the side of the Radwinter Road, where the cars were driving too fast beside them and filling up the warm air with exhaust fumes, made Stella need to breathe in deeply.

'Tell me the truth,' she'd insisted. 'Was it in the flower bed, like you first said? Near where you put Mary down, in the flower bed?'

The thought of Jack taking Mary out of the pram, weaving around the patio – possibly just holding her by the ankles, for all she knew – his insubstantial, bendy arms gentle and reckless, and of how Mary's head might have banged about as Jack put her down on the dry earth, made Stella dizzy and dark with panic. Like she might just fall away. She wouldn't go there, couldn't go there. She'd decided to concentrate on the necklace.

'You don't sound sure. Was it in the paddling pool?'

'Yes, the paddling pool.'

'Not the flower bed then?'

'Yes, in the flowers.'

'Tell me the truth, Jack. Where did you find it?'

'In my pocket?'

Every time he'd given her an answer she'd demanded a different one. She knew that Jack had lost all sense of what might be the truth. He was just earnestly offering up an answer — any answer — in the vague hope that it might be what she was looking for. Perhaps Jack didn't know where he'd found it, perhaps there were no locations in his mind. Children think differently, don't they? Stella remembered taking money out of her mother's purse (she was older than Jack now), stealing money for sweets. When Marie had caught her in the act and grassed on her, her mother had confronted Stella and she'd not been able to give the proper, truthful answer — her mouth sticky with contraband chews and illegal, fizzy shoelace sweets. She'd convinced herself that she'd found the money on the street; she was certain of this fact, and no matter how sympathetic her mother had been, how enraged Marie had become, even when her father had delicately but firmly broached this subject, she hadn't wavered. She had decided that she'd found the money on the pavement between numbers twenty-four and twenty-eight in the close. She'd even taken her dad to show him the crack in the pavement where the coin had fallen, told him how she'd seen it glinting on her way to school, how it had caught her attention. This deception hadn't been stark and guilty, or even purposeful; it was amorphous and shadowy, elastic with possibility, just as the truth had become in her mind too. Perhaps it was like that for Jack? She could remember Marie, though, her fists balled up in frustration, stamping her foot and screaming, 'I saw her take it, with my own two eyes. She's only bloody lying.' And how both her parents had turned to Marie, shocked, and told her to watch her language.

Stella had rung her mother's mobile, but not with any conviction. She knew full well that her phone would be in the drawer in the kitchen, tucked in neatly beside the placemats and the coasters. The thought of the phone ringing and receiving her messages left her with the unsettling image of her voice trapped in that dark kitchen drawer, beside the ironed and folded table napkins.

Zeki and Stella had bought that mobile phone last Christmas, as an invitation for Sheila to join the modern world of instant availability and constant communication.

'Oh, goodness,' Sheila Buttle had said, sitting in her armchair, a purple paper hat sitting awry on the top of her curly hair, cheeks flushed. 'A mobile phone.'

Then she had carefully put it back in the box, and to one side. It had fallen to Zeki to charge it for her on Boxing Day. Stella had been angry with her mother, hissing to Zeki, 'Everyone has a phone. Why is she being so stupid about it?'

Stella had been obstinate about the phone, leaving constant and increasingly irritated messages on her mother's answering service, asking her why she didn't take it out shopping with her, why she let it run out of charge. She'd fed on it, been consumed by it. Eventually she had given up on this stubborn campaign after a calamitous texting exchange. Stella had sent a text saying, '*Hi Mum, cld u pick up some milk 4 me?*' and had received one back three hours later, which said, '*I'm sorry I can't love you. Mum.*'

Stella had stood in her lounge and read it four times, her heart racing and the edges of her vision blurring and darkening a little. She hadn't told her mum that, after the standing and staring, she'd sat down on the settee and cried hot, helpless tears, which had surprised even her in their persistence and their readiness. That evening Stella had gone round to her mother's and stood in the kitchen, looking at Sheila's rounded back at the sink.

'What did your text mean, Mum?' she'd demanded, placing her hands on her newly pregnant belly for support, watching her mother's face reflected in the dark windowpane.

'I couldn't pick up any shopping,' her mother had said slowly, without looking up. 'Sorry, Stella, I had a busy day today.'

And Stella had gone over and shown her mother the text, how it had looked on the screen, stark and brazen, and her mother had peered carefully, screwing her eyes up, hands still plunged in the sudsy water.

'It should say, "*I'm sorry I can't. Love you, Mum.*"' And her mother had started to laugh, tickled by the misunderstanding, so Stella had pretended to laugh along, forcing out a thin, tinny sound, which had reverberated off the shining floor.

'You must have known I wouldn't have written that – just out the blue like that,' her mother had said, her shoulders shaking.

*

When Auntie Joyce telephoned Stella about Sheila's disappearance the following Tuesday, her voice operatically rising and falling, pouring out high notes of terrible news, Stella was hiding in St Mary's Church.

Things had gone strangely wrong for her that morning. She had started with good intentions, ones conjured up in an effort to meet head-on the challenges of her life. She wanted to attend to the small domestic decisions and matters, so as to combat the tired yet dazzling nature of her daydreams. Daydreams that, she worried, were going to overwhelm her. She had done the washing-up, got everyone dressed and ready to walk to the art activity group, leaving behind them the tang of washing-up competently completed, the air in the kitchen soapy and precise.

They had cut down Fairycroft Road, along East Street and then across the market square, up Market Hill, along Church Street and then up Church Path. Puffing beside Dorset House — a line of tiny, ancient houses which had recently been done up in a tasteful green, to look less like the Tudor slum-houses they were and more like objects of historical interest — and then, finally, towards St Mary's Hall beside the church. When she was crossing the road next to Dorset House, Stella stood for a moment, stunned, staring at a man coming out of a house on Church Street. She thought he was Mr Linklater, who had run the grocer's in Market Place with his brother, but the shop had been closed down years and years ago, and even then Mr Linklater had been really old. Had it been him? It couldn't be him. Did she really remember him? Perhaps she didn't, but she could see herself as a child walking with her mother to the shop — her mother wearing her pale-blue mackintosh, the swishing noise the lining had made. Stella's shoes had thick, yellow, rubbery soles, which squeaked on the pavement, and she remembered how Mr Linklater and his brother had worn white overalls in the shop, and the piles of old tins, the ham slicer and the bottles of sweets behind the counter, and the musty smell of the shop. Stella wiped her filmy brow, thinking she could see these hazy memories bouncing around the quiet street, like a stretch of celluloid, flammable and opaque. The man, aware of her staring, glanced in her direction and she awoke with a jolt of embarrassment and quickly kicked the brake off the pram. Perhaps this wasn't her memory at all, she thought, scratching her nose in confusion, perhaps it was her mother's.

By the time she had walked around the outside of the church she felt hot and dizzy.

Stella wasn't sure why she bothered going to Paint&Sing each week, for she much preferred the mums' and toddlers' group at the Baptist church; it was quieter and easier, a cup of tea, a chat, and the children played with the toys from the cupboard, and that was that. The mothers there were friendlier too, more normal. She found the art group intimidating — all the other mothers were much older than her, and they mostly seemed to be ex-lawyers from London, sitting on their tiny wooden chairs, helping to make pasta tractor pictures, and talking too loudly and too emphatically to their children. She thought they judged her, but when she confided this to Zeki, he'd laughed at her and said she was paranoid. 'They're no different to you, Stell,' he'd said, 'they're just mums, like you.'

But they were different. And Stella kept going, stubbornly sitting there, not talking to anyone, smiling slyly, taking her silent part in the coffee rota, encouraging Jack, in a quiet way, to stick the glittery stars in the right place, but secretly holding her ambivalence to her, like a prized memento, not caring if he emptied the stupid stars all over the floor instead.

'This week,' Barbara had told them in her optimistic, sing-song voice, 'we will be making dinosaurs with modelling clay. The clay is quick-drying, and then next week the children can paint them. It's a two-week project, this one,' she'd finished, clapping her hands and giving a startled laugh, as though frightened by her own ambition.

'I don't want to do a dinosaur,' Jack had grumbled, taking his usual seat at their regular table. 'Dinosaurs are stupid.'

'Oh, doesn't he like dinosaurs? I thought all boys liked dinosaurs,' said the woman taking her seat beside them. Stella shrugged and pulled Jack's chair closer to the table. This was Jan, tall and sleek, with long, tanned legs and well-toned calves; she'd told Stella that she played a lot of tennis. 'A lot, mind you, I *train*.' That morning Jan had been wearing a pair of gingham shorts and a bright white shirt, sunglasses balanced on the top of her head. She always smelt fragrant too; one week somebody had asked her what she smelt of and she'd crisply replied, 'I always wear fresh linen', and Stella hadn't known whether or not that was the name of a perfume.

'Come on, Jasper,' Jan said loudly to her son, pointing to the prototype dinosaur sitting in the middle of the table. 'Now what sort of dinosaur is that? Can you remember? What's that dinosaur's name?'

Jasper, hot and fidgety-looking, mumbled, 'Stegosaurus.'

'There,' Jan said triumphantly, looking round at the others taking their seats. 'He knew it. I knew he would. He's mad about dinosaurs.'

Stella didn't think Jasper looked particularly mad about anything; he just looked a bit fed up, and no wonder, with his mother talking so loudly and crisply in his ear all the time. As far as Stella could make out, these ex-lawyers at Paint&Sing were all married to current lawyers, city lawyers, traders or stockbrokers, but had stopped working themselves and were now – they would say to one another, rolling their eyes – going slowly crazy as a result. She guessed they spoke in this familiar, lazy way with each other as a code or shorthand to express mutual professional astonishment at the turn their lives had taken.

One thing she did know was that they were all rich. They talked of private schools and holidays abroad, of rented homes and flats in London, of cars and of parents who had gone abroad for the 'winter months', of skiing and surfing and of luxury hotel breaks with childcare, of nannies and au pairs. The reason she knew they were rich was not just from their speaking of these things, but from the complacent everyday way they rattled through their choices and options: the sun-filled places, breezy plans, quickly awarded treats and domestic appointments were merely a part of the common detail and fabric of their lives.

Stella listened to them carefully, whilst squeezing out glue or sticking wobbly, fake eyes on a hand-puppet. She could treat it lightly, find them funny or even pity them sometimes because of their efforts to impress. Like they had no foundations. But then she'd find herself thinking about how she wanted a new kitchen, with matching units and a smart countertop – perhaps a granite one, she wasn't fussy, just a countertop that wasn't stained white laminate, where the edging had started to come up by the oven, so that it was coated in kitchen grease that she didn't seem able to get out of the sticking-up plastic, however hard she tried. They'd slightly overstretched themselves on the house as it was, especially as they'd bought it when Zeki had only just started working for the estate agent; he'd got a good deal in his first week – his first week – an amazing deal, given the price of property in the town.

Stella had been nervous about it, had circled this 'deal' with a quiet, questioning uncertainty, but Zeki had insisted that in the end there would be greater 'long-term financial gain' if they took on the mortgage. Zeki had started using phrases such as 'financial gain' as soon as he joined the company, and also 'moderate gain' and 'negative equity' and 'long-term security'. They all seemed empty, hollow phrases to Stella, except for 'long-term security' – she liked that one, though it always made her want to ask, 'What about our short-term security then, what about that?'

Stella wanted the new kitchen, but she most emphatically did not want these women's lives.

'I'm Jan,' Jan said to Stella, as she did every week, every single week without fail. 'I keep forgetting your name.'

'I've told you, it's Stella.' She sounded rude and abrupt, without meaning to. Stella looked down at the mound of grey clay on the board in front of her and passed Jack a miniature rolling pin.

The other four woman at the table talked loudly that morning. They seemed so confident, so purposeful, they had so much to say, their words spilling over each other, interrupting one another. Stella couldn't imagine having that many words in her head to start with – what did they do with them all day? She didn't think her childhood in the town had been full of people like this. It struck her that she didn't think her mother would have given them the time of day when Stella and Marie had been young; she'd have stayed at home, never having to suffer the strangeness that was Paint&Sing. Now Stella thought about it this way she wanted to tell Zeki, to make him understand.

If he would understand. She remembered Zeki sitting at the computer late one night last summer, his back hunched, the look of concentration on his face in the glare of the computer screen.

'Bloody hell!' she'd teased him, looking over his shoulder. 'You're not reading nursery-school Ofsted reports, are you? You'll be wanting to send Jack to Firlands next.'

'Why shouldn't he go to Firlands?' Zeki had looked guilty and defensive, holding a pencil in his hand, a piece of paper on the desk beside him – for notes, she supposed, though it was quite blank.

'His nursery is fine. And you're not sending my son to some poncey private school,' she'd said, assuming he was joking. 'Have you seen those poor kids in their blazers? Jesus, Zeki!'

*

'Stella, where's your baby?' Natasha sat down opposite Stella; she was an enthusiastic and bonny presence at Paint&Sing. A sweet-looking woman with a mess of hair and wide, anxious eyes. 'We never see her. Where is she?'

'In the pram,' Stella answered without looking up. She suspected, in spite of herself, that there was a criticism lurking in the question, nestling down in the blades, ready to pounce.

'God, Jasper never slept as a baby, not at all, not for a single minute,' Jan said. 'The doctor thought it was because he was so intelligent, ahead of himself – you know, his brain whirring all day long. Do you remember how he never used to sleep, Natasha?'

'Yes, which means we've been here for over three years. Hasn't it flown by. Three years in Toy Town!'

'Toy Town?' Stella looked up, a flicker of curiosity opening up inside of her. A shaft of sun from the hall's high-up windows lay across their table and fell into Natasha's lap.

'Where Noddy lives,' Natasha explained, shaking her head and looking fluttery. 'You know, Noddy and Big Ears.' She laughed nervously and changed tack. 'How long have you lived here, Stella?'

Natasha always asked Stella questions, each week, tried to get her involved, but it never felt genuine to Stella, never real. These well-intended attempts to accommodate her in their conversations, to try and manage Stella's presence at the table, resulted in her feeling more left out and awkward. An alien at their table. There was something in Natasha's eager, but polite expression that made Stella feel as if she was being interviewed. Normal people don't ask questions like this, she thought, looking up at Natasha; ordinary people don't interrogate each other.

'All my life,' Stella said, a flush in her cheeks. She picked up the mess that Jack had made on the board and pressed the clay together in her hands. It felt damp and solid, surprisingly slow to yield. 'Let's make the body,' she whispered in Jack's ear.

'Sorry? What was that? What did she say?' Jan demanded.

'She said she has lived here all her life,' the woman seated at the end of the table said, speaking each word with cold measurement. Stella hadn't looked over at her, though she knew who it was: the blonde woman with the pastel cashmere tops and strange, foreign-sounding name.

'Well, that doesn't happen very often nowadays, does it? I mean, the places we've lived: London, Dubai, Brussels, London again. I can't imagine spending my whole life in one place, especially if that place was *here*.' Jan snorted. 'I reached a new provincial low this weekend – I was roped into running a cat show at the village hall.'

'Oh, do shut up, Jan,' the woman with the strange name said. 'Shut the fuck up! We're all in the same boat now, Dubai or no Dubai. We're all here in this church hall making dinosaurs out of clay.'

Jolt. Everyone looked up in surprise, even Stella. Nobody ever spoke like that at Paint&Sing. At Paint&Sing it was all wholefood organic purées for the babies and reading schemes for the school-goers, and how marvellously someone was doing with their numeracy, and how wonderfully someone else was proceeding with potty-training, and whether it would be better to go to Verbier or Méribel this year. Nobody said shut up, nobody ever swore.

'Shut up!' Jasper said, delighted, pointing his cutting knife at the woman at the end of the table. 'She said fuck.'

'Don't point.' Jan lowered the plastic blade with her hand. 'Make the stegosaurus, Jasper,' she said evenly, her eyes trained on the bottom of the table.

'Tacita,' Natasha said nervously, 'you shouldn't swear in front of the children.'

'Oh, for fuck's sake!' Tacita glared at them all. 'Why not? God, doesn't it all just seem a bit bloody endless to you? Is this how you thought your life would be? Here again, in this miserable church hall in the middle of nowhere, making a clay dinosaur? It's just so . . . repetitive. Stella knows what I mean, don't you, Stella?'

Tacita laughed and swept her thick hair back from her face, exposing her brittle jaw and flinty eyes. Stella thought she looked Norwegian or Swedish, pale and demanding, like she ought to be wading through a fjord, plunging her hands into pure, freezing water for fish. Stella wondered whether she was one of Dawn's depressed, popped up on Prozac, walking the lonely streets, miles away from any family, marooned on the side of a pavement, trying to make sense of her new life here, away from the ice and ravines and the clear, bright Norwegian air, pushing her pram under the gabled ends, buying coffee from Starbucks, like it mattered.

Stella realised that everyone was looking at her, expecting an answer. Even Jack. The children were enlivened by this conversation, animated. Natasha's little girl had her elbows on the table, resting her chin on her hands, staring solemnly at Stella with green, almond-shaped eyes. Only Tacita's daughter ignored them, her head down, carefully kneading out little discs of clay with her thumb and lining them up in a neat arc on the board. Stella looked around the table, her stomach tightening.

'No, not really,' she said hesitantly. 'That is, I don't know what you mean. This isn't the middle of nowhere to me — it's home. If you don't like it here, then don't live here.' She shrugged, and then surprised herself by hearing her voice say more. She didn't know where the words were coming from, or even why she was saying them; she could only hear herself speaking out, her words afloat in a pure ribbony thread above the craft table. 'It's not London, but if you think it's better there and, well, that the people are better, then live there. Not everyone is like that. Most people – most *normal* people – don't think like that. Some people are a bit quiet; they like to live quietly, you know, just to try and have a normal, quiet life. Because otherwise there's no point, is there? I mean, everything is so big and difficult nowadays, like with the Internet and all that.'

Stella heard the impatient tapping of Jan's tennis-trained feet on the floor beside her. She found she couldn't bring herself to look at Tacita.

'The Internet?' Jan said with a laugh so explosive, so loud and sudden, it made her chair shake. The whole room looked over at their table, as one, like hippos at a watering hole, briefly stirred by a gunshot.

Stella felt Jack's hand on her thigh, and she looked down at the fan of his tiny shining hand, small arcs of green plasticine lining his fingernails. Looking up, she searched for his face, but it was turned away from her – just one red-hot ear. She had to leave. Was Jack ashamed of her? It was unbearable. The lumpen, unformed dinosaur sat on the block in front of them. Yes, she had to leave, now. She stood up, grabbed Jack's arm and hauled him out of his seat. The air around her felt thick, rippling with surprise at her spoken words.

Jack, thankfully, had been more than happy to leave and had padded after her as she'd almost run past the other tables and chairs towards Mary's pram. Stella had only looked back once, accidentally, because she had to turn and go through the doors backwards, pulling the pram after her. Then she saw her table, her empty chair sitting too far back, abandoned, all their heads down together; she saw Tacita spin round to look at her, and – the horror – saw Tacita stand up as though to come after her.

'Come *on*, Jack,' she implored, urging him out into the sunshine with her.

'Why are we going?'

'Quick.' Stella started to run down the path, thinking she could hear the old wooden door to the hall opening again, terrified to think that Tacita intended to pursue her. She ran around the outside of the church, saw the open door; it seemed the safest, most obvious place to hide.

'In here, Jack, let's go in here.'

Inside the church it was cool, clean and peaceful. Stella's heart hammered, the adrenaline rushed in her body and she needed to concentrate on stopping still by a pillar; she put out a hand to steady herself, terrified that she might carry on running down the aisle, Jack watching as she hurtled the pram into the altar, unable to stop herself fleeing. Instead she wheeled the pram over to the right, where there was a carpet and some toys on the floor below high-arched windows. 'Here, Jack,' she whispered, 'here, Jack, they've got toys – look.'

What if Tacita saw her come in? Stella strained to listen for a footfall outside the church, while Jack quite happily pulled toys out of a cardboard box, and Mary silently slept on. Stella walked down the far aisle towards a small chapel to the left and slipped into a pew behind the screen. She thought she'd bow her head if she did hear Tacita come in; Tacita wouldn't disturb her then, not if she thought Stella was praying.

It was peaceful in the chapel. Stella looked up at the dark wooden vaulted roof and over at the glass panels that separated the chapel from the main church, feeling herself start to calm down, a smooth air easing through her body. Through the panels she could see the watery, sedate colours of the stained-glass window at the far end of the church – all that yellow. The floor beneath her was stone and uneven, and she pressed her feet firmly down. It was very quiet. She concentrated on the painting hanging above the small altar in front of her.

'It's a copy of a Correggio painting,' a voice said behind her. 'It's called *The Day* – picture of maternal bliss, apparently. I bought Pevsner when we moved here. Can you believe I did that?'

Tacita sat down heavily beside her. Stella bowed her head, a little too late; it was obvious she was avoiding eye contact, clear that she was not at prayer. There seemed nothing for it except to keep her head down, like a shamed fool. They sat in silence for a moment. Stella dared to glance to her left and watched Tacita restlessly scratching at her knee with a long, pale fingernail. She thought she recognised the French manicure work: Claire at Nails on the High Street. She wanted to bring this up – talk about that, talk about Claire and whether Tacita had chosen the acrylic or the gel, because Claire usually offered the acrylic when she ought to be recommending the gel, in Stella's opinion.

'They said I upset you. Sorry,' Tacita said eventually. 'Jesus looks more like a little man than a baby, doesn't he? In the painting.'

Stella kept her head down, her hands clasped together in front of her, blushing.

'Are you *praying*?' Tacita peered at her. 'So, did I upset you? It was Jan I wanted to upset.'

'No,' Stella mumbled, sullen with embarrassment. 'I'm sorry. I just wanted to leave.'

'Good. I didn't think I had, but they wanted me to come after you and check you were okay. You're the last person I want to upset at Paint&Sing. In fact, you're the only person I *don't* want to upset at Paint&Sing.'

Stella looked up at her then. Tacita laughed, and shook her head.

'Ignore me. It's nice in here, isn't it?'

Stella allowed herself a small nod.

'Are you shy? You didn't say anything wrong in there. Why did you leave?'

'No, I'm not shy.'

'Good. Does anyone go to church any more? Did you come in here as a little girl? Or maybe you got married here? Did you?' Tacita sounded as though she very much wanted this to be the case.

'No.'

'Me neither – go to church, I mean. It must be nice to feel rooted to a place, like you do.'

'Why do you say that?'

'Well, that's the whole thing, isn't it? Like you said: how to live the good life.'

'Is it?' Stella's enquiry was open and sincere, but Tacita ignored it.

'You were right back there – don't listen to us. We're all on the run, making it up as we go along. It takes some resolve to stay in one place, doesn't it? It's all bollocks anyway, middle-class angsty crap.' She grinned at Stella. 'Definitely not normal.'

Stella smiled back. 'I didn't mean it like that.'

'I know. We're not all against you, Stella, you know that, right? Sometimes I sit at the table and hear us through your ears, and I think you must hate us. I don't mind if you do,' she said, quickly putting her hand on Stella's arm and then withdrawing it again. 'God knows, I hate us.'

'I don't hate any of you,' Stella said quietly. 'Sometimes I think you're different to me, but that's me being stupid. We're all just mums.'

'God, yes, that's true. It's all very playground, this conversation, isn't it?' Tacita drummed her fingernails on the pew in front. 'Motherhood – the great leveller.'

Stella knew Tacita wasn't meaning to be insulting; she looked too far away in herself, too lost. She stared at the fine lines on Tacita's stretched, pale skin, the burn of pressure around her eyes, the nervous flick of her tongue against her lips, and was struck again by how sad she looked. Stella wished they could talk of ordinary things, maybe make each other laugh.

Poor Tacita had been told to follow her, and was now making conversation about being middle-class and crap, and how Stella was right and possibly shy. Stella wasn't entirely sure what it was that Tacita was trying to say, but she sensed it was important. Important to Tacita, to hear the sound of her words in the quiet, light-filled weary air of the church. Stella found, to her surprise, that she liked her being there.

'Lila will wonder where I've got to,' Tacita said quietly, standing up.

'It's okay,' Stella smiled. 'It's okay, honest.'

'Yeah.' Tacita ran her fingers through that blanket of blonde hair, smiling back. 'Storm in the proverbial teacup. Load of women with nothing better to think about, eh? See you then, Stella. Thanks for understanding.'

Stella listened to Tacita's echoey footsteps walking back down the aisle, her shoes clipping on the stone floor, heard her say something to Jack. She waited a minute more, staring again at the painting, then stood up and peered round the entrance to the chapel to check Tacita had gone.

As Stella walked slowly back towards Jack, her mobile rang.

'Stella? It's Joyce here. I've called the police. She's gone, your mum, she's gone.' Joyce's words came excited and fast, hurtling high and low. 'I've called the police, they're coming over, in an hour they say – you'd better get over here.'

Stella stopped, looked up at one of the side windows, at the calm, pure light filling the church.

'Are you there, Stella? Did you hear me? Come to your mum's house. She's gone. Stella? Stella? Stella?'

Washed Up – One Woman Swearing at Her Kitchen Sink

<u>The Project – another post</u>

The way I see it, marriage, conventionally speaking, comes into being the wrong way round. The first thing you do is sign the contract – i.e. get married – and then, once the contract is signed – YOU START TO NEGOTIATE. How crazy is that? Of course, you might live together for a long time before you get married – we didn't – but all the same, things change the moment you are married. Contracts have a way of finalising things, and then both parties start to get itchy.

I read all your comments last night. Was really interested in what Salamander wrote: she said she agreed with the idea of The Project. (A rare voice of approval, guys! Only joking.) And that moving here was indeed our new start, that he must think it was a new start too. That sometimes we don't need to say everything to each other, sometimes it's better to keep the gloves on, be thoughtful, be circumspect – be more like our grandmothers and behave with dignity – a sense of self-worth, at all times.

Nobody needs to keep taking each other apart, hollering and screaming about what they're not getting, what needs aren't being met, what failures are being handed out, day after day. It's tiring. Negotiations have broken down. Return to the original contract. I believe it is more elegant to ignore his affair,

48

skim over it, let it lie, let things be, absorb it within the fabric of our lives, move on, move on, move on.

Hence, The Project was born. A new way of living! I like to think we're writing a New Code of Conduct.

124 comments

The holes in her head

'You took your time.'

'Hello, Auntie.'

Stella levered the pram up the step into her mother's kitchen. Jack, hot and sulky after their walk across town from the church, pushed past her into the kitchen and kicked a chair leg, for want of anything better to do.

When Stella had been younger, she and her sister had played a game of deciding what sort of animal someone they knew might be. Their choice of animals had been limited and prosaic: the girl up the road with the high, pale forehead and thick, electric hair who had been good at skipping (and had the board game Dream Phone, which Marie coveted) was a show pony; a boy in Marie's class was unquestionably a gerbil. There were no tapirs or exotic fish, no variety of African buck; they knew only pets and some of the larger zoo animals, elephants and tigers, and so forth. The game pleased Marie, and Stella had played along with it, hoping to please her too, in the dark of their bedroom or in the back of the car, stuck in traffic, a travel sweet lodged in the roof of her mouth, carefully watching Marie's face screwed up in concentration, kicking the seat in front, leaning her head against the slimy window until she'd whisper, 'Jane Forth? Your year? She's a rabbit.' Stella would nod encouragingly, but without really knowing what it was about Jane Forth that made her a rabbit, but Marie's certainty impressed Stella. She never doubted the precision of Marie's judgement – if Marie thought Jane Forth a rabbit, then she must be one, and it would make no sense for Stella to offer up optimistically, 'Elephant?' instead.

Once, Stella, gripping the sides of her skirt, had asked Marie which animal she thought they were. Marie had laughed, pityingly, and said, 'Well, I know what I am, and I know what you are, Stella. You're a frog.' Marie had settled her beady eyes on her, awaiting a response. Stella had stared back, biting her tongue, not wanting to give Marie the pleasure of feeling her disappointment.

Whenever they played this game Stella would always ask what kind of animal their Auntie Joyce was, because she loved the way Marie would lower her eyelids a little, lick her lips and whisper, 'That woman is a *wolf*, Stella.'

It was so outlandish and scary an idea, so deliciously over-whelming, that every time she asked, and Marie answered, Stella would feel her stomach lurch and her face redden.

*

'The police, the police,' Joyce repeated, dropping her voice a little, 'will be here by midday. Noon. I've had a phone call.'

'A call?' Stella bent over the pram to check that Mary wasn't too hot. She was still asleep.

'I want to watch telly,' Jack said to Joyce.

'He makes it sound like a demand, not a request,' Joyce said, smiling, putting one hand gingerly on his shoulder. 'So like a male.'

Auntie Joyce removed her hand and tucked her top into the elasticated waistband of her summer trousers. Joyce prided herself on her slim figure – and on her seasonally appropriate trousers – the cut of her waist, the length of her legs, her upright, cupped bosom and her flat stomach, her curling, dyed-deep-purple but still buoyant hair. Joyce had never been married, never had children. As far as Stella is concerned, Joyce has had the whole of her life to concentrate on maintaining her figure and fussing over hemlines, though it is from Joyce, her mother's sister, and the maternal line that Stella has inherited her own tall, neat figure; though this is something neither of them acknowledges.

Joyce had always been there, determinedly present in Stella's life: at Christmas, at birthday parties, over a weekend, always patting her hair, self-possessed, never apologetic or overly helpful. Never demure, never knowing her place, or whispering when Stella's father came home, *Should I go now?* More like she'd rear up her head of then-auburn hair, look him in the eye, as though challenging him to ask why she was in his kitchen. He never did, of course. He'd say how pleased he was to see her, and kiss her cheek. She had always been there. They are family, and Stella loves her. Loves and fears her.

Once Joyce had met a man on a holiday in Corfu, and then announced to them all that she was packing up her things and moving to somewhere called Annan in Dumfriesshire to live with him. Stella had sat on the stairs, sucking her fingers, banging the toes of her furry pink slippers anxiously against each other, leaning forward to hear her parents discussing this sudden decision, this shot across the bow. *Annan.* The sound of the place had even sounded alarming to Stella, like someone stuttering, struggling to be coherent, failing to communicate properly. *A-N-NAN*. She could feel her mother's disapproval, which was perhaps what caused Stella to knock her feet against one another so quickly.

'She hardly knows him,' she'd heard her mother say from behind the half-closed lounge door.

And her father replying, good-naturedly, 'Well, he probably doesn't know her either, then. Poor man, he's no idea what he's let himself in for.'

Her mother's patient laughter. Then, 'That's not fair.'

A heavy, brain-splitting silence followed, and Stella, ever watchful, had been able to imagine her mother sitting on the arm of the settee, running a finger across her frown-line and saying, 'I don't think this is going to work, you know.' Stella had just caught her father saying, 'You don't say,' before he'd turned on the television quite loud, so that she hadn't been able to hear a word after that.

Her mother's gloomy prognosis had been correct, as Joyce moved back to her cottage almost exactly a year later. There had been one family visit to see her (and her partner, whose name Stella never knew, as she and Marie had been invited to call him 'The Scot', and so they had) in Annan. It was a four-day stop-off en route to a summer holiday in Galashiels – never visited before or since – and The Scot's house had barely room for them all. Stella and Marie had been told to sleep on the landing on mattresses of newspaper, whilst their parents were detailed to sleep in the armchairs down-stairs in the sitting-room. Stella's parents seemed never to say his name, either, except once when her mother had called him 'Mr Scot' followed by awkward laughter.

It had rained solidly and hopelessly for four whole days. Stella had found Annan a dark and forbidding place. The town's streets seemed always to be empty, the miserable uniformity of the dark-red sandstone buildings so unlike the different-coloured friendly houses of home. She thought it cloudy and cold, impoverished and miserable. In the distance, about three miles from the town, were four huge cooling towers billowing out dark smoke. Auntie Joyce had told her, tightly, that it was a nuclear power station, and then Stella had cried at night, scrunching up the newspaper in her hand, imagining they were all being poisoned during their stay, and because she wanted to go home and not away on holiday in Scotland at all.

The Scot hadn't treated them like family. Stella knew he had disturbed her mother and made her anxious. She'd overheard her mother whispering to Joyce that wouldn't it be better if they went to a B&B, and Joyce saying loudly and angrily that she wouldn't hear of it. On the first night The Scot had left for the pub, after they'd eaten a stodgy, fretful meal, without a word or invitation to any of them, not even her father. Joyce had stood on the step of the house shouting up the darkening street after him, 'Go on then! See if I care. You no-good drunk.'

'*Wolf*,' Marie had whispered in Stella's ear. 'That's a wolf howling, that is.'

After Joyce had returned, Marie and Stella had been instructed never to say a word about The Scot nor to ask Joyce questions about him; it was none of their business. So they hadn't, and it seemed to Stella that year in Joyce's life had been washed away, never acknowledged or referred to, completely eradicated, wiped clean from the collective family memory bank. Though Stella imagined that everyone, individually, privately, must remember all the details and feel sad or thoughtful about them. Particularly the grown-ups, because two weeks after Joyce's return she had accompanied her mother and Joyce to the hospital in Cambridge, and though she hadn't known the exact reason, she'd guessed it was something to do with him, and probably the dark misery of Annan; that her auntie had been punished, or become infected and undone by her impulsive and ambitious departure to that dark place with the no-good drunk boyfriend.

*

'Go put the television on then,' Joyce said to Jack, tenderly kissing his cheek. 'I imagine you know how.'

'What's going on, Auntie?' Stella sat down on a kitchen chair, stretching her heavy, tired legs in front of her. She caught Jack's elbow as he trotted past her, 'Not too loud.'

'Your mother has disappeared, darling,' Joyce said with some determination, turning to flick the kettle on. 'I am going to make us some tea. The police are on their way. When I rang them they were very nice, very interested. My call was immediately logged – they asked a lot of questions.'

Joyce seemed to be trying hard to sound sombre, purposeful and practical, but Stella could feel the frills and trills of barely contained panic in her voice. It was clear in those plain sentences, in the way her lively, neat fingers danced over the kettle and inside the cupboard as she reached for two mugs.

As Stella looked at her aunt's back she tried to process those words, but tired gaps had opened up in her head again. Spreading quickly, shadows over clusters of black, blank spaces emerged, blanketing across her brain, tide-like, gaps big and empty enough for a person to fall through. She blinked and tried to recover herself. The room was silent, the importance and the terror of Joyce's news merely a foggy outline. Stella leant forward, pressing her hands against her eyes.

'It's all rather serious, Stella,' Joyce went on. 'The police took a *verbal risk-assessment*.'

Stella frowned and ran her hands across her face, to give herself comfort. She wished she was still in the church, in the dim subtle light, listening to Tacita.

'I don't understand,' Stella managed. 'Disappeared? Where to?'

'Well, I don't know, do I? If I knew that, then it wouldn't be a disappearance, would it? She'd be in the Lake District.'

'Is she in the Lake District?' Stella watched Joyce pull the kitchen blind up, quickly and abruptly, making the metal end of the cord bang loudly against the windowpane. A hot sheet of midday sun flooded the kitchen, making Stella blink again.

'No, she's not.' Joyce poured water into the mugs. 'You can be infuriatingly slow sometimes, Stella. Where's Marie? I've tried calling her – I called her first actually. She is by far the more quick-witted of the two of you.'

'She's in Florida for two weeks. Getting over things.'

'Florida!' Joyce ran her hands down her legs. 'Of course she is. So like Marie, such an adventurous girl. I've always thought her rather like me in that respect.'

The blare of the television from the sitting-room was loud. Stella wondered if it would wake Mary; she wondered if anything would ever wake Mary.

'Mary's been asleep all morning,' Stella muttered, taking her mug of tea. 'Do you think that's okay?'

'I should think so.' Joyce bent over and looked into the pram. 'Mary, such an old-fashioned name. Mary, Mary, quite contrary.'

Joyce looked from the pram to Stella and back again, a quiet, gentle curiosity shadowed her face.

'Are you okay, Stella? You don't seem to be . . . well, entirely usual.'

'No, I'm okay. Why did you call the police?' Stella sat up straight in her chair, trying hard to concentrate. 'Perhaps she's on holiday, or something? I know where she keeps her suitcase – shall I check? I'm sure there's a good explanation.'

'Of course I checked,' Joyce said quickly, nettled. 'Both suitcases are there, and her clothes too. Everything is here, even her car. I went through it all this morning, before I called the police.' She put one hand on the pram and dropped her voice to a gravelly smoker's whisper. 'I've been calling her for days. Instinct told me, Stella, instinct it was. I had a dream.'

Stella sipped on her tea and waited to feel better. She needed the sugar, and when that kicked in, then she'd be able to join up all these glossy black dots circling in the air before her like lost musical notes. She'd grab the impact of Joyce's news, the relevance of her mother not being in the Lake District, the mystery of Joyce's instincts and dreams. All this would happen in a clean moment of upcoming clarity. The dark fatigue would lift and she would return to the sun-drenched kitchen.

*

Joyce and Stella sat on the kitchen chairs, staring at PC Chambers wipe the crumbs from his mouth and jumper. The sweet, tinny sounds of a cartoon came sailing down the hall from the lounge as they waited for him to fill the silence between them. Stella knew that Joyce wasn't convinced by PC Chambers; she could feel her aunt sharpening beside her. Stella felt sorry for him. She wanted to warn him not to call them 'Ladies' again, to ditch the patronising smile and the easy air with which he had finished his sausage roll ('hope you don't mind, Ladies; I was on refs when I took the call'), to abandon this casual, relaxed business of looking through the papers in his folder. 'If you don't,' she longed to tell him, 'Joyce is going to gobble you up with one big bite.'

'It's a worrying time,' he said to them both, smiling and nodding.

Stella shot a look at her aunt, who was sitting ramrod-straight beside her, a glint of defiance in her eye, as though she sensed she had a fight on her hands. Stella looked at the pastry crumbs on his tie and wondered whether she should tell him about them.

'We'll fill in this Missing Persons form, then I'll take a look around the property. I know this is a worrying time for families,' he said again, flatly, running a finger across his shaving rash. 'Let's see if we can get all this sorted out, pronto.'

'Pronto,' Joyce said the word carefully. She crossed her arms. 'Yes, we are very worried. Do you have many such incidences? Here, in this town?'

Stella bowed her head and started running her hands through her hair, pulling her hair over her face, enjoying its smooth feel between her fingers.

'No,' he had to concede, 'no, not really, not many incidents like this.'

The form was long, and interesting to Joyce; she reached for the answers quickly and promptly, as though it was a test she expected to pass. A couple of times she queried a question, demanding a clearer explanation. Joyce didn't want him gliding over any sections either. When it came to Sexuality, she saw the nib of his biro hover over 'Heterosexual' and she snapped, 'You don't know that. Ask the question.'

'Heterosexual, gay, lesbian, bisexual or transgender?' PC Chambers asked obediently, chewing the end of the pen.

'Heterosexual.'

'Habits or peculiarities?' Chambers's finger pointed to the next question-section.

'Well,' Joyce laughed, 'where to start?'

'What do you mean by that?' Stella said suddenly, the gaps in her head starting to shrink. She flung her curtain of hair off her face. 'What do you mean?'

The air in the kitchen was warm and soupy. Her eyelids were heavy. She stood up and gripped the pram firmly to steady herself.

'What's this form? Where's Mum?'

'When did you last see Mrs Buttle?' Chambers asked loudly, his voice suddenly more authoritative and loud. 'Do you know what her intentions were?'

'To go to the hairdresser on Thursday,' Joyce said firmly, one careful eye on Stella. 'Sit down, Stella. Keep calm. I saw her on Tuesday and we spoke last Wednesday night. We were making plans for this week. We talked, as we usually do. I asked her if she was getting her hair done on Thursday morning, and she said yes.'

'And do you know if she went for that appointment?'

'No, she didn't. I rang to ask them.'

'How was she on Tuesday or during the call? Did she seem upset or frightened? Depressed? Did she give any indication that things weren't normal?'

'No.' Joyce looked suddenly tremulous, her eyes filled with unexpected tears. 'No, none at all. We didn't manage to fix a date for this week, but only because I had commitments. But it was all normal – there was nothing wrong with her.'

'I found her necklace in the paddling pool last Thursday afternoon,' Stella said quietly, looking out of the kitchen window. 'She wasn't here on Thursday; I came by after nursery.'

'You were here on Thursday? Didn't you notice she wasn't here, Stella? For goodness' sake, that was four days ago.'

Stella suddenly remembered herself as a small child standing in the garden between her mother's legs – she couldn't have been more than three or four. It was a hot day, brimming with light, the sky a powdery blank blue, the grass faded and soft beneath her bare feet. The memory seemed to Stella to be bleached by the sun, like a Polaroid that has started to fade.

She is standing between her mother's legs and in front of her is Joyce, holding a round red plastic ball, improbably shiny, like a ball from a storybook. And Joyce is bending over, her mouth a coral-pink, wearing huge sunglasses, and telling Stella to catch the ball – she must catch the ball; she's going to throw it, and Stella must catch it, does she understand? And Marie is over by the flower beds, in pale-blue towelling shorts, jumping up and down. She wants to catch the ball, and then it's flying high through the air towards her, and Stella wants to retreat; she doesn't want the ball, she pulls back further against her mother's bare legs, frightened. She is surprised by the softness of her mother's skin, the shock of flesh; and the next thing she knows, her mother has bent down and caught the ball for her. Her mother bends and looks through her own legs at Stella, holding the ball, her face upside down, calm, a rush of golden hair, her necklace near Stella's nose, twinkling in the sun. 'Got it!' she whispers to Stella, passing the ball to her.

'Jack found her necklace – she never takes it off, you see.' Stella turned to Chambers. 'It was very precious to her. I have been calling her. I was going to come round again tomorrow – I didn't want her to think I was pushy.'

These details were suddenly very important to Stella, she wanted Chambers to understand them.

'Did you see anything unusual when you were here on Thursday, other than the necklace?' Chambers asked, and his voice sounded far away and cloudy. Stella blinked at him.

'No. It was clean, like it is now. It looked like it does now. But it was cool. The ceiling fan was on. The back door unlocked. Her bed wasn't made.'

'And that was unusual?'

'The door was locked when I came by on Saturday,' Joyce said pointedly. 'I don't know why you didn't call the police then, Stella, when you realised she wasn't at her house. No instinct!'

'She might have been at the shops,' Stella flashed back at her. 'I didn't know. I locked it when I left.' Stella tried very hard to focus on Chambers. She couldn't look at her aunt. 'I imagine she makes her bed in the morning, that's all. I should have told you. It's all my fault, isn't it? I should have done something on Thursday. I didn't realise I hadn't.'

Stella suddenly clamped her mouth shut. She was worried those clusters of dark gaps in her head might expand again, like dangerous ink blots, if she said more.

'It's okay. Has she ever done this before?' Chambers said, being kind, nodding at Stella, giving her an encouraging smile. 'Gone off without telling anyone.'

'No.' Stella allowed herself to speak through her fingers, shaking her head at him.

'Yes,' Joyce said. 'Yes, once before.'

'When?' Chambers picked up his pen, pulled his chair closer to the table. 'Is this a habit?'

'No, it's not a *habit*,' Joyce snapped. 'She left once before, when Stella was about six months. She asked me to come and babysit. I came round after work. She said she had things to do in town; she picked up her bag, said thank you and that Marie's tea was in the oven. She said Roy would be back from the printer's by six, and Stella's milk and bottles were on the side, and then she left. She just walked out.'

'How long was she gone for?' Chambers put his pen down again, uncertain whether to add this new evidence.

'I don't know,' Joyce shrugged. 'A month, maybe two? She went to the Lake District. She wanted to be near some water.'

Joyce sighed. She looked down at the kitchen table and ran a finger down the pile of placemats in the centre. It was an oddly gentle and sentimental gesture, as though she were absent-mindedly stroking the strings of a once-loved but long-neglected guitar.

'She rang us, though, when she got there,' Joyce went on quietly. 'Told Roy that she needed some time, and she hoped we didn't mind too much. Said she'd be back, just needed to have some time to herself. That was all. She'd been saving up, setting a little aside from the housekeeping money each week. She walked around Windermere and Coniston Water; she wanted to go up Scafell Pike too, but didn't have the time. She said on the morning she was due to walk up there she woke up and thought she'd like to come back. So she did.'

'You're making this up.' Stella stared at Joyce.

'I am not.'

'Did she have a breakdown?' Chambers asked carefully. 'Was she on medication? You said she wasn't on any kind of medication now, is that right?'

'When was it then?'

'I can't remember, Stella. It was the winter – because she didn't take a warm coat. In the winter: January, February. And since when,' Joyce turned on Chambers, 'did wanting a break from being stuck at home with two small children constitute a breakdown? More like she *started up* than broke down, if you ask me.'

In the winter. Had there been snow? Great drifts of snow across the fields, the lakes frozen: thick, sparkling sheets of ghostly quiet. The ground unkind and hard, a pitiless bitter wind. Stella tried to imagine her mother, out in the elements – what had she looked like back then? – marching about the Lake District, choked with despair, or perhaps it was happiness? More calm and solitary than hopeless? Her arms whirling by her sides, walking without a coat, the blades of frosted grass snapping and crunching under her purposeful feet as she marched forever forward, her chin in the air, around Coniston Water, leaving no trace behind her. Try as she might, Stella couldn't imagine it, she couldn't see it. Her mother wasn't like that, she had never heard her express a need to be near water – why should she say such a thing?

'She didn't expect to get all the way up Scafell Pike,' Joyce went on defensively, glaring at Chambers. 'Just a little way. Does Scafell Pike have foothills?'

Chambers shrugged; he didn't know. Stella wanted to leave the kitchen. She wanted to get away from her aunt and her improbable stories. She wanted to see Jack. He hadn't had any lunch, she'd forgotten to give him lunch. She would leave now, walk down the corridor – nobody would mind.

'I'm going to see Jack,' she said.

As she walked out of the room she could still hear Joyce talking with that defensive, wary tone.

'She's in shock. Stella didn't know, and of course she couldn't remember. There are a lot of things Stella doesn't know. She doesn't want to hear them. In my opinion, she's a bit windy, always has been. Very passive, you know? Very passive girl. If my other niece was here we'd have made some progress by now. But Marie's in Florida on a little trip of her own; she's had troubles too.'

Stella stopped in the corridor, leant her head against the wall, pressing her forehead into the Artex wallpaper. Perhaps Joyce had a point about Chambers. She found herself wishing that a proper detective had come into their house. Oh, she knew what he would be like: world-weary, kindly, capable of great insight; he would bring order and understanding to their lives; he'd carry before him the useful humane knowledge of the experienced and the moral compass of a saint, despite his divorce and drink habits and insomnia. He'd be able to stand up to Joyce, tell her to stop talking so much, and he wouldn't have crumbs on his tie either.

'How do you mean, *too*?' Chambers sounded confused, his voice carrying in soft drifts from the kitchen. 'You said Marie had been having troubles too. Do you mean as well as your sister?' He paused. Stella imagined him looking down again at the form, reaching for it because he felt so panicked and undone. 'I thought you said this disappearance hadn't been triggered by . . . a "family dispute or domestic situation"?'

'Family dispute or domestic situation.' She heard Joyce echo his words, then the scrape of a kitchen chair being pushed backwards and Joyce saying firmly, 'You'll be wanting to do the house-check now, I suppose?'

Blogger

Washed Up – One Woman Swearing at Her Kitchen Sink

The civilised web and its discontents:

I think it might be time to address (again) a couple of issues that keep on coming up in the comments section. Some people seem to be really annoyed at me, and The Project.

1 No, we are not just limping along. I haven't undertaken this blog or The Project to hide away or to ignore an ailing marriage. Far from it. I'm trying to save our marriage. Lots of my regular readers and the other blog writers are trying the same thing too – we're pooling our experiences.

2 Honesty. This is a really hot topic. Lots of people are complaining that I'm being dishonest – they think that only the truth can save the marriage. They might be right, that might be true for their marriage. I don't think it is for mine. Sometimes honesty hurts and the truth can be just as deceptive. What's done is done. I don't think we're going to benefit from discussing it.

3 Anger. Yes, I do get angry. We've discussed handling anger a lot (see Archive).

4 Self-esteem. This isn't because I've got low self-esteem! It's the opposite. I'm using my sense of self-worth to try and preserve what we've got, the family we've built, the life we committed to have together.

And in other news: I got an email from a publisher interested to know about the blog! Someone had told her about it, and she's wondering whether there might be a book in it. A book! Imagine! We'll have written it together. I'll let you know what happens.

It's my book club tonight, so must rush. Thanks so much for all your input and comments to the last post. I don't know what I'd do here without my virtual buddies – you're all wonderful. Let the debate continue!

42 comments

The importance of good deeds

News of Sheila Buttle's disappearance spread across the town, carried by a distinct but indolent autumnal breeze. Along the pavements, across the rooftops, weaving amongst a queue at the butcher's or between two neighbours on a street corner, it spread aimlessly, without purpose, or force, without a headwind. Nothing like a forest fire, no heat or urgency. Stealing through an open bedroom window, whispering around the ankles of parents at the school gates, wafting into the café in the market square, cooling cups of tea. There was a light scattering of leaves and a dampness in the air. It was gently disquieting and unsettling. When people heard the news they wondered what it meant, turned over in their minds how such a thing might happen. They warded off the darker ideas, but the urge to speculate and gossip lingered.

'The truth will come out soon enough,' they said in the end, to reassure one another. 'She was a sensible woman.' They argued for a safe, knowable, hopeful resolution, whilst buttoning up their winter coats. 'It won't be anything bad, you'll see.'

The breeze carries past them, lifts overhead, a faint noise, brushing past the houses and their gabled ends towards the clouds, leaving the fallen leaves behind in the gutter. Then the breeze swoops high above the Market Place and towards the town's museum, around the edges of the colourful houses on Museum Street, circles the castle ruins and gamely sweeps through the museum gates and up the driveway, picking up to a gust. It's bringing a newspaper, pages fluttering, through the doorway, rolling down a narrow corridor and into the museum's kitchen. The newspaper collapses neatly on a counter, waiting to be read; waiting to be seen by someone who could imagine more, who might provide a link, be urged towards action, who might say: *I saw her, I saw this woman.*

*

Theresa, humming, walked into the museum kitchen. She was in a powerfully good mood. She'd spent a very enjoyable and profitable morning in the ceramics storage room, her favourite place in the museum. She was in love with that room. Always had been. On her first morning she'd marched up the drive, swinging a new bag from her shoulder, with a pack of specially bought pens inside, and when the curator showed Theresa up the back stairs, apologising for the lack of space, and into the ceramics storage room located off a tight staircase, she had gasped with pleasure and dropped her bag to the floor.

It was perfect. Perfect and perilous. The room itself was not particularly noteworthy – small and dusty, with one low window showing the museum's car park, a stretch of lawn and the feathery tops of trees in the distance. A narrow workbench had been fitted underneath the window. The whole room was dominated by, and dedicated to, three long wooden free-standing shelving units. Theresa had stepped carefully down the narrow aisles between the shelves, her fingers gripped around one another, peering at the collection. Seeing the fissures running deep in the bone china, their cold smoothness and dusty waitingness, she had felt the luminous quiet of the room against her skin. Each piece had looked so precarious, sitting a little too far forward on the shelf, stilled and delicate, yet solid and cold. The iceberg effect of museums never failed to please Theresa – even this small, local museum – the public galleries being just the tip; and how behind it a great archival mass heaved and creaked, shuddering under its own weight.

'Oh, yes, thank you,' she'd said, beaming, surprising the curator with her ardency, unclenching her hands. 'This is perfect. Terrific!'

And so it had been on that morning too. Theresa had spent some time alone, but then had met the museum's restorer to discuss an old china pipe that needed attention, and also attended a pre-meet for the important Museum Society meeting, which would be discussing their bid later that weekend for lottery funding. She liked the restorer's workshop too, and the education buildings, and of course the never-ending glory of the museum's public galleries.

Theresa flicked on the kettle; she was going to have a quick cup of coffee before heading into town. Only working part-time at the museum meant that she had useful amounts of time on her hands for other things. Which was good, because there were a lot of other things that Theresa liked and wanted to do. She brought this brightness and energy everywhere with her. The kitchen was a mess. Theresa grabbed a cloth and wiped down the spilt milk, returned the coffee jar to the cupboard, swept what looked like dried soup granules into her hand, ran the hot water into the sink, wiped that too, then wrung out the dishcloth and hung it over the tap.

Then she saw the newspaper. Theresa's first thought was that she shouldn't have recognised the photograph staring up at her from the counter. It felt wrong, like hearing a favourite piece of music being played abroad; an obbligato across a souk or a rhapsody out of a teenager's car window. Familiar and yet foreign, in the manner of a disturbingly good dream. Theresa inspected the photograph more closely. It was a sweetly domestic picture – the woman looked happy, full of food, sitting in her home and smiling indulgently at the person behind the camera. Though the smile looked a little put-on, Theresa thought. The woman did look wholesome and grounded, though, very much at home in a cardigan, quite unfitting for the headline, which shouted out above her greying hair in alarmingly tall, black letters: MISSING!

Theresa frowned; she shook her head and turned the page to find *The Reporter*'s job pages. Her eye dropped down the columns advertising for van drivers, catering officers, care assistants – and then she remembered. The woman in the photograph wasn't an old, long-lost memory at all and she wasn't from a dream.

This was the woman who had crossed the market square in front of her that morning, the morning that Theresa had woken up too early, her mind buzzing, and had decided to go for a jog to rid herself of some energy, and to feel the morning air about her. This was the woman who had looked so eager and nervous, who had been walking too fast across the market square in her pale-blue speedy cruise-shoes. She was sure of it. Theresa had watched her, from under the porch of the old town hall, as she ran up and down on the spot.

Theresa read the article quickly:

Police today confirmed that Mrs Sheila Buttle (58) of Harvey Way, Saffron Walden has been reported as a missing person. Mrs Buttle was last seen on Tuesday 28th September by her sister, Ms Joyce Harding, of Great Chesterford. 'We did a spot of shopping in town,' a distressed Joyce told The Reporter *last night, 'and went for a coffee together. She seemed her usual self — chatty, very keen to tell me all about her new grandchild. I can't imagine what has happened to her. This isn't like Sheila.'*

Mrs Buttle's daughter, Stella Robinson, who also lives in Saffron Walden, confirmed to the police that she had visited her mother's house on Thursday afternoon, and that the door was unlocked and her mother was not at home. Her family are said to be very concerned about her welfare.

'She's just a mum,' Stella told us last night. 'My mum. I don't know where she is. We've tried all the hospitals. I hope that someone has seen her. She was in good health — I mean, she's quite sane and only takes pills for her blood pressure.'

Police are asking any witnesses who may have seen Mrs Buttle since last Thursday to please contact them on 01799 458567. The police are not, at present, treating her disappearance as suspicious.

Theresa read the article again twice more. She put both hands down on the newspaper and pressed heavily upon it. Leaning forward, she looked out of the door. The corridor was empty. The kettle boiled.

She had a busy afternoon ahead of her: lunch with Natasha from the book group, an appointment with Evelyn at the Oxfam shop, food shopping to do, returning books to the library, a new notebook to buy for her pargeting project, and any number of telephone calls to be made. That evening she had an Arts Society meeting, and the next day was her book group, and she somehow had to find time to read the final three chapters of their chosen book before then. And she'd offered to bring appropriately themed food for the meeting too – Moroccan to fit the flavour of the novel. So that needed cooking and preparing. What should she do about this photograph?

'You still here?' Neil Bartlett appeared in the doorway of the staff kitchen, smiling at her from inside his salt-and-pepper beard. 'Been tidying up again, have you? What'd we do without you, Theresa?'

'You'd tidy up yourself,' she said, with a laugh.

'One challenge too far for me.' Neil edged past her, to feel the side of the just-boiled kettle. 'Is this hot? Can I have it?'

'Yes, you have it.'

'I like your skirt, Theresa.' Neil said, a little awkwardly. 'Is it new? It's very bright.'

Theresa looked down at her skirt. She favoured unusual clothes, either entirely home-made or reassembled from clothes bought in charity shops. She was drawn to the second- or third-hand, frequently rootling through charity-shop rails, alert for any item that carried even the faintest whiff of theatrical potential. Any item that seemed to be waiting to be reborn or refound. By her. Old-fashioned men's dress-shirts, jackets with a satin lining, a dowdy brown skirt – all these would be hoovered up by Theresa, carried triumphantly home, and then she'd set to work on them. She'd replace the plastic buttons on the jacket with home-made fabric ones, cut an opening in the back of the jacket to make a satin flare, get creative with her scissors on the brown skirt and hem on new jazzy, contrasting panels, make patchwork panels for old coats. It brought her enormous pleasure. Her skirt that day was quite bright, she supposed: turquoise, pink and purple paisley, which she was wearing with orange tights and a pair of vintage green shoes (with gold buckles) that she'd unearthed at a recent fundraising bring-and-buy sale.

'Is it too bright, do you think?'

'No.' Neil poured the water into his mug. 'You're our bird of paradise, Theresa. I need cheering up, I've been upstairs with the ethnographic collection all morning.'

'Neil, I think I recognise someone in the paper.'

'Is it a famous person?' Neil asked in his deliberate monotone, running water in the sink and cleaning out a mug. 'They do reproduce photographs of famous people in the newspaper.'

'No, Neil. It's the local paper. It's this woman who's gone missing. Have you heard about her? It says, "*The police are not, at present, treating her disappearance as suspicious.*" Why not? It sounds suspicious to me – people don't just disappear like that.'

'Where's the coffee?'

'In the cupboard. Do you think I should go to the police?' Theresa folded the newspaper over and creased the page. 'They've given a number, they're asking for witnesses.'

'Crikey.' Neil looked at her. 'Are you sure about this, Theresa? If you don't come back again, I'll know what happened. You've been relocated. You're in the programme.'

He looked at her in a kindly way, with a wry smile.

'Don't be an idiot,' she said, a little tightly, annoyed at his teasing. 'I think I should go and see them.' She picked up the newspaper. 'It might be helpful to their investigation.'

*

When Theresa left the police station she stood on the narrow pavement outside, frowning in the light autumn rain. She was not satisfied, not by a long chalk. Thin raindrops drizzled on her jacket and her hair, insubstantial and light. The rain wasn't really trying.

She hunched up her shoulders against the traffic and the exhaust fumes and decided she had enough time, before meeting Natasha, to walk up towards the Market Place and retrace in her mind exactly what it was that she'd seen over a week ago. Passing the tourist information shop, she headed for the safety and shelter of the large strutted porch, with three stone arches, that stood out in front of the town hall, facing the square and the drinking fountain. Theresa half-closed her eyes and tried hard to cancel out the sight of the parked cars and the old man shuffling down the far pavement, the toddler screaming outside the library, his mother standing patiently in the rain, watching him curl himself around one of the pillars.

She concentrated hard on conjuring her up: the woman from the newspaper photograph walking diagonally across the square from the bank on her right. It wasn't raining; it was a light, bright morning. Theresa was running on the spot, trying to catch her breath. She was right – it was the woman from the newspaper, and Theresa had seen her from exactly this shadowy spot, partly because she was the only other living soul in the square, but also because there had been something about the way she walked and moved, about the expression on her face; she'd looked 'afraid, yet proud' or 'appalled, but majestic'. Theresa wasn't sure exactly what it was, but nonetheless she had felt a connection with her because of it.

This was what she'd tried to impress upon the policeman who had taken her statement.

'Wherever she was going, it was voluntary, but difficult. She was afraid, yet proud. Appalled, but majestic. That's what I'm trying to tell you.'

He had asked her for the time, place and date: the specifics, the knowable facts. She hadn't liked his manner. He was sceptical, she thought, as though she were someone subject to impassioned making-ups and foolish fantasies, the sort of person who might waste police time.

'I work at the museum, you know. I am a professional,' she'd said, because experience had told her that sometimes official types were put off by her clothes. 'This woman was late – that's what I thought. And she was going to meet someone, to get away. She was excited, but afraid. It's difficult to explain.'

'In a nervous state then? Did you see anyone else?'

'I wouldn't say nervous exactly. No, definitely not nervous. I don't think that's the right word at all.'

'And you could tell all this from the way she was walking?'

'Yes.' She nodded, for extra emphasis.

'Right, well, I've logged your statement. Thanks for coming in.'

The rain was easing off now. A woman near her peered out from under the archway and smiled at Theresa, before stepping out into the square. She sensed that her information, beyond the specifics, had not sat comfortably on the policeman's form. Theresa wondered whether she should take this further, exercise herself a little, try to make a difference. She still had the newspaper in her bag; perhaps she should contact the family directly, let them know the how and why of what she saw? She glanced at the badly printed leaflet about an upcoming book sale, inside the locked, wooden noticeboard. That was definitely something to remember.

Theresa checked her watch. Still enough time to go into the tourist information shop and buy the book on pargeting she had been circling for the last couple of weeks. One day, when she had the time, she planned to stand all day on Church Street opposite the Sun Inn and its impressive pargeting and observe how the shapes and tendrils, the effect of the mouldings, changed under different light. She was interested to see what shadows might form, what changes the afternoon sun might bring out on the surface texture. *'Good pargeting has sensuous, textural qualities and allegorical dimensions, and its success is usually related to rhythm, scale and proportion,'* she had read in a book last week. Theresa had been thinking of doing a personal project on pargeting. A research project. She'd been looking for something like that since moving here — something local and unusual, something to capture her interest and perhaps an opportunity, at a later date, to share her work and enthusiasm with other local people. That would be perfect. Marrying the traces of the past with the present.

*

Natasha waved at her across the crowded café.

'I couldn't get a table near the window,' she apologised in a rush, as Theresa came towards her. 'Sorry.'

'Don't be sorry. This table's perfect.' Theresa glanced around as she took off her coat. 'It's much less noisy back here.'

The café was crowded, humid with noise and steamed-up windows, lined with beams on the ceiling and exposed studwork on the walls. It was a cosy, lemon-yellow place with bleached wooden tables and spotlights. Natasha sat opposite, looking a little crumpled, running her hands through her fly-away hair, smiling nervously.

'I love your outfit, Theresa,' she said. 'I wish I could dress like that. You look so . . . well, *free.*'

'Do I? Thank you, I guess.' Theresa smiled at her. 'Do you think it's too bright?'

'No, I don't mean that. You look just how you want to be.' Natasha laughed, self-consciously, and picked up the menus. 'What will you have?'

They both had vegetable soup served with triangles of white bread and butter. Theresa flipped open her notebook.

'So, I thought as the book is set in Morocco, that should be the theme of the evening's food. I was thinking spices — you know, warm and earthy food, fragrant yet comforting. Do you think?'

'Yes,' Natasha nodded, encouragingly. 'Yes, that sounds wonderful.'

'I thought I could do a big tagine.'

'Oh, yes, a tagine.'

'With a cucumber raita.'

'A cucumber raita.'

'Then what do you think to my doing two different couscous dishes as well?' Theresa broke off a bit of bread and dipped it in the soup, then sucked on the soggy crust.

'Well . . .'

'And I thought harira for starters, and a bowl of bessara on the side, with some Moroccan bread.'

'Harira?'

'It's a sort of lentil soup.'

'Right . . .'

'Bessara's made with fava beans. It's a bit like hummus.'

'Oh, I see. Well, it sounds delicious.'

'It does, doesn't it?' Theresa smiled and sat back in her chair, warm with satisfaction.

'Yes, except . . .' Natasha ventured nervously, lowering her spoon, 'it does sound like an awful lot. Are you sure you've got the time? I mean, there's only six of us in the group. Nobody would want you to go to too much trouble.'

'It's no trouble at all.'

Theresa would spend the evening in the kitchen, all pots simmering on the stove, her cookery book perched helpfully and eagerly open on its stand, apron on, filling the house with the beautiful, heady, humming smells of industry. And outside the window the world would tilt to the opposite; it would lean back, as outside the window all would be dark and cold and empty. For Theresa, there was no happiness like the kind of happiness that came from active absorption, the kind that filled up your body and your head, sought out spaces and filled them with a warm, heavy wave of purpose; the kind of happiness that brought its own significant peace.

'I've already soaked the lentils.'

'I don't know where you find the energy. I feel tired all the time, and I haven't even got a job. I'm just at home with the children,' Natasha said, looking deflated and exhausted, as though this lunch were suddenly draining her now too.

'Well, that's tiring, isn't it? Children are tiring. It must be very demanding,' Theresa said quickly, sitting forward and smiling earnestly, giving Natasha her full attention. 'But so worthwhile. You're doing the most important job in the world.'

'Do you think it is the most important job in the world?'

'Of course it is. My goodness. Yes.'

'That's what I like about the book group,' Natasha went on, dreamily, almost talking to herself, looking down at her soup bowl. 'Meeting people like you. The only other people I meet are mothers.'

'Yes.'

'Not that they're not nice – they're all very nice,' she said, apologetically. 'I've made lots of friends at school, then there's the Paint&Sing group, and the music group too.'

'Yes, well, that's good, isn't it? Having lots of people to see.'

Theresa stared straight into Natasha's face, willing her towards happiness.

'Yes, yes. I suppose so.'

'And you've got the book group as well, so that's something for you. Not that I have children, but I can imagine you might need time for yourself too.'

She wanted Natasha to feel the force of her optimism, to feel rooted by her focus. Sometimes Theresa felt that if she stared at someone long enough, and hard enough, if she listened and concentrated fully enough, then she could effect this change. Like taking the clay pipe to the restorer's workshop: the two of them had surveyed the pipe so carefully, with such gentle, forensic attention, that Theresa fancied she saw it plump up a little, correct itself; years of neglect were ameliorated by their attention, their plans for improvement, their thoughtfulness. It seemed to Theresa that everyone benefited from time to time by having a spotlight put on them, a warm spotlight, one that might invite them to dance, to whirl, encourage them towards bravery.

'Yes.' Natasha smiled again, brightening. 'I hadn't thought of it like that. I'm lucky really to be at home with the kids. Most mothers have to go to work.'

'Exactly.' Theresa beamed at her and put her notebook in her bag. 'Look, I've got loads to do. Can I leave the money on the table? Do you mind if I rush off?'

'You've only just got here,' Natasha said, shaking her head, thrown by the sudden change in conversation.

'No time, sadly. See you tomorrow night?'

'Yes. Right. Okay,' Natasha said weakly, watching helplessly as Theresa gathered up her things in a spin of colour. 'Bye, then.'

*

As she crossed the square, heading for Evelyn in the Oxfam shop, the pavements gleamed a dark grey after the rain, smooth and blank. Theresa looked down at her green shoes clipping along the pavement. She walked past a boutique clothes shop, the building society, a gift shop. Here on King Street the shops more than lined the street, the shops *were* the streets: three gift shops, a television and hi-fi outlet, the butcher's, a teddy-bear emporium, three charity shops, seven hairdressers. Like a honeycomb of everything. The street and pavement were quiet, but Theresa's head was noisy. Data streamed through in lists. Mostly it was a whirring of lists, spooling and clicking; like an old-fashioned Teletext printer, reams of paper collapsing in elaborate curls on the floor, filled with tiny black lettering of *things to do*.

When Theresa had told her colleagues at the Horniman Museum in London that she had plans to move, someone (who didn't know Theresa intimately, and hadn't heard of her circumstances) had declared, 'Oh, I wouldn't *choose* to leave London.'

Theresa had thought this limited, unimaginative and incapable of discovery. She didn't think she was like that. She thought it a wonderful opportunity. Which it was.

For Theresa, there had been something pleasantly Victorian about uprooting and descending upon a sleepy market town, deciding to make a new, industrious life for herself. To start anew. To hit Refresh. She'd been grateful for the opportunity; it was so precise and forward-looking, shining with optimism and possibility, that it had made her feel light and free — absurdly, almost fanatically, purposeful. This need, this energy, still bloomed against her skin almost a year later. Because Theresa had never felt the urge to explain to anyone her need for peace and smallness, for navigable places and clean, empty pavements, she'd begun to forget her original thinking too. As though it were, indeed, entirely brought about by a desire for the town.

Evelyn was leaning heavily against the door when Theresa arrived at the Oxfam shop. She had to bang on the glass to get her attention, to persuade Evelyn to move and allow her into the shop. All Theresa could see was the length of her straight shoulders, pressed against the door.

'Are you trying to stop people getting in, or bar them from leaving?' Theresa asked when Evelyn opened the door.

'I was surveying the shop,' Eveylyn replied evenly. She turned back, her eyes narrowed, hands thrust deep in the pockets of her fleece. Theresa joined her, casting her eyes across the clothing rails and piles of clothing, the wall-bracket shelves, the corner of second-hand books, all floodlit by the fluorescent lights above. 'It needs work, Theresa.'

'Yes.'

'Are you daunted?'

'No, Evelyn. I'm dauntless.'

'That's what I thought. That's why I asked you.' Evelyn smiled at Theresa, proud. 'I told the other ladies you're one of life's natural organisers. But where to begin?'

Theresa did not exactly regret offering her time to Evelyn. After all, Evelyn gave of her time very readily to the museum; she was one of an army of volunteers without whom the museum could not function. It relied absolutely on the goodwill, tireless efforts and freely given citizenship of local people such as Evelyn. If there was any fairness in the world (or, failing that, in the town), then it seemed to Theresa that she should give just as freely back. Theresa considered altruism to be a particularly delicate, but necessary, balancing act. Evelyn's needs on one side, hers on the other; between them, if they were thoughtful, they might manage to make needs needless.

Besides, Theresa liked Evelyn and enjoyed her company. She saw in her a fellow-traveller, a woman buoyed up by purpose and effort. In her youth she had been a dancer.

'I was a Tiller Girl, Theresa. Can you believe it?'

Yes, Theresa could. Evelyn was tall and precise in her movements, had long soft fingers and still-slender calves. Her white hair was cut elfin-short, which showed off her high and attractively reddened cheekbones. Theresa considered her to be beautiful, and wondered whether Evelyn had always been beautiful or whether it had descended on her with age, an unexpected gift; she'd become illuminated by her white hair, shining in turtle-neck sweaters rather than fading into the dull, misshapen clothes of later years. It was difficult to imagine her with different, more youthful colouring: had she been blonde or brunette? She must always have been beautiful, Theresa concluded. Tiller Girl Beautiful: long-legged and straight-lined. Though Theresa saw that she had the sort of beauty which adapts with age, moulds and changes. The sort of beauty which endures because it wasn't ever clung to or fixated upon, and so was never arrested at any single point in its development. Evelyn was a constant, clear-running and elegant brook.

Theresa made a tour of the shop, assessing the situation, imagining new and different possibilities. She pulled out a notebook and drew a rough plan. Then she looked in the small back room behind the curtain. She dragged bulky boxes out from behind the curtain to see the size of the room, piling them up beside a basket full of second-hand shoes.

'Don't you find it too quiet here?' Evelyn said from behind the counter. She was watching Theresa's tour with interest. 'I always think you might.'

'No, I don't find it quiet at all. So these shelves could be moved anywhere in the shop?'

'Yes.' Evelyn leant lightly on the counter, her head to one side. She was tasting a thought, letting it rest in her cheeks. Then she put her head to the other side, letting it slip over, rolling this consideration around her mouth – a lemon drop of a thought.

'Met anyone yet?'

'No. I promise you'll be the first one to know.'

'But you'd like to?'

'No, not really.'

'Why not? You won't be young for ever, Theresa.'

'I'm not that young now.'

'How old are you? Twenty-eight?'

'Thirty.'

'You never are.'

'Yes, I are. Evelyn, can we talk about the shop, please? I haven't got long.'

Evelyn had been married three times, and couldn't recommend the condition highly enough. She had not been made cynical by her experiences, far from it: she held each husband in high and affectionate regard; indulgent of their mistakes and flaws, and equally kindly and thoughtful of her own. Theresa deeply admired her lack of bitterness. She thought that perhaps Evelyn's generation was better at life than her own. Evelyn made each doomed relationship sound reasonable and without damage, as though she'd glided through life, never bothering to get caught in the defeating traps of self-pity or victimhood and remorse.

'Well,' she would say, languidly waving a hand in the air. 'What did we know? Ralph and I were children when we met.' Or 'James was a charlatan, a liar through and through,' said with a light, warm laugh. 'I believed all his lies. Lapped them up; I lapped *him* up, I was crazy about him. He was marvellous-looking.' The last husband, 'my golden golfing saviour', had proven himself a stayer until he'd died one night, quite unexpectedly in his sleep. 'Oh, my. I've certainly learnt the power and necessity of devotion. It's quite a discipline.'

'You never want to talk about yourself, Theresa.' Evelyn smiled at her now. 'Now, why is that? You're always whizzing about.'

Sometimes, in moments like this, Theresa had the feeling that she unwittingly and unexpectedly failed in her social engagements. As if they shifted out of her range. What she wanted to give – her time and attention to the shop – was not quite right, something else was required of her.

'I want to talk about the shop, that's why.' Theresa surveyed the children's clothing rack. 'It's a question of storage, isn't it? That's the problem. You've everything so bunched up in here, nobody can see anything.'

'Perhaps you're still nursing a broken heart?'

Theresa turned with surprise towards Evelyn when she said this. Evelyn cupped her chin in her palm and looked encouragingly at her.

'I was the same after James,' Evelyn said, as though that explained everything. 'Nothing disreputable in it, of course.'

'Why do you say that?' she quickly asked Evelyn. 'Why a broken heart?'

Evelyn shrugged her shoulders, and a light kindly smile flickered across her face. 'Just wondered. The old tend to be curious – we've nothing else to do.'

Frowning at Evelyn's words, Theresa was reminded of her friend Kate's visit last weekend. Though it had just happened, Theresa had successfully and methodically shelved the memory of her visit on a dark shelf. Not entirely put away, not ignored; just stored, until she had time to attend to its meaning and work out what to do next. But now the memory, or the fact, had seen its chance and broken for freedom. It came streaking across the donkey-coloured charity-shop carpet, courtesy of Evelyn, dressed up in neon clothing, blowing a whistle, waving its arms in the air, like a crazy saying, 'Look at me! Look at me! Remember what happened. You can't ignore me!'

Theresa felt an uncomfortable hot wave of disorientating confusion blow over her, as though she'd just stumbled across a betrayal. She looked across the shop at Evelyn, still poised behind the counter, looking coolly expectant and peaceful.

Theresa had been looking forward to seeing Kate. Her friends came up less and less often from London one year on. Perhaps she'd stopped asking, or they'd visited, taken a check, seen she was happy, and everyone had got on with their lives. Theresa had enjoyed showing Kate around the town.

'I have to say something,' Kate had said, pouring herself some wine in the kitchen. 'I've decided I just have to.'

What was it Kate had said?

'I'm worried about you, Tee. I never hear from you properly. You're always so busy – it's all activity. Are you happy here? Really?

'The thing is, Tee,' Kate went on, gulping down the wine and looking flushed and out of control. 'It's like you're getting louder and louder. Like on the phone. Even your emails. I'm worried about you.'

What are loud emails? How can anyone send a loud email?

Theresa thought, amazed all over again at the memory of Kate's concern. She had taken it well at the time, she'd listened and laughed.

'Yes, I like it. I'm happy. Why is that so difficult to understand?'

'Oh, Theresa, nobody blames you for anything, you know that, right?' Kate faltered, looking for words. 'Please.'

*

Theresa turned her back on Evelyn now, thinking she'd return to the back storage room and look more carefully at its possibilities, having removed most of the bulky boxes. She wanted to take a moment behind the curtain.

'I'll just take a look in here,' she said, pulling the curtain to one side.

She leant against the wall in the dark back room. What is heartbreak anyway? Her heart wasn't broken. Hearts don't break – they're loose, spongy organs, pumped with blood and air; they don't crack or splinter, shatter. There's no brittleness to a heart, only to bones. Theresa could feel her heart rising up, as though summoned, pumping inside her chest, obediently swelling, to magnificently prove her point. She was alive. It wasn't until recently that she tested her heart's elasticity, challenged it to stretch beyond the normal shape, asked it to assume a strange new dimension. She considered her experience. Before Nic, all of her relationships were best measured by their hopelessness. Often of the sweet, collapsing kind. An air of apology draped over those dates at the cinema or the three-month friendships with sex, which were a mark of her undergraduate romantic life. Even as a teenager she'd been more awkward and polite than passionate, and then in her twenties she'd graduated to a maturity that meant she was capable of being both awkward *and* passionate.

She'd made a fool of herself with one of her MA lecturers; written him a demanding declaration of ardent love and attached it to one of her essays on nineteenth-century ceramic restoration in her second term. Why? And then the thrill when he'd called her into his tiny room and pressed her against the bookcase and told her, 'I could get the sack for this.'

How could she have felt such rapture for him − prematurely grey, and creases pleating the skin around his eyes, a decent but passionless man. But she had, and their affair had lasted for eight weeks and two days, until his wife had found out and she'd wanted to meet Theresa to 'talk it through'. Theresa had refused, been appalled and frightened by the idea. 'But there's nothing to talk through,' she'd whispered during an emergency lunch in the university canteen. 'I don't want to come to some weird sophisticated arrangement. That's a horrible idea. I'm so sorry, it was a stupid mistake, a mess. It's all my fault. Let's forget about it.'

And he'd looked at her over his warm chicken salad, his eyes hardening into impatience and disbelief, and she'd put a quick hand on his cardiganed arm and said with earnest sincerity, 'I'm so sorry. Nobody should ever have to go out with me. I truly believe that.'

She had believed it too, Theresa thought, picking up a bag from the floor and shoving it onto the shelf in front of her with a little too much force. Of course you can read a lot into a quiet or reserved person, put things on them and believe them to be true. Quiet people tend to lend themselves to such projections, she knew that now, they seem to take them without question. Quiet people are very accommodating.

Nic had been quiet too, and grave. The first time Theresa saw

Nic she thought he looked like a graphite pencil – a graphite pencil in tan shoes, standing erect in the Horniman Museum's library, banging his briefcase against the table. He was tall, slim, neat with black hair, the fringe of which he kept stroking across his forehead as he watched her come nearer to him. Nic had made a great show of pulling papers out of his briefcase and arranging them on the desk in front of her.

'What I need to know,' he had said, smiling, 'what I need to see, are the types of flowers and plants growing in this area.'

He had pointed rather elaborately – his long finger poised and direct – at a photocopied map, and his anorak had rustled.

'Is that possible? I'm interested in the flora of the Crimean Peninsula in the nineteenth century. I need access to your identification keys and guides.'

'I don't think we can help,' she said, gently, staring at his finger. 'Our collection is very small, and we don't cover that area. I don't work in natural history, but the curators at the European Herbarium or the Natural History Museum should be able to help.'

'Oh, yes, the herbarium at Kew,' he said slowly. 'I don't work in natural history either; I work in unnatural history.'

It had been a joke, apparently. Theresa hadn't realised; she'd looked at him, puzzled. The conversation had been awkward. Later Nic had said he was attracted to her the moment she'd marched up to him. 'I noticed your legs,' he said. 'And your hair, and of course your clothes.' Which was all very flattering, but surprising; at the time he'd barely looked at her.

'I noticed your hands,' she responded, feeling that she was expected to trade formal compliments. But it had been a lie; she hadn't been attracted to that long, precise finger, though she remembered it, and she also remembered the way he had stroked his fringe across his forehead, his hand flat with two fingers separated, as though he were miming cutting his hair, and she had wondered why he did that.

When Theresa had returned with the contact number he needed, all the papers had been cleared from the desk and Nic was standing awkwardly near the door.

'I'd like to take you for a drink,' he'd said, looking down at his shoes, shy. 'Is that possible, do you think?'

Theresa had looked at his crumpled and pale face and, she would say afterwards, had been both so startled and flattered by his invitation that she had accepted. And fifteen minutes later they were in the sunken beer garden of the nearest pub, a sun-trap with white walls and blue parasols and lines of geraniums in pots.

'Shall I tell you a joke?' Nic said, putting the glasses down on the table and ducking under the parasol, slowly pushing a packet of crisps at her, as though he expected them to be rejected.

That had surprised her too. She'd nodded, moved by his effort, a swish of tender affection getting the better of her.

'So,' he said, 'a priest, an imam and a rabbi walk into a pub. The guy behind the bar says, "What is this – some kind of joke?"'

Theresa had laughed, wanting him to feel successful. She'd allowed her laugh to linger between them, to warm him, to make the telling of the joke an event in itself.

She hadn't noticed in the library, but as that first glass of wine, lifting the roof off her mouth, became the second and then the third, she realised that he was surprisingly sexy. He was sexy, but he hid it, behind nasty trousers and grey polyester shirts ('Church of England shirts' she would call them on their third date). And as the sun faded, they got slowly drunker. As Theresa tried to draw him further out, to entice him towards her, she started to notice his high, demanding cheekbones, girlish grey eyes with long lashes and his very red mouth. When he went to the bar to get more drinks, she'd glanced at his neat hips and bottom, and when he returned she found herself staring greedily at his thin wrists and elegant tapering fingers. The next surprise came when they were kissing on the pavement, wrapped up in the warm night air and the balmy orange shadows of the sodium street light, their delicate, thoughtful mouths a mixture of beer, wine and salt-and-vinegar crisps; when Nic stopped kissing for a moment and said, 'You should know – I don't want children.'

'Okay,' she had said, blinking, her mouth throbbing. 'I'll tell you something too then. My last sort-of-boyfriend left me because he said he just couldn't hack it.'

Nic had surveyed her for a moment, weighing things up in his mind. He'd wanted to let her know that he was a patient, serious man, not drunk or expansive or foolish, but solemn and careful about all important things.

'I think I'll be able to hack it, whatever "it" might be,' he said, finally.

And she'd thought him authentic – that was the word which had occurred to her, her mouth fizzing and throbbing from his surprisingly good kissing; authentic.

*

The back room had a skylight.

Theresa walked over and stood under it for a moment, staring up at the grey sky. But then all Nic's 'other' had been just as authentic. Nic's sacerdotal gravity had given way to, or exposed, a general lowness of mood, a difficulty. Those peculiar two months

90

when he had decided to build a model of the Battle of Inkerman out of plasticine. The initial rush of enthusiasm, poring over websites, ordering the best modelling clay, the clearing of a space on the floor. Theresa had been enthusiastic, stupidly so. Then, slowly, the model had failed to take its proper course or shape. Lines of toy soldiers – small plastic ones, their helmets painted in red, green or blue – had waited patiently in the wings for their landscape to evolve. A hundred dead plastic eyes standing to attention, watching as Nic struggled valiantly, failing to construct the Chernaya River, the Careenage Ravine and Victoria Ridge, the Barrier, the Sandbag Battery out of lumps of clay, like some misguided, untalented, clumsy god.

It had been the opposite of what she'd thought it to be. An undertaking of lively enthusiasm then exposed as an act of desperation. And she was, perhaps, the more desperate for not having known that. Which had led in itself to the time she'd walked into the bathroom and found him curled up and unconscious on the floor. (Why always the excruciating politeness of the bathroom?) Then the rush to hospital, and the talks with the doctors and psychiatric staff, and those long empty yellow afternoons staring out at the car park. She had made her loyalties known during that long, collapsing week.

Theresa blinked; her own act of banishment.

Perhaps showing Kate that blog hadn't helped, she thought now, allowing her mind to take a loop skywards. Theresa had stumbled across Washed Up's blog when googling Saffron Walden. She wanted Kate to be interested too – but Kate hadn't been, she'd wanted to 'chat in the kitchen'. Theresa read the blog compulsively and secretly. It made her cross, and sometimes her crossness filled up the room. She'd shake her head, or run her hands through her hair, grimacing with irritation. Honestly, the defences this woman could marshal to justify her bizarre decisions. It was extraordinary. She'd wanted to talk it through with Kate, because she was a stranger, an outsider. Theresa was worried that if she brought it up with anyone in the town, they might know Washed Up or, even worse, be her.

*

'No, I'm really fine,' she said to Evelyn as she stepped out from behind the curtain and back into the glare of the charity-shop lights. Theresa sounded the words out carefully and, as she bent to pick up one of the boxes, the smell of stale second-handedness enveloped her. 'Absolutely fine.'

'Oh.' Evelyn sounded as though she'd forgotten all about her original question. 'Well, that's good news.'

'I'll have a think about the shop, come up with some strategies.' Theresa straightened herself, wanting to get her cheerful, bright footing back. 'I've got some ideas. We'll sort this out for you — it'll be perfect. Just you wait and see.'

'Terrific. You're an angel.'

Perhaps, Theresa thought as she returned a second box behind the curtain, perhaps recently there had been more ebb than flow. Maybe it was this that Kate had picked up on? As though a tide had pulled back and the world was opening itself. Sometimes, but very rarely, she caught the smell of it, of her own life passing. It had a briny, tinny smell. It was not one she much liked. Perhaps, she thought, sometimes life can just narrow itself without you noticing. You fall asleep, cheek soft on the pillow, the air above you wide and full of great stars, but in the morning a ceiling has been lowered, the air around you is darker, a little damper; horizons might become mislaid or lost. And it might take a while before you noticed. She wouldn't like that to happen. She wouldn't let such a thing happen. Perhaps this was what had happened to that missing woman?

'Did you hear about the local woman who disappeared?' Theresa asked Evelyn after she'd moved the last box back. She took *The Reporter* out of her bag and passed it over the counter. 'She's just gone.'

'Sheila Buttle, yes.' Evelyn nodded, looking down at the photograph. She pressed two fingers into her temple, looking uncharacteristically worried. 'She's a friend of a friend.'

'I don't think the police are doing much about it, you know. I went to see them today, because I saw her on the morning she disappeared. The policeman was very relaxed about it.'

'I don't suppose there's much they can do.'

'There's always something someone can do,' Theresa told her. 'Always.'

'Like the photographs of Sheila with the orange ribbons,' Evelyn said thoughtfully. 'Have you seen them? They're all over town.'

Theresa made her farewells. She needed to do the food shopping next – the library books could wait; then she wanted to get back home, as quickly as she could. She wanted to see the photographs and the orange ribbons. How had she missed them?

After a quick rush through the supermarket, Theresa walked home to the rented house she couldn't afford on South Road, slipped in the door, easing it shut as quietly as she could. She stood in the hallway for a moment, as was her habit, fastened quite still, the hairs on her arms and neck standing upright. She turned into the sitting-room, softly pushing the door closed behind her. She'd cook in half an hour; she'd skip the Arts Society meeting tonight, then she'd be able to read the last three chapters of the book whilst cooking. She had time.

Theresa opened her laptop and typed 'Sheila Buttle' into the search engine.

Washed Up – One Woman Swearing at Her Kitchen Sink

The photograph in my kitchen

It's late at night, the house is empty. I'm looking at this photograph in my kitchen. It's the everything, isn't it? The feeling like a fool, the constant suspicion, the wondering why it's fallen to me to carry the load. I don't know how I got here.

In the photograph, I am standing outside the Reichstag, of all places, in Berlin. I am squinting slightly at the camera, a little coy, tired-looking, but sexy too. My hair is all over my face – it was a windy day. Behind the camera is my then-German boyfriend. Who loved me. He loved me so much and I broke his heart. We had long days in bed – he was a student – and cheap dinners out in cafés at midnight. We fucked a lot. And then I broke his heart. But that photograph, oh, that photograph. I was invincible, perfect, desired, desirable, in charge of my life and in love.

If that girl should show up here now, there would be no end to her scorn. Her wrath. Her fury. And I don't know how I get back to being her. How I navigate through this loss and hurt and confusion. With The Project, I thought I'd stick it all back together again, make it work, be sophisticated, take the long view. But I can't. I can't forgive him. I can't move on. I deserve more. That girl outside the Reichstag with her blowing hair, and hands pushed into Carl's coat pockets, with her keen, alive feeling for life – she can't, either.

24 comments

Why they bought
the wrong house

At Liverpool Street Station a man shouted out Jonathan's name as he was boarding the train. Jonathan chose to ignore him, he wanted to get a seat. A twinge of anxiety set in as he mounted the steps, trying to look as though he were in a world of his own and so therefore – understandably – impervious to friendly cries. It wasn't personal. Jonathan felt a surge of hot anger as he entered the dry, stifling air of the carriage: this rushing for seats was unseemly; it smacked of desperation and was forcing him towards unfriendliness. Why had the stranger shouted out his name? He didn't go around accosting other commuters. He understood the game.

Jonathan wasn't sure how he'd got through that afternoon, nor how he would manage the rest of the day. His head was abuzz with disorientating information. He didn't want to talk to anyone, certainly not some random, nameless commuter.

He found a seat and sat down. Jonathan opened his laptop on the tiny plastic tray in front of him. He took out some earphones, so that everyone would know he was not available for conversation. He closed his eyes. He needed to think about what he would say when he got home, how he would handle everything. Keep control. Be powerful. Contain the problem. He really should turn his laptop on and inspect the damage again, keep reading, but as the train pulled out, his mind turned instead towards the small bottle of whisky he'd bought on his way to the station. Small enough to afford relief, and respectable enough that he could take a swig on the train without needing a cup or glass. Christ, when had life got so fussy and complicated?

The whisky worked; the soft, strong fluid dulled his anxiety. His body began to warm and glow, his thoughts relaxed and lay out under the heat, became flat and unfrightening until finally, with a soft, muddled murmur, they fell asleep. His body and mind floated instead towards extended, soft fantasies.

When the train stopped at Audley End it was dark. The narrow platform was shrouded in inky blackness. Everyone who got off the train kept their heads down and eyes averted. Now they were on home soil, they were too tired to talk to anyone. Other commuters walked towards their cars, but Jonathan had decided, the previous summer, to take up bicycling to the station. A decision he regretted this evening. Feeling clumsily drunk, he snapped his clips onto his trousers and pulled a Day-Glo vest out of his rucksack, then fought to unlock his padlock. He was sad to have left the safe bubble of the train and was in no great hurry to get home.

By the time he had made it up the hill by Audley End House and gone past the high school and town-council building, as he was about to turn down the High Street, where the orange street lamps illuminated the trees, he began to feel better. The pleasures of cycling hit him at this time. The sense of movement and silence rose up within him, the whisky fumes evaporated like smoke as he swerved around the corner into George Street, where the smell from the Chinese restaurant hit him between the eyes. The one advantage to living in the town, not the country, he told himself, was that he could cycle home from the station.

He stopped in the car park, his cheeks flushed, and looked across the common towards his house on the opposite side. The downstairs lights were on: thin, warm rectangles. He wanted to think they were beckoning him home.

'Calling you home. Right now, that's some fucking conflict of interest,' he said out loud.

He let himself into the house and with great care put his rucksack down on the floor and eased the door shut behind him. Beyond the closed sitting-room door he could hear the television, and down the hall he knew Tacita was in the kitchen. The walls of the high-ceilinged hall were painted a turquoise blue. Jonathan stood, wondering what to do. He could creep upstairs with his laptop, but then again, he could go and get a drink.

He went to Tacita in the kitchen. He didn't want to say anything just yet; he wasn't sure what to say, but he wanted to look at her. Just look at her.

Tacita was in the kitchen making tea; she was leaning over the stove, inspecting a gloopy red mixture in the pan. He leant against the door frame, looking at her back, her shoeless feet, her hair coiled up on the back of her head, that familiar roll of fat burgeoning out of her waistband. His heart went soft as he observed her.

He watched her draining the broccoli into the sink, the steam making her screw her eyes up a little, and her hand shook as she tried to hold the colander in place with one hand.

'Hello,' he said.

'You're home.' She gave him a quick smile. 'How was the bike?'

'Still working.'

'You look all flushed.'

'It's my healthy look. Do you want a drink?'

Jonathan opened the fridge and took out a half-full bottle of white wine. He fetched a glass from the cupboard. He wanted a cigarette. He could still feel the rush of cold air on his hair, across his ears, which were now absurdly hot.

He felt weak and hopeless. What could he say to her? It was as though they'd never been married; all that built history, the layering of shared joyful moments and mutual pain, the vast webby, knotty jungle of their relationship could dissolve to dust with one wrong word. They were on the brink. It would only take one sentence and everything might unravel. He looked over at her slender bare wrists; he'd always loved her tight, elegant wrists. He felt a spasm of panic turning inside him. Jonathan drowned the glass of wine in one. He didn't want to feel like this.

'I was just thinking, on the train, that I never wanted this house,' Jonathan heard himself say, pouring himself another generous glass. 'You wanted to live here. I wanted that farmhouse. Not that it matters, of course.'

Tacita slammed the saucepan down on the side, ignoring him, and padded over to the stove to stir the pan of pasta sauce. The cost of doing the house up had risen each month, just as the market value of the house seemed to be teetering on the edge of collapse, in the fluctuating and nervous housing market. It was like a bad index, a fiendish and faulty scale. Jonathan could still feel the taste of new paint like a smack of shame around the edges of his tongue.

'And that estate agent ripped us off. I bet there was no higher offer.' Jonathan took another sip. He was beginning to feel indignant and put out, and therefore perversely more at ease.

Tacita turned around, her face red and sweaty, pushing one hand through her hair.

'What? What are you on about?'

*

How had this happened? Why had he bought the wrong house? The one he didn't want? Tacita, even with her opinions and polished certainties, had – he was certain – been just as keen on the move. Well, perhaps not keen exactly. Jonathan topped up his glass with a shaking hand and watched his wife move across the kitchen on her bare feet to fetch something down from the cupboard. No, not keen. She'd never expressed excitement or pleasure or anticipation about the countryside, but then she'd never really strenuously objected, either. She'd just picked holes, insisted she was being reasonable, objective, disinterested. As though she were the adult, the sensible one.

When Tacita and Jonathan had lived in London, a white house in Fulham with window boxes and shutters, he was the one who had compiled, carefully and lovingly, their shortlist of houses to view each weekend. The idea had been to buy a house in the countryside – as far as Jonathan was concerned, that was the whole reason for the move, the headline act. The area they had settled upon was only a fifty-minute commute straight into Liverpool Street and the City. The nearest town to their farmstead would be a delightful market town with a market square, plenty of shops, a mix of medieval, Tudor and Victorian buildings, a prosperous, quiet place. It might appear quaint, but there was history in that town, and it would give his children a sense of themselves, a context. He wanted his children to grow up properly, not in the city, but in the

100

countryside, like he had. Jonathan wanted to fill up all their lives with good things. A desire that emanated from fear.

Each evening he had sat at the computer in their kitchen and gorged himself on all those country houses, the ones with gardens and lawns, elegant willow trees and pretty front doors, the stretches of lush, grassy acreage, duck ponds of beautiful greenish light, sheds, outbuildings. He would fill himself up with them, his heart racing – a sort of frothing passion, which eventually disturbed him and he'd had to take himself outside to their small, walled, dirty London garden and drink glasses of whisky in a bid to control this dreadful, all-consuming want.

Each house had presented a subtly different story to him – a version of a new, plausible and deeply desirable life – and though his imaginings were always buoyant and pleasantly clichéd, he suspected them also of being foolish and so had hid his lusts and greed, shrouded them in decency, in form and purpose; had drawn up masculine-looking spreadsheets, lists and considerations, had talked confidently about knowing the market and making cost comparisons – this his reassuringly sensible vocabulary. It was a language that kept him afloat too at work, a ruthless rounding-up of useful pragmatic, likely-sounding words to contain the terrifying numberless chaos. Nobody knew anything and nobody was listening. This was why – when his head had been full of the bewitching bucolic visions of his girls in wellington boots playing in long grass, or of Tacita taking them to search for blackberries and then making jam, of him digging a vegetable plot or spending weekends doing capable, physical chores in pale wintry light, such as chopping logs and making bonfires – he had suggested that they view the house which they'd eventually bought. The mistake.

Jonathan glanced at Tacita's back. The kitchen was warm and

bright, she was wearing her pale-blue jumper, and he wanted to pull her close to him, whisper in her ear, remind her of all the happy things, tell her they had a good life. He wanted to preserve it, keep it upright, put his shoulder to the facade, allow their goodness to dominate, not for the scene to darken. He didn't want to think about The Problem. He didn't want to be at fault; she was just as much to blame. They'd both had secret lives – this much he now knew. His head swam with contradictions, and a familiar emptiness clawed open inside him.

*

'Do you remember when we first saw this house?' Jonathan asked, gripping his wine glass tightly. 'That day we saw the houses?'

'Yes,' Tacita answered coolly, 'it was raining.'

'Right. But then it stopped raining.'

'Did it?' Tacita stretched her arms above her head, locking her hands together and yawning, the picture of relaxed insouciance. 'Did you hear about the woman who went missing? She lived in one of those houses behind the school, apparently. Just disappeared. Makes a difference to the usual cat-stuck-in-tree headline, doesn't it? Everyone was talking about it at school yesterday.'

Jonathan stared at Tacita; he suspected her of stalling.

'You wanted to buy this house.' Was he sticking his lower lip out, or just imagining it?

'Oh, and the weirdest thing? I know her daughter – she goes to the Paint&Sing group. She's the girl who ran out that time, do you remember I told you? I followed her into the church? Well, that's the daughter of the missing woman. Small world.'

'I don't remember you telling me that. Perhaps you told someone else that? Perhaps you told lots of other people that.'

'What are you on about?'

'The house, Tacita. You wanted to buy this house – you went after it. You wanted it.'

'We did, yes, we did want it.' She wasn't rising to the bait.

Tacita gave him a thin sorrowful smile and turned back to the stove, standing directly under one of the (many) downlighters they'd put into the kitchen, the light bouncing off her hair, creating a halo.

*

The final shortlist for that heady, fateful Saturday had looked this way: two houses in the market town (first viewings), and both purely for reasons of cost comparison and understanding the market, and then the two countryside properties – one farmhouse (second viewing), a barn conversion (second viewing).

It didn't matter how Tacita had been at the first house, not really – they weren't interested in it, but it was on the market for the same price as the barn conversion and Jonathan had insisted they view it to understand what they might, or might not, be getting for their money: a modern, executive home built in a close near the old castle ruins, hidden behind black gates with a driveway so smooth that it looked polished. Inside it was thick and silent, unfurnished and with white carpets across the whole house, making the interior seem both artificial and blank. The state-of-the-art gadgets confused Jonathan, their bright lights blinking at him from every room, their state of eager, expectant and flashing readiness made him anxious.

'Yes,' the estate agent said frowning at the house details in their glossy folder, sounding and looking like a man from another age. 'Yes, all the mod cons in this one.'

It was still raining during the first viewing and the estate agent wore an over-large sports anorak; drips fell off him onto the floor, and his thin hair was plastered against his head. He had struck Jonathan as an exceptionally tired person. In the monochrome kitchen the agent leant heavily against the island unit and pulled at the edges of his nicotine-stained moustache and said, 'Well, I suppose this must be the kitchen.'

'God, they don't make much of an effort to sell around here, do they?' Tacita whispered to Jonathan, pulling her camel-haired coat tightly around her.

The agent must have heard her, because he quickly shuffled across the kitchen in his soft, damp shoes to show them how the multi-source, multi-room audio access system worked. 'You can listen to different music in the different rooms at the same time, by using this — here — this elegant keypad,' he'd told Jonathan, pointing at a slim blue box on the wall of the kitchen.

'How unsociable,' Tacita said. She rolled her eyes at Jonathan and he'd mouthed 'What?' at her across the gleaming black granite worktops and chrome breakfast stools, while the estate agent had fiddled with the elegant keypad, but to no avail.

'Don't worry,' Jonathan said, tapping him gently on the shoulder. 'I don't think we're interested.'

No, that was acceptable, understandable even. At the barn conversion Tacita had agreed that the headroom was dizzying and the kitchen larger than she'd ever dreamt of having. He'd taken her hand then and said, 'I know. And there's a lot of land here too.' Tacita had reminded him, as they were in the master bedroom, looking inside the built-in wardrobes, that they were worried about the flight path and suggested they wait and see just how bad it was. 'You said it might be a deal-breaker, Jonathan, didn't you? What with the new runway at Stanstead, it's only going to get worse.'

So they'd stood outside at the end of the flat garden, beside the fence to the paddock, waiting for an aeroplane to fly overhead. The owner had stayed in the house, Jonathan painfully aware of her staring at them from the kitchen window, her face pressed with concern, staring up too at the empty white sky, waiting for judgement to be passed. When a plane had eventually appeared on the horizon, its undercarriage clearly visible the closer it came, a dull roar filled up the quiet around them. The plane flew alarmingly low across the skyline, only four fields away. Tacita shook her head at him.

'Nope. That's really noisy.'

'It wasn't that bad. It's not like the ground shook or anything,' he said, knowing it was too loud. Looking up the garden at the baleful home-owner, who smiled back from behind the window, he'd given her the thumbs up, and she returned the gesture wearing a yellow washing-up glove, a huge yellow thumb signalling upwards.

'Why are you doing that? That noise isn't acceptable. We don't want to live on a runaway.'

'Runway,' he said. 'I'm just being nice. I'm putting my thumb up to say, Yes, we saw the aeroplane, not to say, Yes, we'll buy your house.'

'Oh, for God's sake. Let's go.'

This brought them to the house Jonathan wanted. A primrose-yellow farmhouse with exposed, weathered timbers, a thatched roof, a white five-bar gate at the end of the drive, small, characterful lopsided windows and sloping floors, surrounded by hedges and trees, and with full well-tended flower beds — the flower heads drooping from the rain — and even a raised vegetable patch out the back. The works. On their first visit an estate agent had shown them around and Jonathan had tried hard to hide his mounting excitement. This time the owner greeted them and offered them home-made lemonade from her fridge, which had impressed Jonathan and he'd congratulated her on having achieved just the right balance of sweet and sharp.

The owner, Sally, was a small, unnaturally thin woman, whose head was too big for her body, with bleached blonde hair and a suntan. She wore immaculate white linen trousers, a floating kaftan top in soft, muted colours and fluffy mules of the sort Jonathan did not want to see in a farmhouse. Sally told Tacita that she was getting divorced and needed to sell in a hurry. Tacita looked Sally up and down carefully during this exchange, standing in the country kitchen with one eye on the green-and-white gingham curtains hanging prettily at the windows.

'I'm sorry to hear that.' Tacita had been polite.

'Oh, no, I'm not sad at all,' Sally told her, kicking one leg behind her coquettishly.

This was news. Jonathan didn't want to buy an unhappy house. He put his lemonade down quite quickly after that revelation and set off alone to wander from room to room, trying to work out whether it was an unhappy house. It hadn't seemed so on his last visit. Now he worried about whether their marital break-up might have infected the beams and wooden floors, sneaked into the deeply set windows or might be found lurking in the pretty sitting-room with its fireplace and long French windows into the garden. Upstairs, under the thatch, he wandered into the master bedroom and leant on the ticking stripe window-seat cushion and looked out of the little window at the wet, pale-blue wisteria flowers bobbing against the pane, and then behind them at the expanse of green lawn below. It looked soft and yielding, sparkling from the rain. He couldn't see that this was an unhappy house; it seemed perfect, impossibly perfect. There was a spare room, and the two children's rooms were painted white, uncluttered, with brass bedsteads and tasteful eider-downs. When we buy this house, he'd thought, I'm going to get beds like these for May and Lila.

Jonathan walked around the garden, sinking his wet shoes in the perfectly cut grass, seeing and imagining his family growing there; in the small barn to the side of the house they could have a ping-pong table, perhaps a teenage den in years to come; and, hanging from that tree, a swing. There was plenty of room for the climbing frame he wanted to buy his daughters, room even for a swimming pool, and they could keep chickens out the front. He'd stood outside and looked seriously at the back of the house, the long wind of wisteria and the proud, thick brick chimneystacks, and his heart had grown and he'd had to concentrate on not smiling too much when he'd returned to find Sally and Tacita.

They'd thanked Sally, and he had ducked out the front door and walked to the car, waiting for Tacita to climb in beside him, a spiral-ling knot of excitement and pleasure in his stomach. They'd driven towards and through the white gate and across the ford, out into the lane, without saying a word – a ford! fishing nets! – and then purred slowly away, banked on either side by high wheat fields. This was when Tacita had started to be difficult.

'You love it,' Tacita said eventually, putting down her window. 'It is very you, very cosy.'

Jonathan concentrated on the road ahead.

'The garden's really big,' he said evenly, not daring to look at her.

'Perhaps, but the rooms are too small and too dark. I hated the inglenook fireplace, it took up half the room and, besides, they're naff. The thatch is dusty — the insurance on that will be a nightmare. Sally said that birds nest in the thatch, and so do mice. The mice come in *off the fields*, Jonathan.'

'Tacita—' he started to say.

'There was no storage space. It'd be a nightmare — God knows where she's put everything. I could hardly stand up in the bathroom; those sloping floors made me feel like I was drunk or had an inner-ear infection. There's damp in the larder cupboard too, a huge green stain all around the bottom. Sally says it comes from a natural well — she says the kitchen, utility room, larder and that back room all need damp-coursing because they're slightly below ground.'

'She doesn't seem very keen to sell her house,' Jonathan said sulkily, irritated with the birdy blonde woman in her clean trousers and fluffy kitten-heeled slippers, so keen to throw off her husband. He imagined that she probably listed her ex-husband's failings with the same candour and glee as she did her house's, ticking them off on her manicured fingers: poor personal hygiene, never fixed the leaking tap, overly interested in cricket, poor attitude towards family engagements, dirty shoes, rings his mother every week — yes, every week. 'Old houses are like that. I feel sorry for her children, with them getting divorced. They had such pretty bedrooms,' he said.

They'd stopped for lunch in a village. The pub had black weatherboarding on the outside and hanging baskets of pink and purple flowers, which under the heavy grey clouds gave it a bruised appearance. Inside it had smelt stale, and when they'd crossed the beer-soaked carpet and asked to see the bar menu, the barmaid had shrugged and said, 'We do sandwiches.' It was as dark and quiet in the pub as Tacita's mood.

'God,' she said, sipping on her warm vodka and tonic. 'It's very Essex in here, isn't it?'

Which had brought them to the final house – the one they had bought. Jonathan had nearly cancelled the appointment.

'I think there's still something to be said for Sally's house,' he'd insisted cheerfully, making notes on his BlackBerry. 'Let's not say "No" – we'll think about it. Shall we cancel the next town house? We don't need to see it. The agent said another farmhouse was coming on the market next week, and he thinks it might be right up our street. That's what he said.'

'No,' she'd said forcefully, surprising him. 'No, I want to see it.'

The house needed a lot of work. The woman who was selling it – a Mrs Hollis, who had sat stuffed-owl-like in the front room during their tour with the estate agent, with the door left open – told Jonathan that she'd lived there for forty years. Jonathan had thought the house was like a cave, large and dark with a hinterland he didn't much want to explore.

The house looked over the common, which lay to the east of the market square and below the castle ruins; it was tall, square, red-brick and imposing, with a high sweeping serpentine roof. To the front was the wide, attractive common, tree-lined at the top, and with a small playground in the near-left corner. They had parked in the market square and walked through the small, red-brick precinct that sat between the Market Place and the common, passing an interiors shop, a children's shoe shop and a coffee shop, until they were out on the broad, green expanse of the common.

'I like it, it's got a proper roof,' Tacita said, stopping on the path to admire the house ahead of them. 'It looks like a merchant's house, doesn't it? It looks important.'

They'd walked past groups of teenagers sitting out on the grass, their shopping bags laid out around them like flower petals. The sun had been shining, all the rain clouds banished; coming across a turf maze cut into the grass, with a labyrinth of narrow paths laid in brick, Jonathan had loped down the small mound to find the start of the maze.

'How amazing,' he joked, but the paths had been too narrow for him and he'd had trouble balancing. 'It makes you quite dizzy,' he shouted up to Tacita. 'I feel odd.'

'You're going the wrong way – the paths just wind in on themselves.'

The kitchen was a deep soupy green, with ancient collapsing Formica units, and the hall and landings were wallpapered in a dark-blue paper cut through with green and gold dashes; the whole effect made Jonathan feel as though he had gone underwater, or was stuck in a marshy landscape, caught and abandoned in the reeds. Upstairs the attic rooms were empty, but covered in stickers and posters, and odd parts of this family's life had been abandoned on the floor: a travel brochure, a yellowing newspaper article that somebody had cut out in 1994, a child's vest.

'I like it,' Tacita had whispered happily to him on the stairs. 'It's very trad.'

'I don't like this wallpaper,' he'd replied grumpily. 'It's awful.'

'Well, we'll take it down, won't we? It won't be here. You've got to look at the house and imagine how it will be – not how it is now, you idiot.'

But Jonathan had done too much imagining at his kitchen table already; he'd imagined escape. Roaring wood fires (and a wood shed), rolling lawns and uneven stone steps. Autumn afternoons in the garden, wild running down a country lane with his daughters, healthy cheeks and icy toes. He had no room or will for imagining how this imposing, draughty, high-ceilinged town house might be turned into his home.

*

Up until that Friday night, watching Tacita meticulously measuring out dried pasta on the scales, and then carefully dropping it piece by piece into the boiling water, he had assumed that buying this house had been a mutual undertaking. It had happened without much design, had been a notion that had gathered a silent, rolling force and become a plan – he had found himself already halfway along the path, pushing back the brambles, looking for the way ahead, fighting through the undergrowth, and it wasn't until he had arrived triumphantly at the end, torn and raggedy, punching the air, that he'd realised he'd never wanted to be on that path in the first place. Jonathan looked over at Tacita. Was it possible that she had insisted they buy this house entirely, and only, to spite him? He now knew that she had her own agenda.

'We should go in and say goodbye to Mrs Hollis,' the agent had whispered to them in the hall. 'It'd be polite,' he'd added as an afterthought.

They had dutifully filed into the sitting-room where Mrs Hollis was sitting in an old frayed armchair. Behind her a large window showed a full view of the common, but the air in the room had been thick, dusty and still. The carpet had patches of bleached rectangles in front of the window. Jonathan thought this room, where presumably Mrs Hollis did most of her living, looked as abandoned as the rest of the house – the armchairs, the patchy carpet, the high, dusty, yellowing ceiling with its cornicing and huge, almost ugly ceiling rose and the small bookcase to one side of the fireplace all looked spent, as though the family that had torn through the attic rooms shedding vests and newspaper articles, and that had kicked against the Formica units and swum up the stairs, had simply eaten the place up, leaving nothing of itself behind. Except Mrs Hollis, who had stood up stiffly as they'd come in, a woman who met their eyes without humour or the pretence of politeness. Jonathan thought she might be one of those old women who have shrunk with age and are surprised to find themselves now so small, stooped and remote from where once they governed.

'Thought we'd pop in to say goodbye, Mrs Hollis,' the agent had said, walking over to speak clearly into her left ear. 'Thank you for letting us in this afternoon.'

The agent had impressed Jonathan; he'd been courteous, easily so, not showy or fake at all. Mrs Hollis had pursed her lips a little and flared her nostrils at him.

'All part of the process, Zeki,' she had said from behind her thick glasses. 'Mr Harbutt couldn't make it today?'

'No, but he asked me to give you his best regards, Mrs Hollis.'

'He says you are married to Sheila Buttle's girl, is that right?' she went on imperiously, ignoring Jonathan and Tacita, who stood side by side, their hands behind their backs, being polite.

'Yes, that's right – Stella.'

'She used to clean for me, ages ago. Pass on my best, won't you?' Mrs Hollis had removed her spectacles and polished them on the sleeve of her cardigan. 'Did you like the house?' she asked, looking at Jonathan, blinking slightly without her glasses, her eyes looking surprisingly bright and vulnerable, a slight wobble to her voice. 'Too big for you, I expect?'

'No, it's a fine house,' he'd said, uncomfortably aware of Tacita beside him. He could sense her fixed, charmed smile without having to see it.

'Are you local?' Mrs Hollis moved stiffly over towards the fireplace.

'No, we're from London,' Tacita said smoothly.

'Oh dear.' Mrs Hollis had looked disappointed and resigned. 'Oh dear. Do you have any children?'

'Yes,' Jonathan said brightly, puffing his chest out a little, grateful at not having to disappoint her further. 'Two girls.'

'Two girls? Well, that's something, I suppose. I had all my children in this house – six of them, all born and brought up in this house. They are all over the world now, of course. It's a family house, isn't it, Zeki?'

'Yes, very much so, Mrs Hollis.'

'I think so too,' Tacita said cheerfully, 'it really is. I like your house very much, Mrs Hollis.'

'She was odd,' Jonathan said, as they'd walked back across the common. 'Didn't you think? Creepy house too.'

'It wasn't that creepy.'

They'd walked in silence back through the precinct and out into the market square. The sun had been shining brightly by then, and Tacita had looked about her with a new sense of interest. Jonathan had watched her pale-blue eyes alight on the library, then the meeting hall, the department store, and gaze dispassionately down the street in front of them as though making calculations, frowning a little. They'd been standing next to the large stone drinking fountain in the centre of the square, close to their car.

'It's very sweet here,' Tacita said. He'd thought her voice a bit artificial, as though she were practising for something. 'Don't you think?'

'Yes,' he replied absent-mindedly, searching in his pockets for the car keys. 'Do you want a coffee before we head off?'

'How much is that house on for?' Tacita made an unnatural movement, leaning across the space between them to place her fingers lightly on his arm. 'Shall we go to the estate-agent offices now? Make an offer?'

'Hang on,' Jonathan had laughed, 'what about the farmhouse?' He'd tried to sound confident and easy, as though he were enjoying himself.

Tacita had stepped closer to him, still smiling. 'Well, this *is* the countryside, isn't it? Won't harm to have the conversation. Just a quick chat? Please?'

'Okay, but just a chat.' It had been curious to see her happy, for the first time that day, that week – for a very long time.

'Agreed,' she'd said, holding her hand out to him, looking flirtatious and like her old self.

And then they'd shaken on it, right next to the old market cross, like traders of old, striking a bargain, their word as good and solid as the stone in front of them.

That 'chat' had become an offer, just to test the waters, and because Tacita hadn't wanted them to lose the option of buying the house, and didn't her opinion matter? Zeki had told them there was a lot of interest in the property – all the developers were after it; it hadn't been on the market for forty years. He'd winced a little at Jonathan's original offer, haltingly proposed; had held his hands up and shrugged. 'I can put that to Mrs Hollis, but it's not near what we've had so far.'

So then the anxiety had set in, a competitiveness, with Tacita urging from the sidelines that they should at least be keeping themselves in the picture, and wasn't it a great investment anyway? Perhaps Jonathan should look at it that way – they could buy it, do it up, make a mint and then sell it on. They'd already agreed that she'd have to leave her part-time job for the move, because it wouldn't be practical with him commuting to the City every day – and so she'd need something to do all day, wouldn't she? The house could be a project. Slowly it had gathered weight in their lives; it was to be a home, a job for Tacita and a great investment opportunity, so when their offer had been accepted and Tacita had opened the champagne, Jonathan had drunk along with her. And then when Zeki had called them and said they'd been gazumped, that Mrs Hollis wasn't getting any younger, and he was sorry, but she just wanted the highest amount she could get; when Tacita had thrown the crockery about the kitchen in frustration and burst into tears – well, then he'd rung the mortgage company, tried to anticipate what bonus he might get that year, and returned with a new and higher offer. Then the house had, finally, been theirs.

Two years later and the renovations were complete. Tacita had undertaken them with a certain boot-faced determination, not enjoying the project as much as he thought she would. She'd said, with a heavy sigh, flicking through her folder marked 'House', that it had proven to be an 'onerous responsibility'. However, she had brought the house out of its dark ages, had reimagined it, renarrated a history with new romantic and yet historically authentic touches.

Jonathan glared across the kitchen at Tacita's back. She'd insisted they buy this house because she hadn't wanted him to get what he wanted. Out of spite. His head rang with frozen silence. She turned around and stared back at him.

'What?' she said. 'Why are you staring at me like that? Don't forget that you've got that Museum Society meeting tomorrow night. You promised Mrs Bird you'd go. For God's sake, don't let her down.'

Washed Up – One Woman Swearing at Her Kitchen Sink

The photograph in my kitchen #2

Sorry about that last post. I don't know what got into me! Just tired, I suppose. If anything, it makes me realise what a huge idea The Project is, what an amazing thing to pull off. It really is a Big Ask.

EvelynW has sent me a book (for which many thanks) together with a tin of muffins (for which even more thanks, they were delicious) to cheer me up and to remind me what The Project is all about. This is an interesting book. It's called SURVIVING INFIDELITY: THE QUIET WAY. Quite similar to The Project, I suppose. Though I never thought of myself as a quiet person, as such. I'll read on and let you know my thoughts.

45 comments

Such delicate structures

Zeki wanted to sit a little longer in his car. He was enjoying the quiet. The afternoon light was thin, the sky white, a damp chill in the air. Autumn was finally on its way, throwing tendrils of cool wind and sharp ending notes into the back of summer. He was grateful to be in this in-between place, not at home, at the office or at an appointment. Sitting in his car felt like a quiet dent in the day, a small hollow of dusty peace, though within his manufactured silence – a silence sliced with the strong smell of pine disinfectant coming from the car freshener – he could hear, and feel, his private worries and concerns, fracturing and splintering inside him, sounding like the shifting creak of heavy ice about to thaw and collapse.

Images of his mother-in-law had sprung up all over the town. He, Stella and Joyce had produced quite a number of flyers themselves, and had bought plastic envelopes to put them in. He knew exactly which ones they were responsible for, as he had first sought permission and then put them up himself: in the newsagent's windows, at the Friends' Meeting House, the entrance to the library, outside the police station, on the community noticeboard at the supermarket, the one outside the old town hall. But now new flyers had appeared. He'd seen the first one walking to work two days ago. It was tied, by a bright-orange ribbon, to a lamp-post on the High Street, and because the ribbon had been flapping in the wind it had caught his eye. He'd stopped, touched the satiny ribbon and peered at the picture. It was a different photograph from the one they had released, which had been used on their posters and in the newspaper, and flashed up once on the local news. Zeki hadn't recognised this photograph.

'FIND SHEILA BUTTLE!' the flyer read in large letters, and there below was a picture of Sheila, laughing into the camera, one hand up in her hair. She appeared to be in the face of a big wind, her hair flying about, the corners of her anorak turned up under her chin. She had an exultant expression of shock and pleasure – she looked youthful and free. Though, on closer inspection, he could see it was a current photograph, for her face was still creased with age, fine veins on her forehead, soft, fallen crêpey cheeks, the same hair. Her face had looked odd wrapped around the pole. Below the photograph, in smaller type, was written: *They say Sheila is missing. If you've seen her, you could contact the police.*

It wasn't an official notice; there was no telephone number, no police symbol. Zeki had stood back, frowning and, gazing down the High Street ahead of him, had seen four or five (maybe more) lamp-posts with the same neon streak of orange stretching away. Who was putting them up? He had been disturbed by the photographs, but Joyce had said, when he'd rung her that night, that she was sure it was an example of the town's concern, their feeling of civic responsibility towards Sheila. She'd said it was a demonstration of neighbourly concern. Still, he'd wanted to know, where did they get that photograph from? Where was she in that photograph, standing in the big wind? Didn't Joyce consider the call to 'Find Sheila Buttle!' a little irreverent, and what about 'They say', what did that mean: 'They say Sheila is missing'? Like it was a game. Or a lie. What was the significance of the orange ribbons – did she know? Joyce had sighed; no, she didn't know, she didn't much care – what did it matter? They needed all the help they could get.

*

Zeki cracked his little finger and checked the time on the car's display panel. He had another five minutes until his appointment. He looked out of the window at the semicircle of low bungalows behind neat hedges in front of him. The narrow pavement around the close was empty; a few tin cans lay on the grass verge, a lump of earth next to them. Someone must have taken a kick at the cans and missed, catching a clump of turf instead, which must, Zeki considered, have been a pretty pointless few minutes in someone's life.

Zeki pulled the orange ribbon he'd taken off the lamp-post out of his pocket and absent-mindedly ran it through his fingers. Sheila. Where was she? He wanted her back. He wished there was more he could do. He was trying to help, support Stella; he was the one who had called Marie, he'd done the notices at work, spread the word around town. He sucked on the end of the ribbon, remembering a conversation with Sheila about six months ago. It had been just the two of them in her kitchen, one Saturday morning.

'Your mother, Zeki,' Sheila had said, leaning back in her chair. 'She left, isn't that what you said? She left you and your dad, when you were four years old.'

'Yeah, she did.'

'And she never got in touch, is that right?'

'That's right.'

'Did she go back to Turkey?'

'We don't know.'

He'd answered her questions politely, truthfully and obediently; it had been the least he could do in the circumstances; he'd have answered any question she'd had right then. Sheila, he remembers, had looked up at him with an expression that he now wishes he'd tried harder to understand. At the time he'd been hovering above her, wanting to leave, but trying very hard not to give that impression, folding the cheque she had just written out to him in half, and then in half again, as an act of respect, wanting to hide away the numbers.

'I gave you my breakdown for the repayments didn't I?' he'd said, knowing full well he had. Knowing that he had copied it out twice for neatness's sake, used a ruler to draw the columns in pencil, filled in those columns to show his proposed repayment plans, week by week, month by month. Knowing that he had done all this with painstaking care, and that his dedication was perversely correlated to the frank impossibility of ever managing to meet those carefully inked-out repayment plans.

'You did.' Sheila snapped the lid back on her pen. And then said, 'My mother did the same thing. Just so we know where we all stand.'

He wanted to leave. 'Your mum left you?'

'Yes.' Sheila looked out of the window. 'Very unreliable.'

'You're reliable,' he'd said quickly, blushing. 'I think you are.'

'I miss Roy.' It was as though she hadn't heard him.

'Stella misses him too.'

'I wish you'd met him. You'd have got on. Do you miss your dad?'

'Sometimes. He wasn't all that reliable, if I'm honest.'

'Reliable.' Sheila said the word quietly to herself. 'Who's to say?'

Her question had caught him off-guard, and he hadn't understood it, so he'd just shrugged and wondered when she'd be done with him. It embarrassed him now to remember how inattentive he'd been.

'It's up to you whether you tell Stella about the loan or not,' Sheila said suddenly, turning back towards him. 'It's not my business. I won't interfere with a marriage, Zeki.'

'Well, thank you, thank you for that, Sheila. Thanks. I won't let you down.'

That was the thing with Sheila, she didn't try to hold anything over you. He loved her for that calmly maintained distance; she never wanted to know too much, she would just take what came. Zeki put the ignition on, and turned on the radio, then turned it off again. He wondered whether that conversation hadn't been important to her disappearance in some way, and whether he should mention it to Stella, but then he'd have to tell her about the money too. A quick, unexpected rush of rage blew through him and out the other side. The thing with missing people, he thought, is what they take away with them from you. How they expose you, make too much space in your life, make everything vulnerable. He pressed the button to put down the electric window, and pressed it to go up again. That wasn't right; Sheila was a good woman, the best, and she had never asked him for the repayments.

*

When Zeki first met Stella, and then afterwards her family, he hadn't been able to believe in them.

He'd been with his mates, doped up and stupid – Ecstasy or

cocaine, he couldn't remember, both probably – and they'd driven up the M11 from the East End, not knowing where they were going, as wide-eyed as the yellow lights of the car filling up the big, dark, empty stretch of motorway. Looking for 'Essex girls', that's what they'd said, like it was an adventure or a safari holiday. Zeki couldn't remember whose idea it had been. They were going to have a good time. They were going to sleep in the car. He'd been flying, feeling dangerous; they'd thought they were being funny going to that nightclub in Harlow, on a spree, escaping something – something which, at that point, he couldn't stand any more.

It couldn't have been less romantic, given the state he'd been in, but when he saw Stella sitting upright on a tiny stool in the nightclub, nursing her single glass of white wine, looking solemn and out of place, running her fingers through her hair, and she'd looked straight back at him through the dark, searching his face with her soft eyes, he'd felt something in him solidify. Whatever inside him was liquid and useless, everything that was messy, inconsistent and sloppy, became stilled, and then solid. He remembered how hard he'd tried to appear sober and reliable – that was a first – and to make serious conversation with this pale, self-possessed girl who didn't dance, and who refused his offer of more drinks and barely smiled. She'd been difficult to read, and it had unnerved him, made his palms sweat. She hadn't indicated that she wanted him to leave her alone, but then she hadn't exactly encouraged him to stay at her table, either. The trip hadn't seemed fun any more. But, despite the sweaty nerves, he'd begun to feel a kind of generosity in her ambivalence; as if she was leaving space for him all the time. So when she stood up to leave with her friends, he'd run after her and asked for her number, his voice sounding odd in the quiet of the corridor after the noise of the club. Then he'd had the urge to do something formal, so Zeki had offered her his hand to shake. That's what he'd done, in the narrow corridor of the club, aware of her friends' mouths all bunched up in an effort not to laugh, and Stella had looked him straight in the eye, smiled and taken his hand.

Then, the slow, courteous courtship that followed, which had been a new development for him too. It had been unreal: the long drives up the M11 every weekend to visit her, perching on the edge of her mother's settee, smiling out of the corners of his mouth and drinking it all in. The house was so clean, the mother and daughter. Such a feminine house; he'd found it heady. The smell of comfort and cleanliness, the central heating, all that hair. Mothers and daughters in slippers and clean matching socks. Sometimes Marie was there ironing behind the settee, laughing at the television and shaking out blouses and hanging them on the sideboard. Joyce making them cheese sandwiches — white bread, thick smears of soft butter, small grey plates with a blue trim. The clean carpets and matching furniture. Zeki supposed this was what most people took for granted. He had found it powerfully seductive and bewildering; he couldn't get enough of them. Like he was always five steps behind. Whiling his weeks away in dead, empty space until he could see Stella again at the weekends. Sometimes he'd felt like laughing out loud.

Stella and he had taken walks around the town, down to Audley End, stopping to kiss on the humped stone bridge, lying on the grass in Bridge End Gardens in the shadow of the hedges. Some weekends he'd come early on Saturday and they'd drive over to Suffolk, or to the Essex coast for the day. Frinton for fish and chips. The time he'd leant against the sea wall, unable to breathe, watching

Stella stare impassively at the grey, swelling sea. He'd wanted to touch and hold the absorbed, still silence that came out of her in that moment. She'd been as cool as silver, distant but present all at once. He'd put his arms around her. He was going to invent his life again, with Stella.

Zeki shook his head. It had been unbelievable. This place was all out of time, it wasn't like anywhere else. He'd hated school, bunked off, hung out on street corners, scrapped in the streets like a wild terrier dog – always on guard, tense and angry at the world. After his dad had died, he'd gone a bit crazy. Drugs, drink, pissing his life away in a snooker hall, chaotic and dead-eyed. He hadn't belonged to the Turkish community, though he'd sometimes hung around with mates outside the barber shops and cafés, trying to look as if he understood or belonged, but he was always caught out. Then he'd started getting his act together, slowly but surely. When you have nobody, you have a decision to make: you either go under or you decide to survive. He'd cleaned up his act – kept drugs for the weekend – started dressing right, found work in the market and realised that he had a talent for it; he could sell.

Zeki felt he understood the value of things, their weight and purpose. He took nothing about Stella or Saffron Walden for granted; he knew the price and the worth of it all. Though Stella's life had been different, very different from his, he thought she understood the importance and value of things too. They both did.

What he'd liked most, apart from Stella – he remembered telling them one evening, stuttering a little – was how when they walked the streets they kept bumping into people they knew. Not just once or twice, but every time. They were sitting around the table in Sheila's kitchen, eating, the oven feeling blindingly hot behind his back because he'd kept his plastic-leather jacket on, hadn't wanted them to see the dirty stains on his shirt. He'd been boiling. The women had laughed at him when he'd said that; kindly, disbelieving laughter.

'No, really. It doesn't happen to me, it never happens to me like that – like it's not an accident,' he said, reddening. 'I mean, I see people I know, but it's different here.'

'Poor Zeki,' Sheila said, passing him some more food, 'poor old Zeki. Our very own Dick Whittington.'

'It's too small, it's dead small here,' Marie told him, folding her arms. She was home on a visit from Kent and impatient with everyone. 'Anyway, there's no one here that I know any more. Except you lot.'

But Zeki saw Stella gazing at him, in that quiet, graceful way she had, from under her fringe, and she nodded at him.

'What you said,' she told him later that night, when they were in the pub, Stella folded into his arm, one hand on his leg, 'I think that too, that's what I like too.'

He'd got a little carried away by it all, Zeki can see that now: making those speeches, not really able to put his finger on it. Easily done, no regrets. He leant across to pick up the folder. He opened it to check the name of this viewing. Mr Wilson. Zeki sighed, feeling sleepy in the heavy quiet of his car. He rolled his head across the headrest and around his shoulders, listening to his bones crack. Jack and Mary. And now he had Jack and Mary too. Love could make even the strongest man's bones crack.

Auntie Joyce had got him the job at Harbutt's & Co. estate agents, she'd pulled some invisible small-town string, because of course in this town Joyce knew someone who knew someone who could fix Zeki up. It had been so easy, tantalisingly so. Everyone had agreed, when Stella got pregnant with Jack, that Zeki being away so much, up and down the motorways of the country selling pharmaceutical products and medical supplies, was not really workable or desirable. They all wanted him closer to home. He'd wanted to be closer to home too. Even then, nobody had blamed him for Stella getting pregnant, there had been no recriminations or judgement from anyone. They'd been understanding and forgiving. Stella had been the same when he'd got things wrong, early on. He'd freaked out once, wanting to destroy all the good things in his life because he couldn't bear for them to be true. He'd gone off, back to his old mates, got pissed and picked a fight. Or that other time he went off for the weekend, after Jack was born, and hadn't called. Stella had been upset about it and hurt, but when he'd apologised, in tears of panic and fear, and said he wouldn't do it again, that he was still learning, she hadn't capsized or staggered about – she'd forgiven him, simple as that. He hadn't done it again, and his good behaviour had not come at too great a price.

*

Just forget about her, forget all about her, his father had said to him, about his own mother. At the time this had struck Zeki as sound advice, and his father had an air of grave and urgent authority about the matter, dispensing wisdom. *Just forget about her*. It seems to Zeki now, imagining himself saying this to Stella, that his father's advice was disastrous, farcical. He's amazed to think he ever thought it persuasive or sound. Zeki and his English father, in their dark, austere flat mourning the absence of his mother. In his teens Zeki had fantasies about trying to find her – he had visions of her wandering through Istanbul, dressed in pink, beautiful and mysterious. She could only have gone back to Turkey, he'd decided.

The fantasies had made him feel ashamed, like he was just a little kid, and he'd been unable to put this vague plan into any kind of real action.

'That's so sad,' Stella had said. 'Something must have been really wrong for her to leave her kid.'

'Yeah,' Zeki had agreed. 'I guess so.'

Just forget about her. His father had never recovered, and had never forgotten about her; he'd wheeled through life like the broken-hearted do — at times enraged and at other times dazed and invisible to himself. Like the wind had gone out of him. He hadn't said to forget her with any kind of malice, Zeki realised; he'd wanted to give his son freedom.

*

Zeki read the papers in front of him now, frowning. Mr Harbutt had stood squarely in front of Zeki's desk that morning, unable or unwilling to meet his eye. 'New property,' he'd said, 'bungalow on the south side, old guy; said you'd go out and value it for him.'

Zeki saw that the bungalow was pretty much as John Anderson had said it would be: an old house, an elderly owner, a bit unkempt and old-fashioned on the outside, and probably on the inside too. Two weeks ago Mr Harbutt had asked Zeki to go and meet John Anderson, a property developer, at the pub; not in the office, but at the pub. Anderson had bought Zeki a drink and ushered him over to a quiet corner of The Angel.

'Here's what I'm thinking,' he had said, sipping his pint. 'A property comes on the market, a place in need of work, you know?' Zeki nodded, he knew. 'Right, some old bird wants to sell; she wants to move out quick, sell the house for her kids or to move into a home – whatever.' Anderson had shrugged, tetchy at the reasons why someone might want to sell their house. 'You give her a low price, a good price, but a low price. You let me know, I buy it, do it up and then give it back to you to sell on.'

Zeki had looked at him squarely across the table.

'You want me to undervalue a property, sell it to you, and then you'll pass it back to me to sell at a higher price?'

'You got it. And you get the cash in hand, on the side, see. We all win.'

'Except the old bird,' Zeki had said reasonably. 'She doesn't win.'

'How did that go?' Mr Harbutt had rung him as Zeki was walking home from the meeting.

Zeki had been able to hear the sound of a television in the background, and then the soft thud of footsteps and a door banging shut.

'Thought I'd ring. Anything interesting being offered?' Mr Harbutt had sounded quite unlike himself, betraying his normal, greying patrician air, more creased and concerned, more keen, than Zeki would have liked.

Zeki imagined him, sitting in his 'den', perhaps smoothing a hand over the green desk lamp or playing with his ornamental fountain pen. He'd only been to Mr Harbutt's house once: a pretty house just outside the town, down a drive decked with rose bushes; a pretty white wooden porch with large, cool stone slabs in the hallway. He'd followed Mr Harbutt into his den that day, trying not to look too obviously around the house, but he'd seen the pale-yellow sofas in the sitting-room, the old beams, the faded but smart Persian runners along the white carpets, the tasteful, gleaming antique furniture. His wife had been there too – Mrs Harbutt, small, white-haired and wearing a pale-blue shirt and jeans. She'd been 'wrestling with the garden', she said, pulling off a gardening glove with her teeth and holding out a vigorous hand. 'Nice to meet you, new recruit,' she'd smiled. 'Come and have a drink.' 'Zeki is just picking up some papers, Mary,' Mr Harbutt had told her sternly, steering Zeki towards the den.

'I don't know,' Zeki had said to Mr Harbutt on the phone, stopping on the street outside the pizza restaurant. 'Maybe. Depends on how you feel about things.'

'Ah, yes.' Zeki had heard Mr Harbutt lighting a cigarette, or perhaps it was a cigar. Neither of them had said anything for a while. Zeki had watched a group of girls on the opposite side of the road; they'd looked gorgeous in their pretty dresses, all brown and blonde. A smattering of clean, pale cardigans and long, floating, shining legs drifting through the warm air.

'Well,' Mr Harbutt had said eventually, blowing his smoke into the telephone. 'Not an easy time, is it, Zeki? Things are slowing up, I can feel it – I've seen it before.'

'Yes.'

'It's a worry. Between you and me, I'm worried about some of our colleagues too. James hasn't sold at all this month; his numbers are really down, and it doesn't look good for him.'

'No.'

'I'll let you get back home, Zeki. Pleased you went to the meeting – needs must, and all that, eh?'

'Yeah.'

Needs must. Opening the door of his car, Zeki told himself now that he couldn't afford to lose his job; nobody could afford for Zeki to lose his job. He had responsibilities now, and he wasn't going to let anyone down. There was still the matter of the money he owed Sheila, which was surely going to come to light soon, seeing as the police were all over her business at the minute. He stood in front of the glazed door and composed himself.

*

Mr Wilson (who asked Zeki to call him Jim) showed Zeki around the few rooms and the garden at the back in silence. He walked slowly across the thin carpets, around the blocky pieces of furniture, under the old, yellowing (and rather dangerous-looking) light fittings, through the dust, stopping by the cracked bathroom suite. Jim was tall, bald, slightly bent and not in any kind of a hurry.

The windows of the bungalow were smeary, and a lot of the floor space in the kitchen was given over to Jim's tomato plants, which were growing – or, rather, had grown – out of compost bags placed in a neat row on the linoleum. After the tour he made them both a cup of tea. Zeki sat patiently at the tiny table in the kitchen, mindfully still because of the plants, which looked a little dried-out now – their fragile, delicate stems at his elbow.

'You a Muslim?'

'Me? No, Jim, I'm not a Muslim.'

'You look like one – nothing wrong with it. Just asking. Name like that.' Jim shrugged.

'Right, uh-huh.' Zeki kept it neutral, but flexed his fingers. This was going to be easy, if he disliked Jim. 'I've been asked that before.'

'A common mistake.'

'Yeah.'

'Where are you from?'

'London.' Then, grudgingly, Zeki decided to give Jim what he wanted, 'But my mum was born in Turkey.'

'Turkey. That'd be it, then – why I thought you were a Muslim. Your mother a Muslim?'

'No, she . . . um . . . isn't a religious woman.'

'How come you're living here then? Do you live here?'

Jim slowly picked up a cup from the side of the sink and shook it dry over the sink, then another. Zeki heard for the first time the ticking of a clock coming from the sitting-room; it sounded ponderous and dull. He wondered if Jim even heard it any more. He tried to age Jim, size him up – a good, healthy mid-sixties, or a prematurely fragile late fifties? His long, rakish body, with the trousers gathered in, the folds and creases of an old man's trousers; another hole in the belt, gathering him in, until he might disappear altogether, leaving his too-big trousers in a puddle on the floor beside his tomato plants. Except that wasn't going to happen, because Jim was going to be leaving this house. Zeki was going to sell it at too low a price to John Anderson, and in the process do Jim out of money that was rightfully his. *Needs must.*

'I married a local girl. Where are you thinking of moving to, Jim? Are you going to family? Or abroad? Have you got somewhere to go?'

Zeki found that he wanted Jim to have an apartment in the South of France, all paid for, or a suitcase of money under the bed or, even better, a new girl-wife somewhere hot, like Thailand – a morally dubious arrangement that would bring respite to his greying years, so that in the scheme of things the fact that he ended up losing tens of thousands of pounds on his bungalow wouldn't matter one bit.

'No, wouldn't live with family. Too noisy. Don't know how your lot put up with it, all living together for your entire lives. A person needs some space.'

Zeki glanced over at him. *Your lot.* Jim was leaning on the counter, his hand in a permanent arthritic fist.

'Get us some milk out of the fridge — save me the bending down.'

'One thing I will say,' Zeki smoothly slipped off his chair and squatted in front of the small under-the-counter fridge, 'is that I'm feeling very confident about selling your home, Jim.'

The fridge was full of meringues. Three shelves of them piled up in neat lines on baking sheets. They were beautiful creations: subtle, puffy and bright white, a mass of air and settled substance, with pale-brown swirls across their tops. It took some self-control not to touch them, to run his fingers across their delicate, perfect architectural mounds, feel the bumps and crevices, catch the yellow bubbles of set sugar. He felt as though he'd put his head inside a cold, sweet sugar cloud.

Zeki shook himself. He took the milk carton out of the shelf in the door and passed it to Jim.

'Meringues,' he said, giving Jim a grin. 'You must like meringues.'

'I bake them,' Jim said gruffly, without turning round. 'People ask me to make them: school fairs, neighbours, charity stuff — all that. Bit of an expert.'

'You don't look the type,' Zeki heard himself say.

'No, s'pose not.'

'They're great,' Zeki said, his heart turning over, looking back at the fridge. 'Great.'

He carefully shut the fridge door and sat down again.

'Actually,' he said, 'it's only since I moved here that I've really been part of a family, Jim — my wife's family, you see.'

'You like it?'

'Sure.'

Jim laughed, a low throttling sound from deep in his throat, and held out a pale-pink teacup on a saucer in his alarmingly shaky hand. 'Poor sod, you don't sound very sure. So, you going to give me a price then, son?'

'Yes.' Zeki reached over to take the cup and saucer, wishing that Jim hadn't called him son. 'I have someone on my books who would be very interested in this property. I'm not promising anything, but I'm confident. The price will need to be right for him, though.'

Jim stayed standing over by the sink. He nodded, waiting.

'Yes.' Zeki poured the spilt tea from the saucer carefully into the cup. 'The market is quiet at the moment – I'm sure other agents have told you this?'

'How much?'

'I'm thinking an asking price of one hundred and forty thousand pounds.'

A silence fell between them. Zeki sipped his tea, trying to look happy and confident. He wanted to take another look at the meringues, to open the fridge and bathe in the white light, drink them all in. The clock was becoming thunderous to his ears; sip-slop from his teacup, tick-tock tick-tock, clunking time.

'You regret much, son?' Jim asked quietly.

'How do you mean?' Zeki sat up straight, alarmed. He decided to look for the joke. 'I regret never having a winning lottery ticket.'

'No, not like that.' Jim waved his bunched-up fist aimlessly through the darkening air of the kitchen. 'Proper regrets. Wasted years. Perhaps you're too young for them?'

'No, I'm not too young for them.' This Zeki could say with confidence.

'Sometimes people make the wrong decisions for the right reasons, son.'

Jim smiled over at him. 'It makes sense at the time, but that never makes it right.'

Zeki pushed his chair back, unclear of where the conversation was going. He wanted to look at his watch. It felt like he'd been there for hours. He wanted to do the deal and leave Jim alone with his tomato plants and meringues and wasted years.

'I guess so,' he ventured, politely. 'Jim, have other agents given you a higher price?'

'Mmm.'

'I'll tell you something, Jim. I probably shouldn't, but I will, because I like you.' Zeki pushed his chair back, just a fraction; he wanted to give the appearance that they were really getting down to business now, to the dirty, thorny truth, and were going to talk man-to-man. Just a tiny movement of his chair. Zeki stretched his legs out in front of him.

'In this business, Jim,' he said, 'in this business, some agents overprice a property. They give you an inflated price because they want your custom. Then, in a couple of weeks, they'll be on the phone saying, "It's not moving at that price, let's drop it a bit, we need to place it more competitively." I'm not doing that. I'm giving you the price I think — I *know* — I can sell it for: this week, right now!'

'Right now?' Jim smiled down at the floor.

'You know what I mean,' Zeki said, pulling his chair closer to the table again, sensing that he'd pushed it too far, and a bracelet of nervous sweat broke out across his neck. 'What do you say, Jim? It's a really competitive price. I have someone on my books — there's no chain, no problems, no property to sell. Cash.'

*

Jim turned around and looked out of the narrow square window above the sink, his hands spread on either side, their knuckles bearing down painfully – or so it looked – onto the draining board. He cut a thin, wire-like silhouette. Zeki glanced past his shoulder at the darkening afternoon sky.

'This local girl you married. What's her name?' Jim said, without turning around.

'Stella. Stella Buttle was her maiden name.'

'She'll be Roy Buttle's daughter then? Used to work up at the printer's.'

'Yes, that's right. Did you know him?'

'He was a pain in the backside, Roy Buttle.' Jim laughed at this, thumped one fist down on the side, making the clean mixing bowls on the side jump a little, startled into music. 'He meant well; used to drive my wife mad with all his plans and ideas. She said they were pie-in-the-sky, the lot of them. They used to sit on some council or other, some organisation. My wife loved all that.'

Zeki nodded, smiled, unsure what to say. He readied himself for Jim to ask about Sheila's disappearance, cringed in anticipation of Jim's interest and sympathy. He might even agree to accept Zeki's offer because of it; he might think later that night, whilst whisking up egg whites and pouring in the sugar, carefully making more meringues for an infant-school fundraiser or the cancer-support stall, that it was the least he could do for the Buttle family and all they were going through. Zeki thought of Stella and the children, of the life he'd created; he hadn't come this far to give in so easily, meringues or no meringues.

'What about that price, Jim?'

'All right,' Jim said, coming over to stand near Zeki, looking down at him. 'I'll think it over.'

'You'll think it over. Well, that's just great, Jim.' Zeki leapt to his feet. 'Let's shake on it, shall we?'

Zeki reached for Jim's hand, curling his fingers around that gnarled-up fist. He hadn't got the answer he needed, but he knew not to push Jim further. Not yet, anyway. Zeki held the thin, cold hand within his warm, generous, guilty grip, awkwardly laced his fingers around Jim's wrist, then pumped it up and down for all he was worth.

Washed Up – One Woman Swearing at Her Kitchen Sink

LOCAL WOMAN VANISHES

Here, in town, everyone is talking about a woman who has disappeared. She's just gone. No clues, no note, no nothing. Nobody knows where to and nobody knows why.

How is it possible for this woman-of-our-town to have vanished, slipped off the side of the world, evaporated under our careful, watchful small-town gaze? We hope that she is okay, that nothing bad has happened, we look sad and thoughtful, we sigh, we raise our hands, shrug, feel helpless, wonder what has happened.

Isn't it sad? I wonder who talked about her when she was here and visible and a part of our community? Her loss has made her the focus of our thoughts just as I've only found a voice by being anonymous. I'm only able to express and say what I want as Washed Up – I'm more myself by not being myself. These separate worlds are difficult to understand sometimes, aren't they? I don't know which is the more real any more – the blog or the me who lives my everyday life.

There are photographs of this missing woman all over town. We see her face on every street corner. The photographs are tied with an orange ribbon. Not yellow, but orange. The town is festooned and garlanded with bright, curling orange ribbons. They look like they're celebrating something. There's nothing mournful or sombre about them. I can't help but find the ribbons wonderful. Joyously defiant. It's as though they are laughing in the wind at us.

You know what this blog was going to be about? The house. The doing-up of our family house. It was going to be all paint swatches and reclamation yards, cornicing and flooring. The first few entries – almost two years ago exactly – are on roof tiles for heaven's sake. I was intent only upon putting the roof back on my house and marriage, but I couldn't keep the blog about the house because all this stuff about my marriage kept seeping out of me. I thought I was expressing it, finding a way forward and I loved all the support and care I've got from everyone here, but really I've been hiding, haven't I?

Listen up. Two years ago, I asked whether a dove grey or a pale, chalky blue might be the more tasteful for our front door? Christ. What have I been thinking? I wish I'd painted the fucking front door orange now.

33 comments

When it fell, she walked

When she was six she'd played on the swings on the common. When she was nine she'd picnicked with Marie and their dolls on the steep, grassy mound behind the museum. The sun had warmed her shoulders, and she'd known nothing except the grass, the pavements and the view ahead of her, the linings of her mind and the unformed shadows of her fears. She'd made friends at primary school, and then more at the high school; she'd cried and laughed and sworn. She'd got drunk and kissed Rick under the wagon-arch on Gold Street on her fifteenth birthday, warm and unthinking. Though the town had emptied of the people she knew, Stella still had her history, nothing had been repeated.

*

'Please,' Stella said. 'I don't know.'

PC Chambers sighed and chewed the end of his pen, looking at her with what he hoped was an even and sympathetic gaze. He wanted to navigate Stella with care and caution, without having to be directly responsible for challenging and changing her assumptions about her mother. He'd heard it too many times before: 'No, my dog is well trained and very obedient', 'My husband never goes to those sort of places', 'But Gary has been studying in his bedroom all week'.

If only people were more honest about themselves and the people around them, it would make my job a whole lot easier, PC Chambers thought, leaning back and crossing his ankles in front of him. He looked around Stella's small, warm sitting-room, at the pile of plastic toys in the far corner and the threadbare carpet beneath his feet.

He had been hoping to speak to Joyce, because for all that she was unnervingly keen to ask demanding questions, she did at least seem to have a handle on their investigation. But Joyce had gone to Bluewater shopping centre for the day. ('Is there news? I am nearing the Dartmouth Bridge. No news? Well, I need things, PC Chambers. Call my niece – she's always in.')

Chambers knew he was lucky to be working in the town: low crime rates, some criminal damage, the odd theft from cars, the occasional house burglary, Friday-night domestic assaults, but few drugs and, generally speaking, good people. Despite feeling mildly impatient with her, Chambers liked Stella; he felt drawn to her. She reminded him of his sister.

You can tell she's a small-town girl, he thought, looking at her balancing Mary against her chest, and quickly using her free hand to smooth her hair behind her ear. There was something peaceful about her – content. This was someone who knew she didn't want or need to travel very far. He considered whether to tell her that the lack of a dead body at this stage in the investigation was a very promising sign. The smallness of the room surrounded them, motionless, and they were both bathed in the quiet light of a table lamp. He looked out of the window and saw that it had started to rain, a drizzly grey, and a scatter of leaves blew past the window. He decided against it. He hadn't forgotten how strange she'd been when they'd first met, how disjointed she'd become, standing by the pram, looking dazed, thinking she'd forgotten things and having to leave the room. Not so like his sister after all then; she was more driven. Stella, clearly, was not as house-proud as his sister, either; no, his sister had an air freshener plugged in every room, handy packets of wet wipes discreetly tucked into shelving units and an army of detergent bottles lined up in the bathroom. Perhaps she was a bit obsessed actually. It was a bit unnatural, her constant cleaning and tidying, now he thought about it. Chambers unlocked his ankles and sat up straight.

'We had a witness come forward. She saw your mother early on Thursday morning, crossing the market square.'

Stella, opposite him, blinked and frowned, holding Mary tightly in her arms against her slim, pale jumper. Jack sat on the floor with his nose pressed up close to the television.

'This means,' he went on slowly, 'that she might have left of her own free will. It's a good sign.'

'She hasn't done that. She'd have told us.'

'Hard work, little 'uns, aren't they?' he said, nodding at Mary. 'I've got two nephews.'

'It isn't that I don't want to talk,' Stella ventured. 'It's just that – most of the time I don't know what to say.'

'This must be a very difficult time for you.' Chambers nodded. 'So, you weren't aware of her various Internet activities?'

'Do you know who is putting up the pictures with the orange ribbons?'

'No, we don't. Would you rather I came back later, when your husband is here? You say he bought her the computer? Perhaps he'll know more about it?'

'What about that?'

'What?'

'The orange ribbons. What do they mean?'

Chambers didn't have an answer to her question, couldn't think of a way to satisfy her need for order. Ah, perhaps that was why she reminded him of his sister; they both wanted things to be knowable and seen, either by dint of polished, pristine clear surfaces or well-answered questions. He chewed the end of his pen.

'I don't know what they mean, Stella,' he said slowly, leaning forward. 'I think it's just someone trying to help.'

'Yes.' Stella nodded, and smiled at him. Comforted. 'Yeah, I think that too.'

'We ran some tests on her computer. Your mother never mentioned anything about any websites she visited or talkboards? No mention of dating sites?'

Stella suddenly grinned at him, a wide, dramatic smile, a strip of sunlight in the drowsy hollow of the sitting-room; it made her look very attractive, almost beautiful.

'A dating site?' she said, laughing. 'My mum? You what? No. She isn't like that.'

Chambers let the silence settle between them. It fell like a snowfall, fast, muffling out all sound. He counted under his breath as the blizzard blew, saw her stop smiling, sit up a little and shake her head.

'Why?' she asked, by the time Chambers had reached eleven. 'Is that what you found? She's been on a dating site?'

'Yes. There's been email correspondence too, but it's been wiped off the machine. Our people are looking to see if they can recover it, or trace it. We've contacted the dating site she was using to ask for the names of the people she's been in contact with. Sometimes data protection can stop these people from being too helpful, though.'

'Do you think one of them ran off with her?' Stella asked, surprising Chambers with her directness. She looked down at Mary in her arms and stroked her cheek with a finger. 'Like, abducted her?'

'Well, no. Let's not jump to any conclusions. Like I say, she was spotted crossing the market square on her own. But did you notice anything unusual about her? Had she got her hair done differently, started taking more notice of her appearance? Suddenly started buying new clothes? Did she seem to be around a lot less than usual?'

'No, none of that. I'd have told you if she had.'

'I'll be in touch, Stella,' he said, closing his notebook and standing up. 'If you think of anything else, then just call me. Ask your husband – he might have given her Internet lessons on the quiet, or something. I'll ask your aunt about it too; you never know, she might have been doing the same.'

'Auntie Joyce? On a dating site? Please not.' Stella smiled, and Chambers grinned back at her, pleased that she seemed to be taking the news in her stride. 'My sister is coming. She's been in America. I'll ask her, she might know something.'

'That's good. I'll see myself out then. See you later – bye, nipper,' he said amiably as he walked past Jack, who ignored him and continued staring at the television, his mouth half-open, one hand distractedly holding and stroking an old bunny rabbit with dark-grey feet.

Stella heard the door bang shut after him, and the house sighed, a small breeze lifting through the lounge.

'I thought you'd be interested in the policeman,' Stella said to the back of Jack's head. 'You like policemen.'

Jack swivelled round and smiled at her, holding the rabbit's plump body against his cheek.

'He was boring. I like firemen more.'

'Yeah,' she smiled back at him. 'He was a bit boring.'

'He just talked.'

'I know.'

*

Stella gently placed Mary down on the sofa, lining her up against the back cushion. She crossed the room to look out of the window. The cement in their small back garden gleamed in the rain. She could hear the raindrops pattering down on the plastic dustbin lids. Rain was falling, the sky full of low, heavy, rolling clouds. Stella leant her head against the window, blew on the pane and drew a finger through the mist. A dating site. *Left of her own free will.* She tried to hold this in her head, to rouse energetic sense out of the words, but they only drifted listlessly through the empty spaces in her head, eventually colliding lightly and rolling to a stop.

It was all anyone seemed to be doing recently: talking – reminiscing, panicking, consoling, sympathising, but all with words. The darker chambers, the internal quiet states, this deadness within her, couldn't be touched upon, for nobody would go there. It was all words. Talking.

It wasn't just with Chambers that Stella had been struggling. Over the last two weeks she had received unprecedented (in her life anyway) amounts of attention; everyone kept asking her questions – so much anxiety, so much concern. She didn't know where to put all their worry and sympathy. It came at her in phone calls, sudden visits, notes pushed through her letter box; from Jack's key-worker and her mother's neighbours, who seemed in particular to want something from her. All their statements ended strangely with a question mark. Perhaps they felt responsible, perhaps that upward inflection at the end was a way of asking her to absolve them, to show they were good neighbours, that they understood that now – after her mother's shocking disappearance – there could no longer be such a thing as a definite answer; that everything was up in the air, and they wouldn't assume to finish with a full stop in case Stella might find it disrespectful or insensitive. 'We do talk quite often, Stella, and I spoke to her on Monday?', or 'She gave me some nasturtiums the week before?', and 'I have spoken to the police, after we read about it in *The Reporter*. We thought we should, because we did notice her lights weren't on, on Thursday night?'

The piece in *The Reporter*. Everyone had been cross with her, after what she'd said to the reporter – even Zeki. 'If you make a point of saying that she's normal and completely sane, then you make it sounds like she's mad,' he'd said, exasperated.

'But she's not mad, she's not gone crazy, she's not got drunk and run off because she's mad.'

This was important. Stella didn't want the town thinking her mother had experienced some kind of a breakdown. It wasn't like that, it wasn't embarrassing; she was scared to think of people reading about her mother and jumping to those kinds of conclusions. Stella would rather the piece hadn't appeared at all. She would rather they'd kept this information to themselves, within the family, and not allowed it out of the door and into newsprint, because after that, she had complained to Zeki, who knew where it might end up? They'd have no control over it now – it was out there, in the public space, on the Internet, in everyone's front rooms, allowing people to think what they would, create their own horrible conclusions. That was why she'd been keen to make clear in her statement that her mother was quite sane.

'We need help, Stella,' Zeki had explained patiently, 'we need the publicity.'

'I know. I'm just saying.'

Stella looked over at Jack, and he looked tired too; they were all of them always so tired. She'd wanted to ask Chambers to write down what he was saying, worried that she wouldn't remember it, or even understand; she might remember the wrong, unhelpful bits.

A dating site. Stella closed her eyes for a moment. She could hear herself breathing slowly under the noise of the television: cheerful people singing in primary-coloured jumpsuits. She leant her head against the windowpane and yawned. This was crazy. She knew she shouldn't even think of sleep, not with Jack unattended and Mary lying with her mouth pressed against the back of the settee. She shouldn't be thinking about sleeping anyway, ever; she should be – what should she be doing? Crawling around the roads of Essex looking for her mother? Haring around the streets for signs: forensic evidence, footsteps in the mud? Was that what people did?

Stella had been overwhelmed too by Marie, with her shrill and increasingly hysterical telephone calls from Florida.

'Should I come back? Do you want me to come home early, Stella?'

'Yes. I don't know. I don't know what we're meant to do.'

'Just tell me; you can't expect me to do this for you, you're so––. Stella, what's going on? We're here for two weeks. I'll cancel the resort after Wilderness. I'm worried sick. I'm going to come back at the end of the week. What do the police say?'

Stella could imagine her tall, slim sister, in her well-cut jeans, gold jewellery and properly curled hair, in her hotel bedroom in the Wilderness Lodge at Disney World. She'd be tipsy on the bottles of vodka bought in Duty Free, swigging back tumblers of vodka mixed with chemical Coke from the mini-bar. Perhaps standing on the balcony squinting darkly at the giraffes, which the video had promised would be outside their window, while her daughter, Jolie, slept peacefully inside the room.

Or Marie on Main Street, surrounded by clamouring children and the whole sky afloat with balloons and candyfloss-coloured clouds, the air thick with heat and the smell of hot dogs. Marie bumping up next to Donald Duck, shouting down her mobile phone at Stella, 'I can't handle this, not on top of everything else. I'm freaking out, Stella, I tell you – this is pushing me to breaking point. I came here to get away, you know, to treat Jolie; she's had such a hard time of it, what with me and Kurt. What does Auntie Joyce say? I haven't told Jolie. She loves it here. Stella, I can't sleep, Stella, I'm worried about her. I can't take it, I don't know how to take on this as well as all my shit. I'll be home at the end of the week.'

Marie and her husband, Kurt, had divorced six months ago. It had come as a huge surprise to Stella. One minute Marie and Kurt were moving into a three-bedroomed executive home near Stevenage – Kurt the model husband with a decent job, Marie the perfect wife, wealthy, tanned and healthy, their kitchen gleaming, their daughter spoilt, their lives the paradigm of perfection; the praxis of the gold standard for a comfortable life. In fact this life had been so often commented upon, by friends, neighbours, family:

how they'd seen photographs of their safari trip, and hadn't it looked amazing? Wasn't Jolie a pretty girl? Wasn't Marie still so slim? Wasn't Kurt good-looking, and wasn't he doing well, running his own company. And wasn't Marie's career going so well too – how did she manage that as well as everything else?

And then the next minute it was over. Marie and Kurt were at war.

'But why exactly are you divorcing? You've not been married long,' Stella asked Marie on the phone one night, when she'd rung up, drunk and maudlin-aggressive. 'That's terrible, Marie. I'm so sorry about it all, but why are you splitting? I mean, what happened?'

'Oh, right, because you think there's always got to be fucking *why*, don't you, Stella? In your goody-goody world, where nothing ever happens.'

In the midst of the highest/darkest/lowest point in the drama, those early fracturing stages, Stella remarked to her mother, 'It's like Marie is making this mess the highlight of her life. Like everything she's ever done has been leading up to this.'

They were sitting outside in her mother's garden, a light, chilled spring day. Jack had been helping Sheila plant bulbs in the ground, and they'd knelt together side by side for an hour, heads bent in concentration, like footmen – the knees of Jack's jeans soaked through. Stella, queasy with morning sickness, perched on the garden bench nearby, wrapped up in her anorak, watching them work. Her face was lit and washed by the spring sun. The plants had been half-flattened by heavy rainfall earlier in the day and the garden was drenched. Everything had looked soft to Stella that afternoon; the lawn so lustrous and damp, the dark, turning earth, the glistening leaves and the buds about to burst.

Once the planting was completed, Sheila sat down stiffly next to

Stella on the bench. This was when Stella had made her careless, unkind and ill-thought-out remark about Marie, born out of an annoyance with her sister that she couldn't hide, but didn't fully understand, either.

'That's a terribly unkind thing to say, Stella. What do you know of what Marie is going through?' Sheila said sharply, a tightness in her voice.

Stella bit her lip, because what did she know? Jack was at the far end of the garden, still armed with a trowel. He appeared to be in urgent conversation with someone – someone he was intent upon hitting with the trowel, someone who should have known better. She watched him wagging his finger in the air and then swooping the trowel through the air in a big clumsy arc.

'The doctor has upped her prescription. He's ever so worried that she's doing too much, and she's not sleeping. He said they had to work together to get her on an even keel.'

'Marie's taking pills? What kind of pills?'

'The doctor thought it best to give her something to see her through. He told her he was very worried about her.'

Stella had felt her stomach lighten, anxious that her mother seemed so comforted by the doctor's interest, as though his concern brought authority to the wild, careering, sloppy mess that Marie's marriage had so dramatically become. Stella thought it best to say nothing.

'It's not her fault, Stella. Or Kurt's.'

'I never said it was. People get divorced, I know that. I'm not a total idiot.'

But deep down Stella couldn't help but feel that life had divided, and they were all entering a new era because of it. An era that couldn't know only soft, wet gardens and hours of silence, but must also accommodate divergent paths and different endings, screaming phone calls and lives rent apart. And because it wasn't her doing, Stella wasn't clear where the paths might go, what it might mean or if it meant anything at all. There had been nothing to say, and everything to say.

'Their divorcing just changes things, doesn't it?'

'You sound like you disapprove,' her mother said. 'But this isn't about you.'

'I know,' Stella said quickly, stung. 'I feel bad for Jolie.'

'It's only divorce. It's not going to kill her.'

Stella looked over at her mother, wary and worried by Sheila's tone. She rarely argued with her mother, tried her very best to avoid it; she preferred the warmth of the consensual overlap. Sheila looked straight ahead of her, refusing to meet Stella's eye, her arms folded across her front. She'd looked steadfast and stubborn, as if she wasn't going to give any ground. It made Stella cross.

'I don't disapprove. It'd just be nicer if it wasn't happening, wouldn't it? That's all.' She shrugged. 'Not many people get divorced in our family, do they?'

This was true. Stella's immediate and wider family were surprisingly, unfashionably, constant in their marriages.

'Marriage is not a question of personal success or failure,' Sheila said, making Stella wonder – not for the first time – whether she could read her mind. 'It doesn't work like that. You should be more supportive of Marie. This is the stuff of life.'

'I know. I never said it was a failure. I just think that . . .' She reached for her meaning, trying to tie the frayed endings of Marie's marriage into something she could understand and contain. 'I just think that . . . it'd be better if everyone stayed together.'

'Yes, well, not everyone is as frightened of change as *you* are,' her mother snapped. 'You're being very naive, Stella. I'm surprised at you. By your thinking, Dad shouldn't have died, either – is that right? He should be here right now, showing Jack around the shed and building him a go-kart. Well, we'd all love that, but life isn't like that, is it?'

Stella had been fourteen when her quiet, gentle father died, and Marie twenty. His early retirement from the printing works had really been a resignation, in the face of a virulent and quick-acting cancer, which he had suffered with the same solidity and fatalistic humour with which he faced all things – that is, maturely. They'd been given enough time to prepare, to say goodbye, to practise for his leaving, but his death was still final and abrupt, and had ruptured them all. His last breath, his faded, warm smile.

Sheila had sought to protect her daughters as best she could, by showing them how to grieve well. They discussed him, cried, held each other, and became more powerfully involved, integrated and triangulated by his absence. Sheila had kept the house as it was, kept Roy's things in the cupboard and his picture on the mantelpiece. They came, slowly, together and found room to accommodate their loss. Sometimes, late at night, Sheila would talk to his photograph and spell out her worries about Stella and Marie, wondering whether his death had accounted for the quick-ness in getting married, their desire to settle down. Then she'd kiss him goodnight and tell him how very much she still missed him, and that they were all doing fine and he wasn't to worry about a thing, because she was coping – just as well as he'd told her that he knew she would. The darkness of the evening would spread around her bungalow at such times, and occasionally she thought she could hear his voice or smell his print overalls in another room. However, Sheila had spread her arms wide, caught and held her daughters as they made their way across the silent canyon of grief; she'd escorted them carefully and thoughtfully to the other side. She'd made sure that Roy was allowed to leave, for all their sakes.

'Stella, you can't expect everyone to balance everything for you. Not all the time, love.'

'I don't! I—'

'Me, Zeki, Marie — everyone. We can't live a version of our lives just to keep you happy.'

'Mum!'

'Who's to say? I'm not sure what I'm about, since Roy's gone. I can't seem to . . .'

Sheila had bowed her head then, and sighed, unable to finish her sentence. She'd picked at the blades of wet grass stuck to her trousers. They sat in silence, staring down the garden at Jack, who was on his knees, sticking the trowel into the ground in front of him. Stella felt the chill of the damp bench on her jeans, and deeply regretted the conversation.

'Marie will be okay,' Stella said quietly, ashamed. 'I'm sorry, I don't know why I said it. I do wish Dad was here, though, yeah. I'm so glad you're here for me, Mum.'

'I know, darling,' Sheila said, a hush in her voice too. 'So am I.'

The sun above the two women tried to burn through the whiteness of the clouds.

'I didn't mean it,' Sheila said eventually, weakened. 'You don't ask people to do that. You're doing very well — Jack's a lovely boy.'

'Yeah.'

Stella knew she'd sounded innocent, and that her outlook was out of step and childish; that she'd sounded judgemental, but this feeling had come from the core of her, and she'd wanted her mother to know that, and to try and understand her. The conversation had left a difficulty between them for a few weeks, each one a little wary of the other.

*

The night of PC Chambers's visit, Zeki and Stella lay in bed, sensing the edges of the other's body, their eyes well accustomed to the darkness. The house was closed down and shadowy, both the children asleep, and they were suspended in time, together. The depth of the night's silence surrounded them; they were curled up in the hold of a ship, refusing to let things change them.

'It's so weird,' Stella whispered, into the dark. 'I haven't cried yet.'

'Yeah.' Zeki's voice reached out towards her. He put his arm out too, resting it on her stomach. 'That's good, though. Perhaps it's because you've nothing to cry about.' He managed to stop himself adding the 'yet'. *Because you've nothing to cry about, yet.*

Stella wanted to say, *Hey, what about the dating site? Hey, do you think she's been murdered, is she dead? Hey, Zeki, what happened to our quiet normal lives that we liked so much?*

'Did you teach her to use the computer? Chambers reckons she's been on it.'

'She never went near it.'

'That's what I told him. Chambers said she might have left of her own free will.' Zeki could feel her shift in the darkness, bending towards him, the faint warmth of her breath on his neck. 'I thought I'd be good in a crisis, but I'm not. It's like I've just flattened myself out.'

'Like a soldier,' Zeki said quietly.

'Dodging bullets.'

154

'That's what I'd do in a war.' He took her hand and squeezed it. 'It's all right, love, we'll be all right. We'll just let what comes come.'

*

And when what was coming came, it was as if it had been waiting to do so all her life. All this time, looking for its chance — a huge wave piled high, massing itself; the rushing of pebbles under her feet, slowly gathering into a towering expectation of an inevitable, deafening crash. And when it fell, it was terrible and terrifying. It knocked her out, knocked her about, sent her spinning across rooms, gasping for air in eddies of white frothing water. It felt like a sickness — like lovesickness — though she didn't think she had ever experienced that before: not for Zeki, not for her dad when he died, not for anybody. It hit. Her heart started racing, and she couldn't concentrate when it came hurtling at her, couldn't eat or sleep; she only felt the need to go out.

And so she would, either bundling Jack and Mary into coats or, if it was later and Zeki was home, she would leap to her feet, trying to ward off this feeling, and shout out, 'I have to go out, I have to go out *now*, Zeki.' And he would rush through to the hall, just in time to see her flapping her arms, looking for her keys and reaching for the door to step quickly outside.

Then she would walk in the evening air. Fast, bouncing on the pavements. She would walk without thinking where she was going. She had to walk to escape this panic inside her, a breaking heart; this all-consuming, mind-bending yearning, this want and desire, this loss. It had never occurred to her that love might be experienced as panic, that it might be something destabilising or vertiginous, that it could be so vital and all-consuming. Like the madness

155

of hurt love — how she imagined love when bruised or damaged might be, or could be.

One night she found she'd walked past her old school, and down the tight narrow pavements beside the high wall that ringed the Audley End estate. It was dark, later than she'd realised. What a lot she had to learn. The commuters' cars picked her out on the raised pavement beside the wall, caught in the headlamps as she leant against the wall, waiting to breathe again.

Another evening she walked down the High Street, and turned left into tight Abbey Lane beside the almshouses, through the residential streets towards the car park. Carly's parents lived on one of the streets near the car park, and she stopped outside their house. Leant against the low wall at the front, her head cocked to one side, her legs humming. She wished Carly was home, not in Portsmouth. She wanted to go into her house and sit in Carly's purple bedroom, like they'd used to, drinking Coke and reading magazines. Wrapped up in problem pages and hair-straighteners. She might find calm there. A figure had appeared at the window — Carly's mum perhaps, or her new boyfriend — so Stella had moved on. Stella and Carly, they'd been a right pair. Everyone had said so.

Down familiar pavements, cars streaming past her, walking outside the busy pubs and restaurants, their windows glowing in the dark air. Past houses sold and resold. The evenings would darken, but she didn't need the light. She knew her way. She was tracking the town, walking down familiar pavements, carried along by the currents of her panic, searching for that which nourished her. There was nothing to discover, but everything to remember. It didn't matter where she went, whether past the Pentecostal church or along the street near the tennis club or past her primary school, near the castle ruins, up by the Catholic church, or outside the council offices or the Methodist church or the golf club, because everywhere held something of Stella. And of her mother. She could trace them both within the fabric of the town. She did not look for ghosts, or fleeting memories; as each foot fell and took her further, she felt herself multiply, as though she were encircling the whole town, containing them all.

One time she headed for the common, one early evening, knowing that she needed to go straight for the maze cut into the turf. She lay down upon it in the rain. She didn't care what anyone thought; she lay on the maze, her head and arms akimbo, her eyes wide open staring at the sky above her, feeling the wash of the raindrops, feeling herself become lighter and lighter, needle-thin.

Stella lay on the maze and waited patiently for the feelings to pass.

Of all the things he didn't know

Jonathan stood by the long window in his bedroom, looking out at where the edge of his property met the tiny lane that separated the house from the common. He leant his head against the window, blowing his cheeks out, and watching the slants of rain through the thick, greenish glass. He caught a flash of white out of the corner of his eye; by squinting and leaning further to the right he could just make out the figure of a woman lying spreadeagled on top of the turf maze. She looked like a wet angel or a human starfish.

Jonathan felt a need for activity. He ran a few steps on the floor, trying to lift his knees as high as he could. He frowned down at the figure on the maze. He willed the figure to move, or get up; getting up would be the best, not lying down in this state of drenched, submissive surrender – he'd really like that to stop, immediately, please. Everything was plenty alarming enough.

The floorboards in the bedroom had recently been stripped and polished, and they felt burnished and slippery under his feet. In a few rooms in the house, such as here, they had decided to keep the old boards, for authenticity and because they were attractively wide, but at that particular moment the boards felt bendy and insubstantial; the old, dark, polished knots and whorls and holes in the wood pressed against his socked feet as he jumped.

The running made him feel sick. He might have a heart attack – that'd show her. Perhaps Tacita would come in and find him strewn on the floor, clutching his arm, and then she'd glance at the laptop, staring mutely and accusingly at her from the edge of the bed where Jonathan had just left it. She would see, Jonathan thought, that actually, indeed, in point of fact there were direct and painful consequences of her decision to thoughtlessly spew her guts about their marriage all over the Internet. He glanced once more at the figure on the turf maze, and turned his back on the window and looked over at the laptop. God, he was pathetic. Jonathan looked down at the floor. He was actually trying to blame Tacita for this unholy mess.

Washed Up – One Woman Swearing at Her Kitchen Sink. However, he didn't feel bad about reading the blog, which was good; it wasn't like he'd snuck upstairs, locked their bedroom door and found and read her diary. An old-fashioned diary for her private thoughts, like people used to write. Then he'd have felt very bad, guilty and sticky at his lack of gallantry. No, this was out there in cyberspace, in the blogosphere; what had once been private had become public, what should be local had become global. Available for everyone to read and comment upon. And it seemed they had. Everyone seemed to know about it – wasn't that what Eve had said at lunch yesterday? She'd said, 'Oh, Jonathan, everyone knows about it. I can't believe you don't.' She'd been cross about having to be the one to tell him about Tacita's blog.

Yesterday afternoon he'd read the blog, frozen and appalled, until the whisky on the train had taken the edge off things. Today it was the comments on the blog that he'd been reading with particular intensity, waves of cold shame washing over him like cooling winds, but then with a pricking kind of irritation too, a growing sense of injustice. He'd found himself glaring, hissing through his teeth, 'Well, no, Coffeespoons; just because your husband behaved that way – and . . . and . . . and *scum* is a bit strong.'

Christ! Did these women have no shame at all? All these strangers, these strangers with their strong opinions:

Thrice Conflicted says,

I love your blog, Washed Up. It makes me laugh and cry. You are a really strong person, you will find the right path soon. Good luck. All I know, whatever you decide to do, is that your husband is lucky to have you – if only he knew it! Your strength is feelable, and your love will triumph.

Your strength is feelable! Your love will triumph! What did that even mean? Jonathan peered down at the laptop and did another bout of jogging on the spot, and then read the comment that Tacita had written underneath:

Washed Up says,

Hey, thank you, Thrice Conflicted. I feel really cherished by that.

Tacita had said she had felt cherished. Jonathan pounded his feet down on the floor, twice as fast, whirled his arms around by his side. As long as he'd known Tacita – for fifteen years now – she had never said she felt cherished, or that she'd liked to be cherished, or indeed that cherishing was ever, in any way, on the agenda.

Jonathan could hear the far-off sound of his children downstairs, screaming about something, followed by a harsh, violent banging and then silence.

Tacita's blog was angry. Jonathan wondered whether his daughters would grow up to be as angry as his wife. It couldn't be right to be brought up by such an angry person, could it? That would surely breed a vitriolic kind of emergency in a small child. Jonathan wondered whether there was someone he could talk to about that, someone he could make an appointment with? Express his concerns. Perhaps Tacita needed an anger-management course?

Jonathan remembered a colleague from the Risk Department at the bank who had been sent on an anger course. He'd picked up the wastepaper bin in his corner office and smashed it, first against the desk, and then he'd thrown it – fifty times, they said – against a window of reinforced glass, all the while screaming and bellowing like a trapped and frightened bullock – incoherent words streaming out of his mouth in vast terrible purple plumes of instinctive, inarticulate rage. No harm had been done, except to the bin, which had buckled. Jonathan had inspected the bin; lots of them had, they'd gathered in the corridor and watched silently as the colleague was ushered upstairs to somewhere quiet and shadowy in Human Resources. His head had been bowed, his shoulders trembling, and if Jonathan remembered correctly, the head of Human Resources had led him – rather sweetly, he'd thought – by the hand to the lift. They'd all peered in the corner office then, expecting to see the place wrecked, the floor ripped up, the computer in pieces, ceiling tiles lying on the ground, paper and cables leaping up through the carnage, erupting through the walls. But no, just one dented wastepaper bin. On his desk. That was all.

He didn't know whether the course had worked. This colleague had continued to stalk the corridors for another month, seething in his suit, his fists balled up and his eyes flinty bright, his barrel-chest tight against his striped shirt, until he had decided (or had it decided for him) to retire, even though he was only thirty-eight. He'd told Jonathan, who had made a point of asking, that he and his wife were going to buy a smallholding on the Isle of Sheppey and grow organic vegetables. He was going to leave this sickness behind him, the City and all its fucked-upness behind him, and start over. He was going to learn to relax, to become mindfully aware of the rhythms of nature, reclaim his life and his right to happiness — he had expressed himself this way, leaning against the wall by the toilets; he would get back on the Isle of Sheppey what he'd lost, he told Jonathan, blinking his watery, furious eyes.

Everyone had expressed surprise and pretended to be jealous, though really as a turn of events it was utterly, depressingly predictable. Everyone had wished the colleague well, and some wag had bought him a spade as a leaving present. A gift Jonathan had considered particularly foolhardy and rash; what if he bludgeoned his wife to death with the spade, when devastated and infuriated by the first blighted carrot crop? It didn't bear thinking about. It would be all their fault. People didn't change all that much, in Jonathan's opinion, organic smallholdings or not. Now *there* was a wife who might have a good, just cause to write a blog.

Jonathan walked back and pressed his head against the glass again; the strange figure lying on the maze was still there. Perhaps she was drunk. Disorderly. He padded across the floor, sat on the bed and picked up the laptop.

This blog had, it seemed, been going for two years now, since they'd moved into this house — this house he hadn't wanted to buy in the first place. There was a thing! She hadn't mentioned that on her blog, had she — oh, no. Jonathan cringed as he eyed up the many archive entries. It was all so unfair. He winced: listen to him/ feeling sorry for himself/when he was the idiot who'd created this mess in the first place. Jonathan stood up and ran on the spot, wanting to keep moving, needing to escape the collisions of guilt, shame and fear inside him.

*

'Her blog is all about The Project, that's what she calls it – The Project,' Eve had told him at lunch.

They'd been in one of those utilitarian City restaurants built for quick, effective lunches in an age when people didn't lunch any more – two water glasses; bright glaring lights bouncing off the black marble-effect floor; discreet, speedy waiters lined up by the far wall like ballboys. Eve looked very neat and precise, her white shirt matching the table linen, dark hair sitting in a perfect helmet across her head; those slim wrists, her small chin.

'This is kind of awkward, Jonathan,' cool, professional Eve had said. 'It's one of those frustrated-wife, half-mad, provincial-mummy blogs. Apparently it's quite popular – she's been approached to do a book deal, or a film, or something.' A book, a film. 'Anyway, the point of it – this Project – the point of it is that she's trying to make her marriage work, despite her husband's affairs. She's decided not to mention them, not to talk about it, just to carry on, be old-fashioned about it; and everyone is talking about how to do this, and whether or not it's a good idea. And the thing is,' Eve sipped on her water, shifted a little on her chair, her talkative congeniality hiding an awkward, nuggety truth. 'The thing is, she's furious and it's not really working out and recently she's started to name names. She thinks it's me you had an affair with. It says my name, Jonathan.'

163

'I haven't had an affair,' Jonathan said automatically, dead. 'Nothing happened. What do you mean, The Project?'

'You did — you had one with Polly Wade.'

'Pippa Wade.'

'Right — well, her. Not me, that's the point, not me. But if you google my name, that's where I come up: on Tacita's blog, only as your bloody mistress. I can't have my clients reading that. Or my husband.'

'I see,' Jonathan had said slowly.

He did not see, he could barely even look. Eve was cut from glass: all neat angles and precise lines, her hair falling in a neat black curtain across one shoulder; a diamond stud earring glittered at him from one exposed ear, her mouth was a red glaze. He'd been trying to listen, unable to eat his dish of pasta — pale, swelling and white — that sat untouched in front of him, but he struggled with the sense of what she'd been saying. He'd concentrated on Eve's perfect red bow-mouth, moving and talking; had wanted her to stop talking for a minute, so that he could catch up, but she'd looked determined, unstoppable, unquashable. He'd stared unthinkingly into the whites of her eyes.

One night three years ago, when he and Eve had still worked in the same bank, he'd left work with her. Walking along the pavement on that bitter, dark night, with Jonathan feeling the brush of her cashmere coat against his hand, he'd felt happy. He was heading back to Fulham, back to Tacita and the toddlers. He and Eve had stopped on the corner to make an awkward goodbye. Over her shoulder Jonathan had seen a group of people getting out of a taxi. It was a family, a large one; then another taxi had drawn up behind, and more people dressed in suits and coats — their children too, hair brushed, best coats on — had spilt out of the cars and onto the pavement. It must have been a special event. He'd watched the grandfather helping his wife step onto the pavement, his hand shaky but courteous, and everyone had looked nervous and excited, all dressed up.

'Look,' he'd said to Eve, turning her around by the shoulders. 'Look at them.'

'What?' she'd laughed. 'What about them?'

'They're all going out together, as a family. They've made such an effort, haven't they?'

And Jonathan had felt warm and moved, because of their nervousness and their hope, their specially done hair and posh, nicely cut coats; how they were trying their best and making an effort for this big night out.

'O-kay,' Eve had said slowly, smiling at him. 'You're so sentimental, Jonathan. I can't think how you've survived this long. It's very sweet. Are you sure you don't want to come to the bar? A load of us are going.'

And he'd watched the family, absent-mindedly touching the heads of their children, smiling at one another, adjusting their dresses; he'd watched them stepping down the pavement, and he'd wanted to race after them and thank them, or wish them the very best.

Thinking of this family, and of his daughters at home getting ready for bed, in clean pyjamas with brushed hair and sweet-smelling skin, he'd felt a wave of generous tolerance, as though they were all about to be rewarded for something. So he'd agreed to go to the bar with Eve, just for one drink — and that was the night he'd taken his chance and started this careless, surprising, yet passionate affair with Pippa Wade.

In fact it was more than a surprise; it was something of a revolution. Jonathan did not consider himself the sort of man who had affairs, or even an affair. He was not, by his own estimation, the type. Consequently once the affair had staggered to an open-ended closure four months ago – Pippa had surprised them both by falling pregnant, by her husband, by her husband, by her husband, definitely by her husband – he'd stashed the memory of it in a cloudy, indulgent and deniable place. Even now it was difficult to make sense of it all. Sitting at lunch, trying to retrace the fragments of their relationship – those spiky, intoxicating hallucinations that had filled his days – made him feel sunk and foolish.

He'd thought Pippa was something else. That they weren't like the others. Like anyone else who had committed adultery, ever. He'd felt this deep, wobbly connection to Pippa Wade. She was the one person who made the air thick when she walked into the room, who enlivened his dark, empty days with the electric sparks and static of charged desire.

It was his secret – one he had tried very hard to disown – a secret he'd lodged so far from his reality that he now half-doubted whether it were actually true. The affair only made sense to Jonathan when seen as a tangent to his life, an isthmus of imagination and possibility, and as a glorious secret rebellion.

However, after the event the lasting sense of their relationship, which had endured for almost two years, on and off, was that even when they were booking into expensive hotels – the more expensive, the better – and ordering £50 bottles of wine and strawberries from room service, rolling around in the sheets or making out like teenagers in the hotel lift (because theirs was a passion so intense and ardent it couldn't wait for the third floor), he could never shake the disturbingly insistent and odourless tang of the unreal.

However much they phoned or texted, however ardently they told each other that they were not as others – they were the more alive, the more glamorous, the more risky and adventurous, the more in love – it had been, both in its beginning and its ending, an airless and uncomfortable undertaking. Despite the half-light in which he had willed himself to be in love with her (and willed himself he had, with a readiness and urgency that had caught him unawares), the reality of Pippa Wade too often made itself anxiously clear to Jonathan. She was funny and sweet, but also overweight and prone to gulping tears, her voice always slightly too loud, her needs too transparent. She was always ravenous. For food, for Jonathan, for excitement, for love. Sometimes he thought of her as a warship, a great hulking warship, steaming through neutral waters, zeroing in upon her target: to remind herself, and him, that Jonathan was the love of her life. She was disappointed with the safe regularity of her own empty marriage and devastated to be three years off forty and still crying down a telephone. Some afternoons she'd stretch in the bed and groan with alarming, bored dissatisfaction. She would talk of how empty her life was, her marriage a mistake, and what did she do anyway? What contribution was she making? What talents did she have?

And Jonathan would creep into the bathroom, unable to look at himself in the mirror, feeling hollow. Dark plumes of desperation billowed up around him at this time, around his ankles, his knees, his waist, enveloping his raw skin in the hotel bathroom, clouding and darkening his just-emptied mind, catching him in a net of sick hopelessness. Sitting naked on the side of a strange bath at one-thirty in the afternoon, a film of champagne stuck to the roof of his mouth, staring at his feet, his head in his hands. Trying to keep afloat, to avoid the painful realities of his everyday life, his terrifying job, which was now completely out of control and bumping downhill at electric speed. Possibly Pippa Wade was just a stepping stone over the dark crevices of his being, not the great chemical, romantic, true love affair no man could be expected to resist, but simply a tacky, banal and horribly usual midlife crisis? Even if this were true – and he could not tolerate the notion for long, standing up, splashing cold water on his face – he knew he had doubled inside himself. He wanted, yearned and longed for her (for the idea of Pippa Wade) because she was shoring up and adding to his life in new, inexplicable and positive ways. He'd discovered that it was after all possible to be with two people at once; he had never stopped loving Tacita. His life had divided, and it felt the better for it.

There had been the constant terror of discovery, but the longer the affair went on and the less Tacita seemed to notice, the more invisible Jonathan felt himself become. He could distance the true, dark, canyon-like horror of discovery by allowing this loosening inside himself. Like a martyred superhero whose true identity must never be known; he could do anything. He was dazzled by the deception. Jonathan had become addicted to the double-life: what it seemed to say about him, what he was capable of, the way it made him feel.

The way Pippa looked at him, her eyes aglitter with admiration. Was it admiration? Perhaps it was tears. Either way, she'd throw herself onto the silken eiderdown like a B-movie actress and make greedy demands of him, or then at other times behave like a chilly and bored princess who deserved to be spoilt, who insisted on indulgence as her birthright – the way she never paid for the hotel room or for a single restaurant bill. It had been exhilarating and exhausting.

Because he rarely thought of Pippa Wade, or those strange, half-known, delusional afternoons, it filled him with an odd, unexpected kind of sadness to do so now. When Pippa had told Jonathan that she'd leave her husband for him, he'd been shocked.

'No, that's not what I want,' he'd told her, laughing it off. 'Christ, no! I don't want to leave Tacita and the girls.'

Surely she'd been joking. Pippa had told him he was nasty (a childish word) and then she'd called him a cruel man. Him! Cruel! He'd spent his life doing everything for everyone else; polite and compliant, that was Jonathan Cresswell. God, it wasn't that big a fucking deal! He wasn't the first, and he wouldn't be the last, so why should he be made to feel so bad about it? Compared to others, he was practically a saint: he didn't take coke or visit prostitutes – he'd turned down every invitation to lap-dancing clubs. He had never – not once, ever – thought about leaving Tacita, and he'd gone to great lengths to protect her from the truth. Leaving Tacita hadn't been the point of the affair.

'Jonathan!' Eve had waved her napkin at him impatiently. 'You're not listening. You've got to do something about this blog. Look, it's her business. Your business. But now she's outed me as your mistress.'

'Right,' he said, the word feeling thick and furry in his throat.

'Everyone knows about it.' She flapped her hand across the table at him, looking furious. 'It's not my fault I told you about it. Shit – everyone reads it! She's got to take my name off, you've got to tell her.' She paused and sat up straight, pulling at the cuff of her shirt. 'It's extremely damaging for me professionally and personally. Unless you sort this, I will have to consider legal action. I mean it, Jonathan.'

*

Jonathan lay back on the bed and balanced the laptop on his stomach. He listened for the sounds of the house. This blog was crazy, properly crazy. He clicked on one archive entry:

Birthday party now all done – thanks for all the suggestions. It was a great success. Husband wasn't there; he called and said he couldn't catch the early train, something had come up at work, it was very urgent and scary. That's what he said. 'It's something scary' – like he wanted my sympathy! I said, 'Not nearly as scary as having thirteen six-year-old girls in your house, Jonathan; not nearly as scary as being a dad who can't be bothered to come home for his daughter's birthday party. That's scary!' And he said, 'I can't talk to you now. I can't talk to you when you're being like this' and then, and then – HE HUNG UP.

108 comments. One hundred and eight people had read about his failure to be present at May's birthday party, and had all commented on it. A hundred and freaking eight people. One commentator, whom he had noticed before, appeared to have worked herself up into quite a pitch about it all. '*Your husband is suffering from a classic Narcissist Personality Disorder,*' OliveOhio's comment read. '*You must get him into therapy. You are being abused. This is emotional abuse. PLEASE get him into therapy. I'm worried about you and your children.*'

Jonathan considered googling Narcissistic Personality Disorder, but then worried that might be a narcissistic thing to do. He sat up on the bed, his arms behind his head. Christ, why on earth was she making such a big deal about it? It was hardly the crime of the century. Emotional abuse! It hadn't been like that. He wanted to tell OliveOhio that he'd been looking forward to his daughter's party very much, had wanted to be there, but his job had prevented it; to tell her about the extraordinary pressure he was under at work, and perhaps she didn't have a job, but for some people – people like him, who worked in the Credit and Risk Department of a vast, terrifying bank – life was not full of carefree, irresponsible choices like he assumed hers must be, out there in Ohio.

He sat up and, swinging his legs off the side of the bed, decided with a pulse of sludgy dread to look at the most recent post:

Washed Up – One Woman Swearing at Her Kitchen Sink

Let's start getting this shit down, shall we? Bugger circumspection and dignity. There's been nothing dignified about this blog anyway, has there? As I started here, I'll start the end here too.

OK. The OW (other woman). Let's bring her out of the shadows first. Her name is Eve Hashall. She worked at the same bank as him. I knew it was her because he kept talking about her. It was 'Eve said this' and 'Eve said that' and he'd get this far-away look on his face whenever he talked about her. I was certain. Then what followed was all the usual stuff: put a lock on his phone, kept it near him at all times, would text at odd hours and walk out of the room when it rang saying, 'It's work' like that explained everything in the world. 'I must take this, it's work.' Decided he wanted to lose weight, started buying new shirts, going for drinks after work, becoming on some days more critical and angry about our home life, and then on other days more loving and appreciative. He looked softly shifty all the time, indulgent and needy. To begin with, at the start, I did ask. I did. I thought if he told the truth first off, then we might find a way through. But he lied and denied it, but not enough. He didn't deny it enough. That's how I knew it was true, I didn't need any proof.

Then, of course, I made some decisions. Too frightened to

persist, not wanting to confront it, wanting to keep our family together, not sure how I'd survive alone when the girls were so young, I only wanted to keep us afloat. I wanted to keep the roof on, preserve what we had, build us a home. We would move house, I'd start the House Project, which of course became the Marriage Project.

Enough now. I'm going to take all the strength of your support to stop writing the blog, and slowly start moving towards my real world. Whatever that is.

2 comments

Christ! Eve had read that, about how he talked about her all the time with some stupid look on his face – how excruciating. And he'd needed some new shirts! Yes, it happened that at the same time as he was seeing Pippa Wade, purely by coincidence, a shirt outfitter's near the bank had a three-for-two sale on. And forgive him, women of the world, for this sin, but he'd decided to buy a few new shirts. Did their husbands never buy shirts then?

Some of the most appalling things he'd read so far were the early blog entries. The ones where Tacita was whining on and on about how she hadn't wanted to move here. That's what she'd written; she'd only agreed, she'd written, because – it seemed – it was part of her Project; she thought they'd needed a new start, was prepared to 'sacrifice' everything for The Project. *Sacrifice*. Christ, this blog, this private life of Tacita's, was cruel bordering on the psychotic. How humiliating.

Jonathan could feel a cold brittleness, a film of chilly filth, settle around him. He didn't want to be alone in the bedroom any longer – he couldn't organise his thoughts, support his evidence or collect himself. He shivered; the chilly white duvet cover was too bright, the huge bare room so draughty. He stood up and wandered over to the window again. All was brittle and stagey and untruthful. Artificial. He wanted to break something, break out of something; he imagined being the kind of man who might pick up a bedside lamp (or a wastepaper bin) and hurl it at the window. He wanted to see the glass break, to hear it break, and outside the window he wanted there not to be a rain-drenched, eternally quiet Saffron Walden, but warm rays of light and sunshine, a blinding, swooping, bathing, rollicking warmth – an evening beach party, beautiful women in kaftans with tanned bare legs and wild manes of hair; stiff cocktails, loud music and brave, capable men who knew the world and were unafraid. A lapping warm sea around his toes. Or, even better, a wild, real, earthy land where people screwed people they weren't married to and nobody wrote anguished blogs about it, or lived in fucking Saffron Walden in the wrong house; and where if you worked in Risk you took bloody risks, without waking up in the middle of the night soaked in a cold sweat.

Jonathan leant his head against the glass; he was not that kind of man. He was a caught, pathetic man. Perhaps he should have left Tacita for Pippa, then his rebellion might have been real, and he'd have undertaken a truthful, brave course of action instead of this secretive mess. He couldn't even be unfaithful properly. Tacita knew he'd had an affair and hadn't left him or confronted him. Christ – they were as crazy and scared as each other.

His secret had been exposed, the bubble popped, leaving a desolate, shameful scene scattered in debris and litter – nothing natural about it, a ruined stage. An empty stage, with Tacita with her fingers in her ears on one side and Eve Hashall on the other threatening legal action. He decided to go downstairs.

Sitting at the kitchen table, watching Tacita empty the dishwasher, the waves of outrage and hurt fell further off Jonathan in limp folds, leaving him painfully exposed in the bright kitchen lights. Tacita held the house together, she held him together. He was a fool. He loved Tacita; he couldn't tell her about Pippa, that was impossible. The heavy weight of what they weren't saying bore into him. He wanted to smoke.

'I wish we still smoked,' he said.

Tacita turned round and laughed; a sudden lift to her cheeks.

'Oh, God, me too,' she said. 'I think that every day.'

'I could go buy us some.'

'You could. Yes.'

'I could buy ten.'

'That'd do.'

'We could have a bottle of wine and five cigarettes each.'

'We'd smoke outside.'

'Of course.'

The aroma of tobacco in Tacita's bedsit flat when they were twenty-five, the tiny candles she insisted on burning in dark-green jars, him drunk and in love, relishing the decadence of Tacita's overcushioned bed and long, slender body. He'd just started working in the City, was making money and had felt vivid and important, and breathless at his good fortune in persuading Tacita to sleep with him. Tacita with her extraordinary thick hair and terrifying history of intellectual and demanding German boyfriends; Tacita with her strong opinions on modern art; Tacita who had been surprisingly quick to cry, unexpectedly vulnerable and soft late at night. Tacita.

He would buy them cigarettes, they'd talk about the blog, about Eve Hashall and Pippa. They could clear this up; she'd forgive him this, because she'd already decided, madly, to ignore his affair.

'We won't, though,' Tacita said, banging a cupboard door shut with her foot. 'We're too bloody well behaved.'

'Are we?' Jonathan shifted on his chair. The temperature in the room had changed.

'Well, I bloody am,' Tacita said bitterly. 'Jonathan, we need to t—'

'Muuum!' Their children, May and Lila came storming into the kitchen, carrying their strong sense of injustice up the hall to their parents.

Jonathan was struck by how small and slim and delicate they were, like strips of pale, vulnerable light.

'She won't let me have the TV buttons,' May announced. 'She's hidden them.'

'Have you hidden them, Lila?' Tacita asked, squatting down beside the dishwasher. 'Have you?'

Lila looked stoutly rebellious and triumphant. She glanced over at her father and smiled. He smiled back.

'God, you two. You told me to come and tell you when she's annoying me. You said you'd sort it out,' May said.

'We are sorting it out,' Tacita said, sharply. 'That's what we're doing.'

'Right! You two can't sort anything out. I wish I'd hit her.'

'You were right not to hit Lila. I'm really proud of you for not doing that.'

'You're proud of me for not hitting my sister?' May said, rolling her eyes. 'Oh, right, yeah – well done me. I just want the TV buttons. Dad! *Dad!*'

'For the record, I never wanted to buy this house,' Jonathan said abruptly, without knowing he was going to.

Tacita stood up, her face pale and pinched with bright fury.

'For fuck's sake, Jonathan. Will you please stop saying that?'

Before he could answer she stormed out of the kitchen, her bare feet slapping on the newly laid stone floor, banging the door shut after her.

'I'll give you the buttons,' Lila said quietly to her sister. 'Come on.'

Jonathan watched them both leave the kitchen, hand-in-hand, and cringed. He couldn't remember seeing his parents fight like this. Were they fighting, though? Their exchanges seemed to be all sudden flashes of misery and slamming doors. He understood why now. They weren't capable of proper face-to-face fighting where dreadful truths and untruths might be traded. He didn't dare follow Tacita.

No, Jonathan's parents had always seemed very happy to him, very sedate and at ease in their clothes and their environment – effortlessly so. They were both alive, recently retired to the Isle of Wight to a modern house with floor-to-ceiling windows – 'we adore the light' – and watercolour prints on the walls. His mother had always seemed calm to him, as serene as the summer sea out of her window. 'Too bloody calm,' Tacita had once said darkly, 'I've seen in her bathroom cabinet.' But this mean stab was untrue, Jonathan knew it was; his mother wasn't chemically happy, she was just happy. Jonathan's father had once told him that his wife, Jonathan's mother, had a gift for happiness, that she had *chosen* happiness.

This had struck Jonathan as deeply memorable, important even. He and and his father had been walking down a cobbled street in Sea View. His father walking a little stiffly, but still upright, still with his military bearing, his face permanently tanned, wearing a dark-blue guernsey, still giving off an air of vitality and superiority. 'Thing about your mother, Jo Jo,' he'd said, banging his walking stick on the pavement. 'She has a gift for happiness. She has chosen happiness, Jo Jo. Damn fine gift, I'd say.'

'I am trying,' Jonathan said out loud to himself. 'At least in the face of all this, I am trying.'

His mobile beeped and, picking it up off the table, he saw it was a text from Eve. Without reading the text, he quickly turned his phone off.

Later that night, after the Museum Society meeting and the drink with Theresa at the pub, he looked at Tacita's blog to see whether their latest conversation had made the daily bulletin. It hadn't.

At the Museum
Society meeting

Jonathan walked slowly across the common towards the meeting, grateful to be out of the house. His mind twisted in the dull, shallow waters of indecision and self-justification. The path cut diagonally across from the top right corner of the common near his house, straight down towards a car park. Street lamps burnt above him. His head was down, hands stuffed deep into his pockets.

Stella was the earth, the rain and the light wind in her hair. Dizzy from lying down so long, she too walked slowly home back across the common, ten paces behind Jonathan. The feelings had passed, and she was returning, drenched and washed-through. Things were starting to change.

Theresa was due at the Museum Society meeting. She stood in her hall peering at herself in a mirror, disturbed by her reflection. She went to the bathroom and splashed cold water on her face, to shock the red patches on her skin into leaving, and tore off a strip of loo paper, pulling it across her eyes, trying to remove the smudges of make-up.

The street was soft and grey after the rain. People were coming back from trips out of town, shopping bags in hand. There was a long queue of cars going down Victoria Road towards Thaxted Road. One of the London–Cambridge trains must have arrived at Audley End, spilling people into their cars.

The town at that time in the evening looked too small and old for the size of the cars that drove through it. All the people-movers, the weirdly bug-eyed space-wagons, offroad vehicles, even the normal saloon cars looked too long. It seemed to Theresa that the roads weren't wide enough, the way the buildings seemed to cower over themselves, all the wood and beams, the narrow pavements. It was better up this end of town: the Victorian terraces and the post-war bungalows behind them, all laid out in neat streets, could just about withstand the traffic. But over near the museum, on Castle Street and Museum Street, with all the pretty coloured houses, and lopsided mullioned windows and wonky door frames – Theresa wondered how the buildings could stand the force of all these huge cars, with smoky blacked-out windows, rumbling past, making them shake and tremble every day. Some of the cars were probably bigger than the houses.

At the meeting Theresa took the seat away from the long table, to show and demonstrate to everyone that she was aware of her lowly, only-three-mornings-a-week-in-the-ceramics-room posi-tion. She had six polythene bags of mixed nuts, chocolate-covered raisins and yoghurt-covered bananas in her bag, which she'd bought from a stall at the market. They burnt a hole of possibility in her bag; she was not actually imagining that she would spontaneously produce these snacks and force them upon people, but should the opportunity arise, she liked to imagine she could humbly offer them around in a reserved and graceful way.

The meeting room was small, and she watched with interest as members of the Museum Society took their seats around the table, storing plastic bags under their chairs, shrugging off jackets and nodding to one another, talking about the weather. This is how these small-town meetings are, Theresa thought warmly, they're convivial and comradely, everyone buoyed up by a sense of common communal interest, under the bright lights of this meeting room. She saw Evelyn opposite, bending towards an elderly gentleman in a mauve shirt, listening intently to what he had to say. Evelyn saw her and glided a hand through the air in greeting. Theresa waved back.

'Oh, yes,' Evelyn smiled at the man, approvingly. 'That's very amusing.'

One board member paced by the window, in little wavery lines, his hands behind his back.

The chair next to her was taken by a latecomer, who arrived just before the meeting began.

'Can I sit here?' he demanded. 'Jonathan Cresswell.' He passed her a business card, which she took with some surprise. 'I'm supposed to be offering advice on the trust fund they want to set up. I'm afraid it's not my area of expertise. I work in Risk.'

'Oh, right,' she said with a shrug, handing the card back. He worked in Risk.

'You're meant to keep it,' Jonathan said smiling. He surveyed her face carefully. 'I've got hundreds.'

'Everybody! Let's call this meeting to order,' a voice cried out from the far end of the long table.

Ten people were sitting around the table, while Theresa and Jonathan sat next to the wall, like aides-de-camp at a summit meeting. Everybody shifted a little in their chairs.

'But I don't need it,' Theresa whispered in his ear, not wanting to be rude, but wanting him to understand that she wasn't involved in the lottery bid, that she just worked in the ceramics room for three mornings a week; that in fact she wouldn't assume to take his card and was only here because, well, because, she'd been asked.

Jonathan was listening carefully to the chairwoman reading through the agenda. He turned to look at Theresa, shaking his head, smiling slightly, not understanding. He put his hand on hers and pressed the card, squeezing her hand slightly, as though he was bestowing a great gift upon her.

Jonathan was introduced by the chairwoman, Mrs Bird, to the room. She described him as a 'City hotshot with know-how', which made Theresa take another quick look at his card. Jonathan stood when Mrs Bird said his name, though he hadn't been invited to do so, and then he sat quickly down, pulling a face at Theresa that was supposed to convey casual self-deprecation. He didn't strike her as gauche. She thought, too quickly, that he was one of those rich City types, a show-off with a fast car and old-fashioned, right-wing values, and that as a person he would be arrogant, remote and careless. A product of his upbringing. She'd taken in his smart striped shirt, his 'weekend' jumper and chinos, the battered green wax jacket thrown over the back of his chair; this was the uniform she'd seen a lot of men wearing in the town when they weren't at work. The one surprise had been his shoes. She'd expected to see tassled loafers or boating shoes, but instead he was wearing huge trainers, with air-pumped soles and long, neon-yellow laces. Jonathan caught her looking, and looked down at his shoes too, perplexed.

After that Theresa knew she was being observed by him and it made her feel restless. She tried very hard to concentrate on the slow, courteous meanderings of the meeting instead.

When Jonathan spoke, in answer to a direct question from Mrs

Bird, Theresa glanced at him again. His voice was polite and tentative. She noticed how he took in everyone around the table as he spoke. Despite this ease, he now looked messy and easily hurt, and she felt bad for being so quick to dismiss him. You can't judge a man by his wax jacket, she told herself. All the same, she decided that when the meeting ended she would leave his card behind on the seat.

But Jonathan was having none of it.

'Hey, my card.'

Theresa blushed, caught in the door frame, jostled by someone walking out beside her. She felt she had to turn around and go back into the room, apologising to everyone for walking the wrong way as she did so.

'The more you want to leave it, the more I want you to take it,' he said, crossing his arms. 'Isn't that perverse? There is probably a rule, or a law named after it, like Murphy's Law.'

'Murphy's Law says that if anything can go wrong, it will,' Theresa answered carefully, unnerved by his seemingly bottomless persistence. 'I don't think that's got anything to do with insisting that someone take your business card.'

'Oh, I don't know,' Jonathan said, smiling at her. 'We could go for a drink? That might go wrong.' Then he added quickly, seeing the look on her face, 'That was a joke. I'm joking.'

'Oh, don't joke about it. Ask her properly.' Evelyn appeared at Theresa's side, zipping up her fleece. 'Gerald and I are going on somewhere now.' Evelyn nodded towards the figure of the white-haired man in the mauve shirt, who was struggling to get into his coat. 'Why not make an evening of it?' Evelyn smiled at Theresa, squeezed her arm and stepped lightly over to rescue Gerald from the impossibilities of his overcoat.

'Ignore her,' Theresa told Jonathan. 'She's desperate to marry me off.'

Jonathan's eyes scanned her face.

'Not that *I'm* desperate,' she went on slowly, under the bright strip-lights and Jonathan's stare. 'I don't want to be married.'

'Whatever,' he said, putting his hands in the air, affecting an innocent face. 'My wife'd probably say the same.'

Theresa smiled at his attempt at a joke. She knew she should leave, nod briskly, make her goodbyes and walk out of the door.

'So,' Jonathan said eventually, to fill the silence of the room. 'Right. They'll be locking up soon.'

'We could go for that quick drink, if you like,' Theresa said, as much to herself as to him. 'Let's see what goes wrong.'

*

As they walked out into the dark night air, Jonathan felt uncertain, a stab of guilt, about the whole undertaking. He was underscoring his life with Tacita's blog, as though her scrutiny and analysis were everywhere, even where she was not, as though he was on CCTV being filmed walking down the street with Theresa, and Tacita's blog was providing the background music, his theme song: a rising, banging symphony of betrayal and disloyalty. He'd lost all confidence in himself, in his ability to make the right decisions, because of those all-seeing fingers that fossicked through his life, and seemed to draw the most damning conclusions from innocent actions. He decided to have one quick drink, make polite conversation and then go home. He'd tell Tacita that the meeting went on longer than expected, wouldn't mention the drink – not that there was anything suspicious about it, he told himself quickly, but because he thought it might set off another chain of events that he'd rather avoid. Besides, why did Tacita need to know everything in the first place?

They went into the first pub they came to, then stood in silence at the bar, waiting to be served, awkward, but both pretending the opposite. It was dark and quiet in the pub, the ceiling low; a fruit machine in the corner flashed orange, and a group of regulars stood around the bar, idly chatting.

'What will you have? I hope your wife isn't wondering where you are?' Theresa said. She wanted Jonathan to know she had caught that bit of information. 'What time is she expecting you back?'

'No, it's fine,' he said, startled to think that she could read his thoughts. 'I work hard, so it's absolutely okay to go for a drink. Nothing to worry about there.'

She watched the rising flush in his cheeks.

They took their drinks to a small table in the far corner. As it turned out, they found a lot to talk about, which surprised them both. Jonathan was grateful for the opportunity to escape the shattering, pressing hopelessness of his marriage and Tacita's blog, and Theresa was still caught in the surprising current of possibility, a luminous strain, which had made her suggest the drink in the first place.

'I've had the oddest couple of days,' he told her. 'Everything is a bit out of control.'

Theresa smiled, and sipped on her gin. 'Just a bit? Well, that sounds okay. Would you like a chocolate raisin? I've got loads. I don't know why I bought them.'

She was enjoying herself; this drink with Jonathan was unexpected and all the sweeter for it. She wondered whether perhaps Evelyn was right about her always rushing about the place, never stopping. She looked around the pub.

'That's what I like about living here,' she said, matter-of-factly. 'The meeting, then going for a drink. It's a very neighbourly place. Don't you think?' Without waiting for an answer, she carried on. 'Same with the museum. It's small, but I feel I can make a difference there. I used to work in London, but it's better here.'

'I could tell you weren't from around here.'

'Makes you feel as though your work matters, you know?'

'Yes.'

'Get out of the rat-race.'

'God, yes. The rat-race.'

'I wanted to get away from all that flabby materialism.'

'Flabby?'

'You know, all that – shit.'

'Right.'

'This is fun, isn't it? I'm surprised we're getting on so well. Are you?'

'Well,' Jonathan said.

'I wasn't sure about you at the meeting, to be honest.'

'Let's have another drink.'

As Jonathan walked back from the bar he took in her pink brocade skirt and bitten-down nails, her earnest expression and eccentric earrings; he wanted to ask how she knew she didn't want to marry, but couldn't find a way to bring it up jokingly. Perhaps she thought marriage flabby too, he thought, tensing his stomach muscles.

But there was something about her bright, watchful eyes, and her keen-to-please smile, that made him falter in the asking and convinced him there was no playful answer to his question. Tacita hadn't met anyone like this in the town. He wasn't sure whether he found Theresa attractive or not. She was certainly unusually positive. The only people they socialised with were parents from the school. And, as far as Jonathan could see, the only people *they* socialised with were also people from the school. Everyone caught in an eddy of arrangements and dinners and new friendships forged at the school gate: similar people with familiar problems. He and Tacita had not yet managed to break out, crack through those layers and into the town. Though wasn't he doing that right now? Yes, he was! Meeting someone new. Tacita would approve.

'I wouldn't have thought you were the sort of person who wanted to live somewhere like this.' Jonathan shifted his weight in the chair, and took a handful of raisins from the bag on the table.

'You're about to ask if it's too quiet for me, aren't you?'

'No,' he lied. 'It's just—'

'Either the town is too quiet, or I'm too loud. I send loud emails, apparently.'

'How do you do that?' Jonathan shoved the handful of raisins into his mouth.

'I have no idea.'

'But you like it here?' he managed to say, wanting to add: *without children, without a family.*

'Sure. Though that's confusing to everybody.' Theresa sipped her drink.

It was time to go after they were two drinks down. On the street outside, as they were making their goodbyes, Jonathan was filled with an urgent need to say something to her; it fired up inside of him, like a compulsion to kiss a first date – the moment couldn't be tolerated if he didn't. Perhaps it was because he wanted not to avoid any more issues, though she was not his concern; but still there she was standing in front of him in an extraordinary plastic coat with large fabric buttons – or perhaps it had been the respectful cordiality of the meeting, or even the chocolate-coated raisins. He took a risk and put his hand on her shoulder.

'If you need anything – anything at all – you have my card. You can call me, whatever you need. If you need something.'

'Thanks,' she said, taken aback. 'Thanks, but I don't need anything.'

The tooth fairy isn't real, either, Stella

The doorbell rang. Stella opened her heavy eyes and saw Jack's face swim into focus; he was bending over her, his knees pressed against the side of the settee, his nose very close to hers.

'You were asleep,' he whispered, blinking. Stella could feel his warm breath on her face, and she stared into his eyes.

'Yes, sorry, I was, yes.' Stella stretched her arms up above her head, to break the spell. 'Not for long, though, Jack. It was a nap.'

'It was for long. I've been watching you.'

'Where's Dad?'

'Your hair's wet. Where did you go before?'

'Is he with Mary?'

'You've got grass on you,' Jack laughed. 'You do.'

'You what?'

Someone hammered on the door, and a voice shouted through the letter box.

'The door,' Jack pointed. 'They want in.'

'Okay.'

Stella got up and walked stiffly and slowly down the hall. She recognised at once the silhouette outside the smoked-glass window in her front door – all that unmanageable hair; Stella imagined that she could smell her too, could almost see the fumes of her heavy, duty-free airport perfume creeping in under the door.

'Marie.' Stella was half-asleep, but she opened the door wide and leant against the frame. The sky outside was low and a steely grey, and she could feel a restful, unfocused dampness in the air. She realised she had no idea what time of day it was. 'How was Florida? Where's Jolie? I thought you were coming tomorrow.'

'Jolie's with her dad. I wanted to come straight here. Tell me everything, everything that's happened.' Marie pushed her way through the door, stopping to hug Stella, hard and with meaning. Stella could feel the dig of Marie's large, chunky bracelet on her shoulder. 'Tell me everything.'

Stella followed her sister into the sitting-room. Marie picked up Jack in her arms and kissed him firmly on the cheek.

'Hello, Monster,' she said loudly. 'You still up? And more handsome than ever. I've brought you presents from America. All the way from Mr Disney himself.'

'Thanks,' Jack said, bending backwards in her arms to get a good look at her face. He looked solemn. 'Granny's lost.'

'That's why I'm here.' Marie put him back down on the floor then, tenderly. She squatted down so that she could be on eye level with him.

'Are we going to find her?'

'Well, we're going to try,' Marie said softly, placing her hand on his cheek.

'Everything is under control now,' Stella said from the doorway, and then quickly laughed, thinking it came out more sharply and unkindly than she had meant it to. Marie had this effect upon her

– a light powder of unease, a disloyal dusting, fell on Stella whenever she was in the same room as Marie. Stella felt annoyed and ashamed with herself. She imagined brushing it off, gathering herself, trying to focus.

'Don't be like that – don't get all like that, Stella.' Marie stood up. 'I'd love some coffee. I'm knackered. Kurt came to get Jolie from the airport and I drove straight here. Where's Mary?'

'Zeki's giving her a bath.' Then, more gracefully, 'Sit down, you're tired.'

Stella didn't think Marie looked very tired. She looked fantastic, as usual. There was a hard, glittering brightness to her, everything about her seemed to gleam: her leather jacket, her jewellery, her skin, bronzed and shining in the early-evening gloom of Stella's little sitting-room. Stella imagined that Marie sat at home and actually polished herself, with a rag, her tongue between her teeth, ardently, madly rubbing and rubbing at her skin, her teeth, her hair and her accessories, until even she was so dazzled by the sheen that she needed to stop, exhausted and blinded. It occurred to Stella that if she was ever to try this on herself, she would simply erase herself, wipe herself out, like a cartoon person being attacked by the illustrator's eraser.

'So Zeki's home? I thought we might go up to Mum's house, look around together. On our own.' Marie came over to Stella again, her head on one side. 'This is crazy, Stell.'

'I know. I'll make that coffee first,' she said, walking into the kitchen. She also wanted an excuse to check what time it was. Jack said she'd been asleep 'for long', and perhaps she had.

*

The bungalow looked unnaturally dark. Stella sat upright in the front of Marie's Land Rover, looking steadily out of the windscreen in front, refusing to be impressed by the all the gadgets and the smell of newness and polish. When they arrived Marie switched the engine off, and neither of them made an initial move to get out.

'Here we go then,' Marie said, flicking the car keys in her hand. 'We're here.'

'Is this a new car?'

'Yes.'

'What was wrong with your last car?'

'Nothing.'

'Did Kurt give it to you? Was it part of the divorce?'

'Stell. I'm tired. I'm sorry I wasn't here when all this happened. Are you cross?'

'Why would I be cross? I'm not cross. I'm coping. So what happened in Florida?'

'Nothing happened. Jolie took the rides and I felt bad about not being here. That was it. That was all.'

'So how come you get divorced, but Kurt buys you a new car?'

Marie shrugged.

'Are we going in, or not?'

*

They crossed the empty road together. Stella kept her head down, furtive; she didn't want to meet any neighbours again, not with Marie. She feared the neighbour would wring her hands, tell them she felt responsible, guilty at not being more vigilant, more nosy, that she'd failed to keep their mum safe, had failed to track her every movement successfully, and could they ever forgive her? And

Marie would look down at the neighbour and suggest that perhaps it would be good to talk that through.

They stood in the dark alleyway by the back door. The light was almost gone, but Stella could see the fallen leaves which had gathered in small piles at their feet and in the guttering. The flowers in the hanging basket had withered and died. Stella had trouble unlocking the door to her mother's house.

The kitchen looked much the same as it had almost two and a half weeks ago. Stella knew the police had been back with Joyce, but they didn't seem to have moved anything. As they both stepped into the eerily quiet kitchen, Stella knew that the house smelt unlived-in now, unloved. It was feeling her mother's absence.

'Oh, God,' Marie said, under her breath.

Stella walked across the kitchen and opened the fridge wondering whether Joyce had thrown out the milk. She hadn't. Stella picked up the half-empty carton and, shaking it, felt the congealing, curdling lumps thud against the side.

'Should I throw the milk out?' she said.

Marie did not answer, but wandered down the corridor towards the lounge, flicking on the light switches as she went. Stella held the milk tightly for a moment, looked at what else was in the fridge: one leaky tomato, some cheese in a Tupperware box, a tube of tomato puree, three eggs sitting in the green egg-holder in the fridge door, and a butter dish. A curiously empty domestic picture. Stella hoped that expectancy also sat on those clean and shining shelves, as though waiting for the moment when her mother would march back through the door to attend to her groceries. She took the sour milk and poured it down the sink, pushing the lumps against the sinkhole, wrinkling her nose.

Stella followed Marie down the corridor, where she leant against the door, watching Marie standing in the middle of the dim, hollow lounge, her hands on her hips.

'Did you think she'd be here?' Marie whispered, looking over at Stella. 'I did.'

Marie took her padded gold bag off her shoulder and threw it onto their mother's favourite chair. They both looked at it sitting there.

Marie walked over to the cabinet and picked up her own wedding photograph, in a huge frame, and peered at it.

'Why has she still got this up?'

'I don't know. She liked Kurt, didn't she?'

'Did she?' Marie put the photograph down, wrinkled her nose and scratched her elbow, like she used to when she was little. 'I didn't know that. I thought she just pretended to, to be nice. She didn't seem upset about us separating.'

'Well, she was.'

'She thinks we married too young. That's what she told Joyce.'

'And Joyce told you.'

Marie grinned. 'Yes, but she has a point. I did marry too young. That was part of the problem.'

'Well, I don't think that's a problem. It's not a problem for me and Zeki.'

Marie crossed the room and switched on a lamp; a dull pale-pink light filled the room.

'I couldn't wait to leave here,' Marie said quietly. 'I liked college. I loved my job. The freedom, you know? I gave it up too quickly.'

'You've still got your job.'

'Yeah. Whereas you married Zeki so you could stay here. That's the difference between us. One of them, anyway.'

Stella walked over towards the window, the street lamps were on outside. She leant against the wall and pressed the arch of her back into it, feeling its support. She pressed her hands flat against her sides.

'Mum told me she was proud of me.' Marie sat down on the arm of a chair. She fiddled with her gold lucky-charm bracelet for a moment, and her long, well-manicured nails tripped across the boot, the heart, the curly, shining spirals. 'She said I was brave to leave Kurt. I think she was pleased to see me doing something for myself.'

Stella looked over at her, uncertain what to say.

'Do you think she really wanted all this?' Marie waved her arm through the air.

'What? Her life? Yeah, of course. Why wouldn't she want her life? What are you on about Marie?'

'There's something about her though, isn't there? About Mum? Something secretive. Joyce said as much.'

'Well, Joyce says a lot of things.'

They smiled at each other.

'*I have instincts!*' Marie said loudly, tossing her head. '*It came to me in a dream!*'

They both laughed. Stella reflected a moment.

'The police said she'd been on a dating site.'

'I know. I wondered about that too.'

Stella looked over at her tall, dark sister sitting in the shadows.

'You knew?'

'Yeah,' Marie said casually, 'we talked about it.'

'She talked to you about it.'

'Yes.'

'She didn't talk to me about it.'

'Well, she didn't talk to you about lots of things. We talked a lot. She was lonely.'

'She was not lonely,' Stella said quickly. 'How could she be lonely? She had me, her grandchildren; she had Joyce, her friends, all their friends, all the people she knows here. She's lived here for years.'

Marie shot Stella a dark and accusing look and smoothed down the front of her tight jeans. She sighed.

'After Dad died, you know, it's not been easy for her. I think she wanted something else.'

'Like what?' Stella felt angry with her sister, unaccountably angry. She pulled herself off the wall and turned to look out of the window to calm herself. She leant heavily on the narrow ledge, pressing her forehead against the cold glass of the window.

'Or perhaps I just think that to make myself feel better,' Marie said quietly. 'Last night, on the plane, I just sat there wondering whether she was in a ditch somewhere. It was awful thinking that.'

'I asked Zeki if he thought it was terrorists,' Stella said into the window.

'Stella!' Marie snorted, the mood broken. 'Of course it's not bloody terrorists, you nutcase. What would al-Qaeda want with Mum?'

'The times we had growing up here – they weren't all bad Marie.'

'I know that, but we're grown-up now, though, Stella, aren't we? Jesus.'

'You turn up here and think you know what to do. How to make everything better, but you don't – you don't know everything. Just because Mum told you she wanted to go on a few dates. It doesn't make you an expert on her, on her life, on anything. I'm the one who stayed here with her.'

'She's the one who stayed here with *you*, more like.'

Stella ran her finger through a felting of dust on the windowsill.

She wanted to stop talking, to be left alone in the silence of her mother's house. She didn't want to speak and then to hear Marie's voice saying things like that. It made her burn inside. If she was never to hear her mother's voice again, she would prefer always the smoothness of silence. She would curl up inside her world, this town, and be silent and sheltered for ever.

'You think you're so perfect Stella.' Marie went on behind her. 'You think everyone else is abnormal. You don't know the half of it. Mum wouldn't tell you, she thought you couldn't handle it.'

'Like what?' Stella turned towards her sister. They seemed always to repeat their conversations, the same petty, rivalrous patterns.

'Like the money she gave Zeki, for instance – you don't know about that.' Marie said quickly with some triumph, in the same way she'd said fifteen years ago, *The tooth fairy isn't real, either, Stella.*

'What money?' Stella hated asking the question. However skilled she'd become at negotiating Marie, however careful to fold herself away from her, the bullets she fired, Stella knew she had to catch this one, and know it. It sat there now, in her hand, burning hot and scalding her skin. 'What money, Marie?'

'Sorry. Look, I probably shouldn't have mentioned it.' Marie looked down at her feet.

'Yes,' Stella urged her. 'Yes, yes, you should. What money?'

'Zeki asked her for money. She gave him a big loan. That was all, it wasn't a big deal; he said he was having difficulty managing things. Me and Kurt said we'd help, but then our shit happened. Look, she didn't mind doing it, she told me that. She said it was okay with her, that Zeki was doing his best and he needed a little help. That was all.'

Marie tipped off the arm of the chair and collapsed into the chair cushions. She looked up at Stella from under her thick lashes, she ran a finger across one high eyebrow, watching Stella carefully.

'Worse things have happened, Stell. It's no biggie.'

A stranger, and all that

Theresa, warmed by gin and comradeship, let herself into the dark house. There were the doors, the floor, the dark window of the kitchen. There the stairs, the threadbare runner beckoning her towards an empty bedroom and a cold bathroom. There the table lamp on the floor, with the plug that needed a new fuse; there in the corner of her vision an empty cupboard. Theresa dropped her bag to the floor. This was the house she couldn't afford to stay in much longer. She was full of emotions that nobody else knew of. For the first time in a long while she allowed herself to stand alone, in the dark, her eyes unfocused, hypnotised by isolating waves of silence.

What should she do? Theresa snapped on a light, marched into the sitting-room and picked up the sheaf of papers, covered in her careful writing, which sat on top of her unfinished, untouched PhD thesis.

She flipped through to make sure they were all there. On the end page she had underlined Stella's address three times, then she'd drawn a box around it, and some steps with bannisters going up the box. Then an arrow, which she'd coloured in. She put the papers in her bag.

Banging the front door behind her, she navigated her way under the broad beech trees beside the language school, one hand stuck deep in the pockets of her jacket, pressing Jonathan's card flat against her palm. In the other hand she held the piece of paper with Stella's address written on it.

Larger, villa-like houses were on her right, each with a Ford Focus parked on the neat driveway. At the bottom of the hill Theresa took the left turning into a small close of post-war, cramped-looking houses, dark brick below and black cladding on the upper parts of the thin, narrow houses. She found number twenty-four quickly and easily, and stood outside on the pavement for a moment. She hoped it wasn't too late; she'd rather lost track of the time. There was no grass out the front, for it had been paved over, and no Ford Focus either. There was a small knee-high creosoted fence at the front, empty dark windows, a neat line of bins down the side alley. Theresa took a deep breath and took three steps up to the front door. She thought she could hear some noise inside, voices perhaps, a television or radio; she sensed there was life inside.

As she was raising her hand to knock on the door, a woman walked up to the house next door and looked over at Theresa as she searched for her own front-door key.

'Is this where Stella Robinson lives?' Theresa asked, 'Is she in?'

The neighbour shrugged.

'I don't know, usually she is,' she replied. 'Sorry,' she said as an afterthought and then stepped quickly into her house and kicked the door closed behind her.

Provoked by the sound of the neighbour's door, a child's face appeared from behind the curtain at the front window – it was a boy; he pressed his whole face up against the dark glass, snatches of light from the room fell out onto the path and he stared at

Theresa. She smiled at him and waved, and he stared back at her, with alarmingly round eyes.

'Is Mummy in?' she said loudly, pointing at the door.

The child was still staring at her. He placed one hand against the window now too, so that he looked as though he were trapped in there, suffocating or pining for escape. It was like an eerie shot in a high-class Hollywood thriller – a child's face staring up from under clear, dark water; this child even had dark hollows under his blank eyes.

Theresa took three steps over towards the window.

'Hello,' she said, bending down slightly. 'Is your mother in?'

She mouthed loudly at the glass, pressing her face up close, and she thought for one wild moment that perhaps she might kiss the glass, land a fairytale kiss on the impassive face of the drowning child, and that once she'd done that something magical and significant would happen: the glass would shatter, he would wake up and reclaim his kingdom, his birthright; or a thousand roses would spring up around her feet; or she might turn into a frog – any of those options, or all of them.

Behind her a large car swooped into the close and braked. The strong beams of the car lights fell into the garden next door, and the purr of the engine filled the close. Theresa turned and saw a young woman climb out, then without a word to the driver she slammed the car door shut and walked towards Theresa. The car reversed back out of the close and they fell back into the orange-dark.

Stella walked up the path towards Theresa, looking at her with an even, steady gaze.

'Are you Stella Robinson?' Theresa asked, announcing herself, feeling awkward at having been caught hovering by this girl's front window.

'Yes.'

'I read about your mum in the paper. My name's Theresa Ford.'

She held out her hand, but Stella just looked at it blankly, as though nobody had ever offered to shake her hand before. She smiled a little uncertainly at Theresa, who could see her slightly crossed-over front teeth, her pale, freckled nose and her long, slim arms in the light from the sitting-room. Theresa faltered, wondered if she smelt of gin, suddenly wanted to go home. What had brought her on this mission, what was it only fifteen seconds ago that she'd been so certain of what she had to say?

'Is he yours?' Theresa tried to smile, to appear like a sane and well-adjusted stranger. 'I was just talking to him through the window.'

'That's Jack,' Stella said slowly, waiting.

'I saw your mother,' Theresa said, moving towards her. Was she mistaken, or did Stella take two simultaneous steps backwards?

'You've seen her? Is she here?' And Stella looked around, up and down the street, expectantly, her child-like face so quickly lifted and animated by hope, by an unexpected present.

'No, she's not here. I saw her on the day she went, in the morning, in the market square. Look, can I come in? There's something I want to tell you.'

Inside the house, Stella seemed resentful of Theresa – that was what she thought, that Stella resented her. She wasn't sure why she would, or why she did, but her slow, sluggish movements, Stella's expressionless eyes taking in Theresa, her shrugging shoulders and unenthusiastic offer of tea or coffee, and her mute invitation to follow her down the hallway towards the kitchen all seemed to breathe resentment, a resistance bordering on a banal kind of hostility. And just as Theresa was deciding to say her piece, and get out as quickly as she could, was mentally kicking herself for this foolhardy trip – a symptom of her own messed-up state of mind and woefully incorrect idea of duty – Stella turned towards her in the kitchen, and said, 'I thought you'd come.'

'I've been doing some research,' Theresa said, feeling hopeless. 'I've been investigating your mother's disappearance. I wanted to help.'

Stella was not surprised to have this stranger in her kitchen telling her about her mother. Her head was still swimming with Marie's words about her, Zeki, her mother, her life. It felt appropriate that Theresa should arrive that evening, just as she had fallen out of Marie's car, her body tingling with giddy panic that all she had known was not as she'd thought, that her safe world had been breached, that everything was crashing on the rocks, splintering, heaving, sending the goods overboard, washed into a cove, that she was awash. She felt strange to herself. Then she'd got out of the car and there was Theresa, and Stella knew that Theresa was a lifebuoy – an unlikely one, but a lifebuoy all the same.

Zeki appeared in the kitchen doorway, carrying Mary in his arms. He gave Stella a worried glance.

'Hello,' he said, looking Theresa up and down, suspicious and wondering if he was supposed to know her. 'How are you?'

'She's come to see me, Zeki,' Stella said. 'Can you leave us?'

'Sure. Why don't I put the kids to bed.' He nodded at Theresa, who smiled back. 'You all right, Stell?'

'Yeah.'

'Is everything okay? Where's Marie?'

'She's gone to Joyce's. She's staying there.'

After Zeki had left, Stella relaxed. She leant back against the unit, crossing her arms in front of her, waiting for Theresa to speak.

Theresa felt foolish, and wished she'd expressed herself better. It was clear to her that this girl, who was looking at her so openly and expansively, who had expected her to arrive, thought Theresa must have something concrete to tell her. Theresa, who was no stranger to the odd injustices and failed expectations that other people hand out, winced.

'I didn't find out very much,' she said. 'I wanted to help. I was sure there was something I could do to help. Sorry – I've got some notes. Hang on.'

'No,' Stella said, 'that's okay. Don't worry.'

'I just . . .' Theresa pulled the papers out of her jute bag. 'I just wanted you to know that I saw her one morning and . . . that . . . I told the police about it. I've also made some notes, I went on the Internet.' Theresa held the papers up in front of her.

'How did you hear about Mum? Do you live here?'

'I work at the museum.'

'Oh, right, I don't go up there much. I used to as a kid, y'know. I should take Jack.'

'I'm sure he'd like it.'

Theresa looked down at her notes. She was sure that she'd had a proper story to tell Stella, that she had created some valuable and plausible ideas, had scoured the Missing Persons network, had a list of hostels, suggestions of places the police might like to look. She'd been going to ask Stella whether she'd asked the police to check the railway-station CCTV cameras, and give her a list of procedures for action, which she'd copied down and cross-referenced. She'd been sure that her lists and thoughts and suggestions had amounted to something important.

'I like your coat,' Stella said, smiling at her. 'It's weird.'

'Yes.' Theresa looked over at her. 'Yes, people seem to think so.'

'I bet.' Stella laughed, then checked herself. 'I don't mean anything by it.'

'This must be a difficult time for you,' Theresa heard herself saying.

'I don't know. Like this is difficult, but that's not all it is. I can't explain what it's like really. I'm not doing what I'm meant to be doing, that's all. It's like everything has turned weird. Zeki, Marie —I dunno, everything is different than I thought. It just kind of makes sense that you'd turn up. A stranger, and all that.'

'I don't live far from here,' Theresa said. 'We're almost neighbours.'

'Neighbours,' Stella said.

Theresa felt a lurch inside her. Standing in Stella's narrow, dimly lit kitchen made sense to her too. She held the papers up in the air.

'I thought I had something to tell you, but I don't really,' she said. 'I just wanted to help.'

'It's okay.' Stella smiled at Theresa from under her fringe. 'It's okay. I'm pleased you came.'

Nothing is more hopeless
than planned happiness

There were other ways to die. The suitcases were piled up in the front hall, beside the door. An air of expectation hung about the house. Of course it did, it was half-term, they were away to be happy on holiday in Norfolk. Marriages end, people change, lives grow, secrets are shared. Jonathan had become vague under the barrage of Eve's texts and messages, which arrived daily, with increasingly rabid threats. He stayed over in London as often as possible, never answering his phone. A feeling of defiance empowered him; he wasn't even trying at work; he got drunk with colleagues, called up old friends, the usual.

He had something of a gift for avoidance.

If he and Tacita both continued to ignore, refute and delude themselves, their marriage might continue. It could work. Tacita hadn't been able to confront him, had tied herself up in complicated knots – she didn't want to end it, either. They were both trying to protect themselves, curling the truth inside their heads, far away from the bright lights of reality. Inside their co-created spell, the tension of this silent complicity grew: on the blog and in their stilted exchanges. The dreadfulness of his secret mounted inside Jonathan, until all he could do was nothing. Do nothing. His thoughts remained circling inside him, hitting moments of light, only to bounce back into confusing, dreary dimness. His head was full of bullshit.

May appeared at the top of the stairs wearing her wetsuit, dragging a vast cloth bag down the stairs.

'I'm taking my bedroom,' she said, watching the bag slump down behind her, one step at a time.

'What, all of it?' Jonathan was about to pick up the suitcases to load the car.

'Yes.'

'Okay. Where's Mum?'

'Writing on the 'puter.'

Jonathan picked up two suitcases and went outside. He opened the boot of the car, and threw in one suitcase and then another. A tide of threat was around him, promising destruction. He tried careful, controlled breathing. He started to sweat. Walking back into the house, he picked up his laptop from the luggage pile and crept into the sitting-room, closed the door and, sitting hunched on the cold sofa, turned it on. He needed to see what Tacita was writing.

We're off to Norfolk for half-term. I can't keep this up any more. I've been a coward, I see that now. I was too frightened to confront the truth, but this is like the worst kind of lie inside me, eating away at me. I'm going to have it all out with him on holiday. I'm sorry to those who believed and invested in The Project. I think I got carried away with the blog, and the attention it got – I let the blog replace the man, and the truth. But this isn't an exercise, this is my life.

Now it had started. She was going to blow it. Beads of sweat broke out on his temples, a cold fear ran through his body. The door opened and Tacita walked into the sitting-room. Jonathan hurriedly shut the laptop.

'What are you doing in here?' She was putting on her coat; she smiled at him and absent-mindedly pulled her hair out of the collar, and a golden wave fell across her shoulders. 'Have you done the car? You won't believe what May's packed.'

'I can't go to Norfolk.'

The room was cold. Mrs Hollis's sun-bleached carpets had been torn up, the ceiling rose painted, the bookshelves hurled into a skip. The room was now emptily tasteful – the colour accent was pale grey – and draughty. They stood in the chill air for a moment, frozen. Jonathan opened and closed his mouth. He was a goldfish. A stupid, orange, useless fish, swimming around his tiny bowl, bulgy-eyed. Even worse, he was a cowardly goldfish, the most point-less and wretched creature on the planet. A nothing – a boneless, spineless, flicking-tailed, stupid, lying, frightened, adulterous fish.

'What?' Tacita said slowly. 'What did you just say?'

There was the deep, unexplored life of this moment between them, and their other known, lived and talked-about life. There was the life that this room had seen before them, and now this redecorated life – this colour, this look, this being the Cresswells' dreamt-about and manufactured sitting-room. The layering of confusions and falsehoods and false identities rolled around Jonathan, their structures fragile, but precious.

'Work called. I have to go in.' He took a deep breath. 'There's an emergency.'

'Don't say that.' Her look was imploring, tired. 'Don't say that.'

'There's nothing I can do.'

Tacita pulled herself up in that moment. She started to button up her coat, her fingers shaking, her whole body and face trembling. 'Fuck you, Jonathan. *Fuck you!*'

She glared at him, and he sat immobile on the sofa, opening and closing his mouth. She stormed out of the room shouting, 'You always let me down', and he followed her into the hall, aware of his children's wide eyes by the front door, soulful headlamps following their every move. He watched her bang up the stairs, glimpsing her ankles through the bannisters, struck by how thin and pale they were, how bony and fast. Ten minutes later she and the children left.

*

The mornings were white and cold. It amazed Jonathan how nothing in his world seemed to have changed.

'Are you in Nofuck?' Bill Thayer was on the phone.

'No. Yes. I don't know.' Jonathan stared out of the kitchen window at the slanting grey rain falling on the garden. He looked at the open sandpit filling with rain; someone should have put the lid on it.

'We're waiting for that report. The Turkish one.'

A couple of months ago Jonathan and Bill Thayer, Head of Risk, had got drunk together, and Thayer had told him about his wife's cancer, her treatment and her remission, and how she'd suffered. 'It's a dreadful thing to watch that,' Bill had said, looking shy, large and sprawling in his seat. 'That's what I was afraid of – the suffering, much more than the dying.'

'Send it to me today, or you're fired.'

Jonathan could hear Bill breathing heavily down the phone, waiting for his response. Jonathan knew that sagging bravado, the accompanying bullishness, puffy face and red eyes; he knew the swaggering, pugnacious routine was an affectation. He affected it too. They both did, just so that they could get up in the morning, walk through the doors of the bank, take the lift six floors. Jonathan had rated Bill too. Thayer was good at the numbers – the best, some said – was experienced and had good judgement. Recently, though, over the last few years, he'd given up. Given in.

'It's a bad loan, Bill,' Jonathan said eventually, deciding to try being honest. To give it a whirl, see how it felt, for novelty's sake. 'I can't give it a rating – the information is too opaque, they're a risk, one of those emergent-market companies. Their published accounts are from some hokey-cokey accountancy firm, and the financial officer was the head of some bankrupt company. They don't provide enough information.'

'Everyone wants this to happen, Jonathan,' Bill said, lowering his voice slightly. 'Everyone wants this loan to happen. Give it a rating, you'll get your reward. Okay?'

He'd get his reward. Nobody understood risk, real risk; if something appeared to be a real risk, then they needed it to not be – it must be magicked into a state of safety, just like that, with the swish of a magic wand, the press of a button; avoided, denied and argued away. Well, he'd tried being honest. Recent events had proven to them all that nobody was in charge. The banks could go bust, ask for help and then carry on exactly as they had before. Nobody was going to stop them, nobody was in charge.

'Okay, Bill, I'll change the report and send it to you.'

'Terrific.' Bill sounded hearty. 'That's terrific. Give my love to Tacita and the girls, enjoy your break.'

'Thanks.'

It occurred to Jonathan to ask Bill Thayer to tell the department to pretend he was at work, if his wife called during the week. He played briefly with how to make this request, nerveless and sane: '*I have a departmental request*'; or needy and insane: '*I'm going to die*'. As far as Tacita was concerned, he was at work. Except for Thursday and Friday, when — emergency over — he was now expected to attend a management-team bonding exercise at a golfing hotel in Kent. It had brought him a small flick of pleasure to read OliveOhio's response to this plan on the blog: '*Golf! I could have written that myself — it's a narcissist's game; corporate male bullshit, money, the expensive kit, the high self-regard despite so little ability — they love it. Seriously.*'

He'd been checking Tacita's blog every day. He'd learnt that she was 'grateful' to be away in the 'wilds' of Norfolk, 'alone', and that she was realising she needed to find some 'closure and peace'. OliveOhio had been effusive in her praise for this, but had warned darkly that Washed Up wouldn't be getting any peace 'anytime soon' unless she made it clear that either she was leaving or he agreed to go into therapy.

Reading the comments, which were now beginning to far outweigh Tacita's blog entries, Jonathan was struck by how many people seemed to have an urgent, needy stake in watching his wife's nervous breakdown take place on the Internet. Her situation was terrible. There must be some gratification for them in seeing the cracks finally begin to show, to see it in stages, a dramatic story arc; to know that their marital stasis was not, could not, stay the same, and that things would inevitably come to a head. They'd been watching them both fumbling in the darkness, lunging out across rooms, their heads covered in heavy dust-filled blankets, but here now were a fourth and fifth act: exposure. A well-made, well-lit play. Tacita only had praise and thanks for them: '*Your support means so much to me.*'

He missed her, he wanted to hold her, he wanted to be the one to support her.

Tacita had posted photographs of the girls on the beach, both in matching fleeces and with their rat-taily hair swinging out in the wind; behind them were great stretches of wet sand banked by vast dunes, which looked ready to shift and slide. Their faces were bright and clear. They looked happy.

*

Jonathan was now alone in the big house that he hadn't wanted to buy. He went out walking. He left the house and walked the streets of the town, surprised at how quickly he would come to the town's edges, her skirts, out in the fields, the pavements dissolving into hedgerow. Then he would turn back and walk towards the centre. On Castle Street or Museum Street he would stop and stare at the pink, yellow and white houses, which he thought beautiful under the turning leaves of the autumn trees; they seemed bent with history. And he felt in those moments a yearning, a dreadful rapacious desire and longing, for something he couldn't quite pin down.

He went to the tourist information shop in the market square and bought three books about the town. He needed to place himself, find out what was real. He demanded of the woman behind the counter how long she had lived here and, taking him for a tourist, she had smiled neatly at him.

'Four years. There's lots to see and do here, even if it is a little off the beaten track.' She pressed her hands down firmly on the Uttlesford District Council plastic bag that she had put his books in. 'I think you'll find there's plenty to keep you interested,' she added firmly, and Jonathan had nodded vigorously, aching to please her/to not let her down too.

In Crumbles, the café next to the kitchenware shop, Jonathan ordered the soup of the day, which when it came was a weak, fatty and tasteless broth-like confection served up with three triangles of buttered sliced bread. His mobile rang, and looking at the screen he saw that it was Eve Hashall and decided not to answer. His favourite of the three books was a book of photographs. He read the back six times before even opening the book, sipping on his thin soup.

This fascinating collection of old photographs will enable the reader to take a nostalgic trip around old Saffron Walden. It was once a town of small shops run as family concerns, where 'The customer is always right', and most of the customers were treated as old friends by the shopkeepers.

Family concerns. When he opened the book, Jonathan found that the photographs showed shocking levels of pastoral poverty: scowling children in petticoats and aprons, a van piled high with old furniture and tin buckets, the narrow dusty streets, medieval slums. It looked a harder place than the blurb had suggested. The shopkeepers were there all right, more recently in white coats and horn-rimmed spectacles, their shelves stacked with old packets and tins, with irritated-looking women in herringbone coats waiting patiently in line for their turn.

As he was walking home, Tacita called, in surprisingly high spirits. They hadn't talked all week.

'You won't believe this. Vicky Clover's sent me porn, along with photos of the birthday party,' Tacita said, laughing. 'By God, you should see his cock. It's extraordinary. Shall I forward it to you?'

Jonathan stared out at the stretch of old houses falling down the street ahead of him, old-fashioned street signs hanging off black wrought-iron brackets; at a huge lorry causing trouble in the middle of the road, so that nobody could get around it; and at the rolling clouds above him, presaging calamity.

'Tell me again. Vicky Clover has sent you porn, along with the photographs of her daughter's birthday party? I'm surprised at them, aren't you? Those photographs – it's not of them, is it?'

'No, God, no, it's not them. It's weird, though. I click on one photo and there's Lila and her friends sitting on a rug with that dazed, party expression they get, and then the next photo – oh, my God, I've found another one. What is she doing to this guy?'

'Just close the email, Tacita. I'll deal with it when I get home.'

'I bet you will,' Tacita laughed. 'Shall I ring her up and say, "Thank you so much for emailing me pictures of your daughter's enchanting birthday party, Mrs Clover, but as it happens you've also sent me porn?"'

'No, don't do anything. Don't do anything.'

'Where are you?'

'On the golf course,' he said. 'It's near a road.'

'Are you having fun?'

'No, not really.'

'Okay, I should go,' she said. 'Jonathan?'

'Yes?'

'When I come back, there are some things we need to talk about. Really talk about.'

'Rightio.'

Nothing is more hopeless than planned happiness. The phrase pops into Jonathan's head as he puts the money down on the counter for a bottle of whisky. He isn't sure where he heard it first

– perhaps in a documentary, or a magazine, his mind reaching for tenuous, shadowy links, something to do with American suburbs of the 1950s. The Age of Eisenhower. Perhaps. Jonathan had never understood what it was about those lines of houses built on a grid, the cliché of the picket fence, the conformity, the safety, the empti-ness, which seemed to upset people so. He'd always found them rather attractive-looking, wholesome, glistening and safe; also the pressed shirts and smart suits, the briefcases, the porches – oh, the porches, so large, wooden and expansive; and a creek, there was always a creek nearby where the children rode their bikes to, and where perhaps a neighbourhood tragedy might take place. Anyway, now he thought that about Mr and Mrs Clover and the planning of their child's birthday party, and what hopes and dreams might have gone into that planning – a storage jar of memories for the future – only to be shattered in the final stage by sending out pornographic pictures to parents. Jonathan sighed. It was hopeless: preservation was hopeless, restoration was hopeless. He decided to get mindlessly, violently, depressingly drunk.

He walked slowly back towards his house. He stopped by a lamp-post on the far side of the car park near the common; an orange ribbon, crumpled from the rain and then drying out again, lifted a little in the wind in front of his face. He put up a hand to touch it, and inspected the poster more carefully.

Sitting in his kitchen, a pile of plates in the sink, the house silent and dark, Jonathan poured out a generous glass of neat whisky. He remembered a woman he'd seen on holiday in Cornwall, last year. A hot summer day. They were on the beach, the sea unnaturally flat and silent. The woman had taken her lilo – an inflatable meant for a swimming pool – out into the sea. She wore sunglasses and a bikini, her body shining with high-factor suncream. She'd pushed the inflatable out into the sea and lain back, her arms behind her head. Jonathan had watched her: she was pretty, poised, a little showy, decadent. And he knew that once the inflatable had floated out past the rock on the far side, the sea would be sheltered no more. But he hadn't done anything about it, hadn't called out to her, or swum out; he'd sat patiently while May buried his feet, his legs, his stomach in the grainy sand, feeling the sun prick his face, watching her, lying back, a complacent smile on her face, awaiting disaster.

I know someone who can take us to Harlow

Stella took the call from PC Chambers, in the rain, on her way back from picking up Jack at nursery. Mary was in the pram, staring above her with an amazed expression barely discernible under the creases of the rainproof cover, where the raindrops fell and splattered. Jack was making an effort to get as wet as possible, stopping in puddles and kicking them, with a serious look on his face, and then, when drenched from the waist downwards, looking up at Stella, shocked.

'It's wet.'

'Yes, they're all wet. They're puddles. Every puddle you go in, it makes you wet.'

'Every time.' Jack shook his head with some satisfaction. 'Every puddle.'

She didn't want to tell him to stop, she didn't care that he was wet. When they were home, then he could put on some dry clothes. Stella refused to have strong feelings on this. She didn't think it was a crisis, she wasn't going to pretend it was, though it was cold, and they were being slow, and she didn't have a hood on her coat.

She could feel the drips of rain down her neck and back, a coldness on her cheeks; she stood on the pavement in the falling rain, watching Jack spraying dirty water up his jeans, and wondered what was different. Ever since she could remember, this was where she wanted to be — here, on these pavements, following the familiar, raising her own children as she had been raised.

Last Christmas, sitting in her mother's bedroom with Sheila, who was in a fluster about the lunch, and a few presents she hadn't yet wrapped, and nobody had thought to take the turkey out of the fridge the night before, so perhaps the cooking times would all be off. And her mother had been trying to change, out of her cooking/preparing clothes and into her best top and skirt, and she'd managed the top, but it was the skirt that was difficult; she had the zip stuck, and she was turning around, bending over trying to see what the matter was, and at the same time she was yanking and yanking at the zip, her face flushed and quietly furious. Stella had sat on the side of the bed, watching her, and telling her all about what Jack had said when he'd opened his stocking, what he'd thought about each present, in detail, until finally Sheila — her face blotchy and complicated — had thrown her arms up in the air and said, 'Oh, fuck it! I can't be bothered any more.' And she'd let her skirt fall to the floor, in a defeated puddle at her feet, revealing her startlingly thin and fleshless thighs in colourless tights.

'Mum!' Stella had been shocked, but in a way that pleased her. 'Here, let me help you with it.'

'I don't want to wear it, Stella. I don't want to cook the lunch, either.' Sheila had turned to look at herself in the mirror. 'I can't be bothered any more,' she repeated emphatically into the mirror. 'I'll cook lunch like this.'

'In your pants?'

'Why not?'

'You're too old to be cooking in your pants.'

'I'm not *that* old. Who's to care?'

'I care,' Stella said softly.

And a moment had passed between them, a vast drifting moment that was nothing to do with Christmas lunch but everything to do with a ridged-up history of lunches and stuck zips and expectations. This was how it seemed to Stella, as she knelt on the floor and slowly pulled the skirt up her mother's legs, put her hand flat against her thigh and tugged the zip up over its broken teeth, until it held.

'Oh, Stella,' Sheila had said, looking down at her, resigned. 'If you could help me with the sprouts then?'

Perhaps, Stella thought now, looking down at Jack kicking the puddle, perhaps she should have let Sheila wear just her pants, like she'd wanted to.

*

'Stella? It's Chambers here, PC Chambers. Are you alone?'

'No.' She heard him sigh, the wrong response, again. 'I'm with the children, walking across London Road.'

'Stella, I've got some news. I'll call you back later? When you're at home? I'd like to come round personally, but we're short-staffed.'

'No.' She took Jack's cold hand and pressed it against the pram handlebar, wanting him to cling to it. 'Tell me now, it's okay, I want to hear it now.'

'A body has been discovered. We need you to go and see if you can identify it.'

Stella looked down at Jack, who was making faces at Mary through the plastic cover. A single, silent tear ran down her cheek; a fissure had opened within her quietness, and behind it lay something dark and rich. She took a deep breath. Below her the town was awash with rain, but it looked asleep, washed through and soft. As though it too were dazed. She looked down the hill of the High Street, at the trees losing their leaves, the wide pavements, that bow-windowed house, the pizza restaurant with its wide, inviting windows. When there had only been mysterious and terrifying absence, Stella had emptied herself out too, lain flat, unthinking and vacant. She hadn't known herself, walking the streets in a condition of quiet, internal panic. Now a kind of strength developed within her.

'Where?'

'Bishop's Stortford, but it's been taken to Harlow for a post-mortem. Look, I know this is hard – it might not be your mother, Stella, there's every chance it isn't. They ran what they knew about the body through the system, and your mother came up, so we just have to be sure.'

'You've got a photograph.'

'The body is . . . um . . . a bit disfigured. We can't be sure.'

The body. *'Oh, fuck it!' her mother had said, 'I can't be bothered any more.'*

'How will I be able to tell, then?'

'Well, we'll be getting dental records, but often relatives can tell – they know the shape of the person, their skin. From what I understand, it shouldn't be too difficult for you, but the photographic comparison isn't strong or firm enough. It'll speed things up, that's all, if you could go and look.'

'Speed what things up?'

'Stella, go home, I'll call you at home. Get your auntie to come round, okay, or call your husband? Then we can make the necessary arrangements.'

Stella squeezed Jack's hand firmly against the bar and turned the buggy around and went left up the Debden Road instead. It would only take her ten minutes to get to South Road, and that was where she should go, she was sure of it.

'We're going to visit someone, Jack, you must be good.'

'I don't want to,' he said, blinking in the rain. 'I want to go home. I'm thirsty.'

'You can have a drink there,' Stella told him, trying to smile. He looked up at her, suspicious and disbelieving. 'Come on, it's important, it's about Granny.'

'Is Granny going to be there?' Jack picked up his pace, looking hopeful. 'I want to see Granny. Look! My feet are all wet.'

Stella walked up to the door, and rang the bell. She positioned Jack just in front of her, by her knees, one hand on his little curved shoulder, to hold him back or drag him in, whichever was required. Mary behind in the pram, under the plastic cover. She waited, expectant, stroking her hot hand against her head, putting her hair behind her ears, her head buzzing.

When Theresa opened the door, just a crack, Stella put her foot in the crack; she wasn't sure why, she just felt that she had to – otherwise she knew, from its first hesitant, worried opening, that Theresa might try to close the door again.

'Stella,' Theresa said, with half her face showing, looking down at Stella's foot, 'careful, you'll get your foot hurt.'

'Not if you open the door, and Jack's soaked through. We need to come in.'

'Come in? It's not really a good time, I . . .' But Stella nudged against the door, gently, and pushed Jack in front of her, so that Theresa could only open it.

'Oh!' Stella pushed her wet hair back from her face. 'What's happened? You've been crying.'

Without thinking she reached out and touched the red swelling around Theresa's eyes, stroked her face. 'What happened?'

'It's nothing,' Theresa said.

'I didn't know if you'd be in,' Stella said, remembering herself. 'I got a call from the police.'

'Come in. Leave the pram in the hall.'

Stella followed Theresa, pushing Jack in front of her. Jack had fallen silent listening to the two women, concerned by the undertow of incomprehensible emotions flowing between the two of them. They followed Theresa into her kitchen.

'Can Jack have a drink? Your kitchen is nice, I like your units.'

'Oh, well, thank you. I'm only renting.' Theresa wiped her nose on her sleeve, and reached over and took a glass out of the cupboard for Jack and filled it with water.

'I don't like water,' Jack said flatly, staring at Theresa's swollen eyes.

'Oh, oh. I don't know what else I have,' Theresa said, looking intently at Stella, who was looking out of the window and ignoring this exchange. 'I might have some orange juice, do you like that?'

'Does it have bits in?'

'Bits? I don't know.' Theresa felt herself give a little giddy fake laugh. She wished Stella would intervene. 'Let's see, I'll get the orange juice and we could check it for bits, or if it does have bits in, perhaps we could sieve them out?'

'Just give him the juice, Theresa, it'll be fine,' Stella said, turning round. 'You've got a load of stuff, haven't you?'

The three of them surveyed Theresa's kitchen, taking in the dusty jars of dried fruit lining the windowsill, the pieces of paper stuck to the wall covered in lists, the piles of unread books beside the kettle.

'I want to watch telly.'

'Oh, Jack,' Theresa said. 'I don't have one.'

She was struggling to keep up with the events unfolding in her kitchen. Moments before, she'd been sitting on her bed, holding and then putting down a letter from Nic. She couldn't bear to hold it for long. How like him to write on proper thick, ribbed paper, and with an ink pen. How like him to tell her he understood, that he didn't blame her, that he thought she'd done the right thing. His careful words, his forgiveness, his understanding. She'd tried to picture him, sitting at a desk — perhaps in a library — picking his words carefully, his tongue stuck between his teeth, stopping to smooth his fringe down. Posting the letter to her, as light flies, as forgiveness comes, pouring down on her. There was a confidence to the letter that she couldn't quite place. He said he'd been out of the hospital for a while, that he was 'rebuilding' his life. He said things were better now that he'd finally cracked; he could put the pieces back together again. He said he thought everyone probably needed to crack up at least once — it might be the sanest thing to do. Then there'd been an exclamation mark. The dreadful, chipper sight of that ! had made Theresa angry, and then she had started to cry.

'You don't have a telly?' Jack said, astounded, feeling a wave of sympathy for her. Perhaps that was why this lady was so upset.

'I just feel that I can live quite comfortably without one. I have a computer.'

Stella had opened the back door.

'You don't have to tell him so much, Theresa. He's only three. Jack — out!'

And Jack obediently walked over towards the back door, the orange juice still in his hand, and peered out into the wet garden. He took careful, one-foot-at-a-time steps out of the door, turning sideways, concentrating on his glass of juice.

'Isn't he lovely,' Theresa said weakly. 'Should he be in the garden in the rain?'

'I've had a call from PC Chambers,' Stella said casually, putting her hands on her hips, casting a glance after Jack's slim, hunched back plodding down the path. 'The one in charge of my mother's case. He thinks they might have found her.'

'Stella—'

'In the mortuary in Harlow.' Stella wandered over and took down a glass for herself and filled it at the tap. 'He wants me to go and identify the body. I was wondering if you'd come with me? I'd like to go with you. Marie's gone home, and Zeki is at work, and I don't drive.'

Theresa stared over at Stella, watching her coolly sip from her glass of water. She had one foot up against the units, and it struck Theresa as an odd pose, as if she was in a bar, or a saloon perhaps. Was it shock that made her seem so composed? That night in Stella's kitchen, Theresa had thought her vulnerable, battered and wide-eyed, like a doe. All wobbly-legged, gentle and affectionate. Now, she seemed to possess a certitude, a straight line of common sense running through her, allowing her to speak these terrible sentences with such calmness.

'My God, Stella! But that's terrible, I'm so sorry,' she managed to say. 'Is he sure it's her?'

'No, he's not. The body is quite disfigured, he said. That's why I have to go.'

As if on cue, her mobile started to ring from the hallway, from her soft bag hanging on the back of the pram.

'That'll be him again, I expect. What shall I say?'

'Say you're going, of course – now, this afternoon.'

'Okay.'

Stella walked down the hall and answered her phone.

'Yeah, no, I'm not at home, I'm at a friend's house. She's going to drive me down to Harlow. Are you coming? Oh – okay – who shall I ask for at Harlow? Have you got an address? Me? I'm fine, yeah; really, I'm fine. I'll call you from there, shall I?' She gestured to Theresa, miming writing in the air. Theresa passed her a pencil and a piece of paper, watched Stella as she carefully wrote down the instructions, looking relaxed, as though she were taking the address for a party, not a morgue. Theresa shivered a little and drew her cardigan around her.

'Stella,' she said slowly, when she'd finished with the phone. 'I haven't got a car. I could call you a taxi? I'm so sorry.'

Stella smiled at Theresa and waited.

'Your husband? Have you called him?'

'Theresa, I don't want to go with him. I need . . . I need to go with a stranger. You wanted to help.'

Theresa was convinced then that Stella must be in shock. However, there was something in the set, certain way in which Stella spoke, with such conviction and hope – as though for some reason Theresa had become very important to her, and because Theresa had made a point, an emphatic point, of wanting to help – Theresa felt she had no alternative but to say, 'I'll find someone who can take us to Harlow.'

It was wonderful, in its way

'Welcome aboard,' Jonathan said, opening his front door and smiling broadly to show he was coping, despite his hangover.

'Thank you so much for doing this. Are you sure about it? We thought about getting a taxi,' Theresa said, frowning.

'Come on in. Don't thank me, I'm pleased. What are neighbours for? I said if there was anything – and here I am.' Jonathan held his arms wide and aloft. He wondered when, exactly, he'd become this comic figure. 'At the end of the pier all week, matinées on Wednesdays. BOOM-TISH. Tell your friends. Hang on, I'll just get my things, be right with you.'

Stella and Theresa entered the dark, cavernous hallway and watched as Jonathan gamely sprinted up the stairs, two at a time. A storm was gathering outside, and as they'd walked across the common to his house the wind had started to build, ravishing the bare trees and sweeping leaves around their feet. Dark rainclouds hung low above their heads, a greenish light had descended, and the first clap of thunder.

'What are we going with him for?' Stella whispered, looking around the hall. 'He's a right plonker.'

'He can drive and he's got a car, for one thing. You didn't want to ask Zeki, or your aunt.' Then Theresa said, 'In the circumstances.'

She felt the unlikelihoods carpeting the ground around them. She had thought of Evelyn, Natasha, Neil at the museum, of everyone in her book group, her mind swirling through a surprisingly inadequate shortlist of possibilities. A taxi. Calling a taxi would have been the right thing, even if too expensive for both of them. Then she'd remembered Jonathan's card, and him saying he would help, that he would like to help, if there was anything she needed. Anything she needed. She called him on the off-chance, presuming he'd be at work, if only to strike him off her list, because her mind had become spongy with the responsibility of a stranger's needs. When he'd answered, she'd been so surprised that she'd just come out with it, in a rush of words, without apology, and he'd told her he would be 'honoured'.

She looked over at Stella. 'I really don't know him. We had a drink once. Are you sure about this? Wouldn't you rather go with family?'

'No,' Stella heard herself say. A hurricane had blown through her head. 'No.'

Then they were off. The car went slowly down the road beside the common and turned out onto East Street, their pale faces caught inside the windscreen and windows. Outside, the life of the town continued as they drove slowly at first and then faster, spurred onwards past the streets: people shopping, leaving, walking, talking, the town filled with affectionate harmony and normal life. They were invisible. They drove past the hairdresser's, the car showroom, the pizza restaurant, the optician's, the Oxfam shop, until at the outer reaches of the town they broke through an invisible permeable bubble, a dome that hung over them and the town. Pop! They stole away, slipping quietly from the town's enchanted grip.

*

In the car, Jonathan was the first to find the silence awkward. He wanted to ask more about Stella's mother in the morgue, but he couldn't find a way to do so without appearing inappropriate or peremptory, or ghoulish. Theresa had rung him and asked for his help. It was a crisis. It was the best thing that could have happened – he'd been able to say, 'Whatever you need. I can help.' It was wonderful, in its way, driving them both to Harlow. The chauffeur, taking the right turns, the click of the indicator, swinging around the roundabouts, the whish of the windscreen wipers. Cars streamed past them, and the storm was above them now, blowing thick sheets of heavy rain; an early, pressing darkness had descended. Jonathan looked at Stella sunk down in the back seat, wrapped up in her pink anorak, staring out of the window, her face quite blank. He didn't know how someone should look on their way to view their mother's body in a morgue.

'Theresa said you had kids,' he said, wanting to make gentle, solicitous conversation with her. 'Have you left them with someone?'

'No, I left them at home on their own.' Stella caught his eye in the mirror for a moment, a slight smile.

'Yes, Stella's husband works in town,' Theresa put in quickly. 'We left them there. He's looking after them.'

In the front seat Theresa stole a look at Jonathan to try and gauge his reaction. The exchange in the low-ceilinged office had been embarrassing. Zeki had been at his desk, an elderly man opposite him, when they'd hurried in the front door of the estate agent's.

'I'm sorry, Jim. Excuse me a moment,' he'd said, alarmed, getting to his feet as Theresa and Stella had trooped towards his desk with the children.

Zeki had stared, uncomprehending, as Stella explained about her mother's body in Harlow, and how Theresa was going to take her there. His bewilderment had quickly tipped into mistrust and then slid towards panic.

'What? Why are you going with her? Who is she? Are you joking? I'll take you, Stella. We'll go now.'

And Theresa had been ready to agree with him. She'd wanted this amiable, eager man with his shiny forehead and tightly knotted tie to take her place. She would bow out, had done what was asked of her.

The elderly man, wearing a very clean mackintosh, had leant back in his chair as they talked and looked them all over, gently, nodding his head. He'd given Jack a quick, wry smile.

'I need to go with Theresa, Zeki. Just take the kids, okay? I'll call you when I know. I need you to call Joyce and Marie. Let them know what's going on.' And Stella had placed her hands on either side of his face and kissed him on the mouth, and Zeki hadn't been able to say anything, only nod with a bemused, querying acceptance. There was a bravado about Stella, Theresa had thought, watching her gather Jack in her arms and then bend over the pram to place her cheek against Mary's, as though she had steeled herself to try something out. They had left swiftly, leaving the two men with the children, before Zeki could marshal any further objections.

The rain continued. Jonathan, unable to bear the silence, put on the car radio, so that he could hum along in this car filled with mute women.

'How long do you think it'll take?' Theresa asked him, to stop the humming.

Stella's mind emptied again. She moved into the space behind it, the deep, silent absence. Watching the raindrops on the window, the grey wet sky behind, she closed her mind from panic or grief. She sat remote and still in the back of the car, felt only her breath rise and fall, heard only the occasional rustle of her anorak, located a soft, round scoop within her stomach. Somewhere to sit. Theresa and Jonathan's voices were a vague, comforting background murmur. None of this would have been possible if she'd been with Zeki or Joyce.

A subtle heat ran through Theresa's body. She wanted Jonathan to share in the responsibility of this trip – she wished it hadn't fallen to her to ask him. She was uncomfortable about this indebtedness, what it might imply. She leant forward and turned the radio down a little, but did not look over at Jonathan or apologise.

'Is your wife at home? Did she mind you coming?'

'No,' he said. 'She's away.'

'That's nice. Where's she gone?'

'It's half-term,' Jonathan volunteered, bending down to peer over the wheel. 'This rain is incredible.'

'Yes,' Theresa said. 'It really is. I heard thunder earlier too.'

'Thunder?'

'Yes, didn't you hear it?'

Why were they talking like this? It was unbearable. Theresa leant forward and turned the radio up again.

'Shall I take the M11 or the back roads? Which will be quicker?'

Theresa shook her head.

'Whichever,' she told him. 'So, why didn't you go too? On half-term, I mean.'

'Work,' he said.

'Oh,' she said.

*

When they arrived at the police mortuary there was no escaping their surprise at being in each other's company. Jonathan thought it best if he waited in the car. On the other side of the road was a newsagent's – he might go and buy some cigarettes, smoke one or two while he waited. Stella got out of the car and looked down at him, still sitting inside, with surprise.

'Come on,' she said, opening his door. 'Come on.'

No longer contained by the car, the three of them walked slowly across the car park, their heads bowed against the wild sheets of rain, towards the ugly, grey concrete building. As they entered the reception area Theresa and Jonathan both hung back near the door. Stella, running her fingers through her wet hair, approached the desk. She was told to wait; someone would shortly come and get her, and take her away to view her mother's body.

'How old is she?' Jonathan whispered in Theresa's ear. She shrugged a response, smiling apologetically at him. 'How do you know her?'

She wanted to say that she didn't know her, hardly at all. That she just had some information on her mother and she'd decided to deliver it personally, and that perhaps her decision to do so, that night, was in itself a consequence of the drink they had had together. That what followed afterwards felt out of her control, beyond her reasoning, because Stella had pulled her – Theresa – in from the edge, towards her, with a careful, unspoken intent. She wanted to tell him that her doing so felt, peculiarly, like the most natural thing in the world.

'Do you want me to come with you, Stella?' Theresa asked as a man in a white coat came towards them in the reception area. She couldn't let Stella go alone, she saw this now. She was supposed to be offering support.

'I'm okay,' Stella told her, steadying herself for the man's approach. 'I'll go alone.'

Jonathan and Theresa sat down in the orange plastic chairs after Stella left them, dutifully following the man through the double-doors to their left, down a long, shining corridor. Jonathan sniffed the air.

'Have you ever seen a dead body?' he asked, crossing his legs. 'I've only seen the one. One proper dead body. She's very brave, isn't she?'

'Oh, God, poor Stella.' Theresa gripped the side of her chair. 'Poor Stella.'

She bought them both weak brown tea from the machine, the liquid scalding inside the inadequate plastic cups. They sat in silence. Jonathan needed the toilet and went for a long, hot piss, the tang of his urine comforting him inside the artificially clean morgue toilet. He stared at himself in the mirror as he zipped up his trousers. He was unshaven, his eyes bloodshot. He saw a face collapsed by failure and regret. He washed his hands with great care and nodded encouragingly to himself before leaving.

'I had a friend,' Theresa said. 'I had a friend who was in hospital for a while. It smelt the same as here – you can feel the smell of the place settle on your skin.'

'The morgue and the hospital. Go figure.' Jonathan crossed his arms.

'Oh, don't. What do we say when she comes out? What words are there?'

'I have no idea.'

When they saw Stella's pale face come into view through the glass of the double-doors, they both stood up. Theresa took a few steps forward, her hands by her side, searching for details. Stella walked through the doors alone, her eyes wide and her face pale against the pink of her coat.

'It wasn't her,' she said to them, her voice wavering and faltering. 'It was someone else.'

'Oh, thank God,' Theresa went over and hugged her. 'Thank God for that.'

*

The three of them stood in the car park. The storm had passed, and the car park was floating in puddles. It was late afternoon, but dark, quiet and turning cold. Theresa stood close to Stella, her arms hanging limply by her sides, but ready to catch her if she fell. Stella took great gulps of air, blowing her cheeks out. She rested her hands on the bonnet of Jonathan's car and lowered her head. Jonathan leant against the car door, watching them both carefully.

'That was – nasty,' Stella said to Theresa, shaking her head. 'That poor woman.'

Nobody spoke. It was a clutch of time, the three of them in the drenched car park, wordlessly together, considering what Stella had seen.

'You were very brave,' Jonathan said, quietly.

'I'd better call Zeki.' Stella gathered herself together, allowing herself to open out to the world again. 'I'd better call Zeki and Marie.'

She fumbled through her bag, searching for her phone. Pulling it out, she switched it on and saw that she had two texts from Zeki, three from Marie and one from an unknown number. Favouring, for the first time, the possibility of the unfamiliar, she clicked on the little yellow envelope for the unknown number and read: '*All is well. Come to Southend as soon as you can.*'

Stella blinked, and read it again. The outside lights of the police building were now on, the asphalt was wet, there was a distinct breeze in the air and the sound of cars rushing past filled her head. She passed the phone to Theresa.

After she'd read it, Theresa handed the phone over to Jonathan.

'It's from Mum,' Stella said slowly into the air. 'I must go to her.'

The three neighbours peered at each other in the dark, grainy light of the car park.

There was seemingly nothing to protect them from one another, from the quiet, peculiar strings that had gently bound them together. They were exposed by their circumstances, and united by their own common absurdity. They were encapsulated, tied together by a ribbon of community, which was, inexplicably, tightening around them in a mortuary car park in Harlow. The silence of possibility flowed between them, until Jonathan said with a shrug, flipping his car keys in his hand, 'I'm not busy. I've nothing to get back for.'

'Okay,' Stella nodded, slowly, the idea of a trip integrating in her head. 'Okay.'

The three of them stood in silence. Theresa looked around her. This was ridiculous, they couldn't all go to Southend now. She had things to do at home, so much left undone: extended unfinished lists fixed to her kitchen wall, the Oxfam shop to sort for Evelyn, the untouched PhD thesis, that new jacket she'd bought, which she wanted to try and make into a waistcoat.

'Stella,' Theresa said. 'Do you mean you want to go now? With us?'

'Yeah.'

'Right,' Jonathan said, rubbing his hands together, looking from one to the other. He felt no hesitation or fear. 'Southend it is then.'

Traffic jam

Jonathan looked over at Theresa, sitting beside him, but she didn't return his look. She turned her head away from him, and he could see the delicate tendons standing out on her neck, her feathery earrings hanging against them, like birds.

'I'll just put in Southend,' Jonathan said, switching on his satnav and punching in the name. 'Then we'll take it from there.'

The road out of Harlow was clear and fast, but the traffic on the arterial road around Basildon, and towards Southend, was at a standstill. They sat grid-locked on one side of a dual carriageway for two hours, staring out at the large warehouses that flanked the road, seeing the light fade, and the lights from the warehouses and cars on the other side get slowly brighter.

'Why do all these people want to go to Southend?' Theresa wondered.

'Perhaps there's a Missing Mothers convention,' Jonathan said, and then regretted it.

'We should have brought food. Perhaps we should have gone back home, and then to Southend tomorrow.' Theresa felt responsible for them all. 'We should have thought about that.'

What was she doing? This thought hit Theresa when they were sitting in darkness on the A127, occasionally illuminated by the headlamps of the cars allowed to take small jaunts forward on the other side of the road. Stella and Jonathan seemed keen to go; they'd all believed, a little too quickly, that the text was definitely from Stella's mother. Theresa looked around; this car was very clean, like a rental car. She'd sold her car, littered with wrappers and bits of paper and small squidges of plasticine, when she left London, to raise money and because she'd thought she wouldn't need a car in Saffron Walden. *What was she doing*, allowing herself to be taken up by other people in this way? But there was no point going back because they were stuck now. On this dual carriageway. Together.

Stella stared out of the window into the darkness. Her mother was alive. Her mother was in Southend. She repeated these words to herself over and over again. She missed Mary, missed the weight of her in her arms; it was like an ache, all over her body. She wished she'd brought her. She could feel the milk growing solid and uncomfortable in her breasts. It would leak out. It started to leak out just because she was thinking about her soft head, the brush of her cheek, that pursed mouth and perfect, oval brown eyes, those thick dented wrists, the perfect shell of her hand. Her desire to have her made Stella breathe in deeply, a heavy snow-filled sorrow. She thought she might cry, and was pleased that she was alone in the back of the car. She should ring Zeki; he would have to go and buy Mary some formula and a bottle. He'd have to gently coax her into taking the hard rubberised teat into her mouth, as opposed to her mother's soft breast. Oh, Mary! Her mother was alive. Her mother was in Southend. She wanted her children near her, and Zeki.

The thought of being on her own — she was never on her own, not since Jack and Mary had been born. Sitting in the traffic in this car with Theresa and Jonathan, Stella wished more than anything that she was back home in her house, waiting for Zeki, holding her children near to her, making their tea. She closed her eyes, knowing also how much she wanted to be exactly where she was.

Stella kept trying to call her mum but there was no answer — and she didn't know what to leave as a message.

'I don't know why we've got two cars,' Jonathan said, shifting about on his seat, annoyed. 'I cycle to the station every day. Tacita has the family car. I don't really need this car.'

'Shall we play a game?' Theresa stretched her legs in front of her. 'What games do you both know?'

'Marie used to play this game where we had to think of someone, and then say what kind of animal they were.'

'Okay,' said Theresa. 'Let's play that then. You start.'

'Denise in the optician's.'

Jonathan burst out laughing. 'Who the fuck is that?'

'Denise in the optician's.'

'I don't know who Denise in the optician's is. Aren't you supposed to say David Cameron or Prince Charles, or something?'

'If she works in the optician's on the corner of George Street, then she's a llama,' Theresa said thoughtfully.

This made Stella laugh. 'A llama?'

'Yes, she's got that thick neck, hasn't she? Big eyes, a little on the glum side.'

'You know who Denise in the optician's is?' Jonathan was incredulous. He shook his head. 'How can you know that?'

'Come on,' said Theresa. 'You do live there too. You'll surprise

237

yourself. How about the woman with bright-yellow hair in Waitrose. You must have seen her?'

'Nope,' Jonathan said.

'How about the guy who has the flower stall on market days?' Stella tried.

'Nope, again,' Jonathan said, beginning to feel uneasy about himself. 'Let's play something else.'

His headache returned with a heavy, rolling thud across the front of his forehead, bearing down on his right eye. His skin itched. Did he even know where the optician's was in town? He should have bought those cigarettes back in Harlow. He might get cramp in his right leg any minute – perhaps he should turn the engine off for a bit. He yawned, his stomach rumbled. He hadn't eaten. He felt sick. He needed food, and sleep. Or a drink. Jesus, why wouldn't this traffic move. Denise in the optician's, for fuck's sake.

'Check your phone again,' he said, feeling impatient with everyone.

'There isn't a text, all right?' Stella snapped. 'I think I'd bloody know if there was.'

'Let's keep calm,' Theresa said. 'We must keep calm. Keep ringing the number.'

'I am.' Stella obediently called the number again, and they both swivelled round in their seats to look at her, her face glowing from the light of the phone. She held it up. 'It's just ringing.'

'There might be an answer machine,' Theresa said.

'There definitely will be.' Jonathan nodded.

Stella hung up.

'She'll get in contact when she's ready,' she told them.

'Oh, great,' Jonathan sighed, banging his hands on the steering wheel. 'That's just great.'

'Keep your hair on.'

'Shall we play "I spy"?' Theresa suggested loudly, her voice rising above the others. 'In the dark.'

Stella's mobile rang. Theresa and Jonathan felt their hearts lift for a moment and they turned around again, in unison.

'It's Marie,' Stella mouthed at them, rolling her eyes.

*

It was dark when they eventually arrived in Southend. The desperate nature of this entire undertaking had become increasingly clear to all three of them, as they'd waited for the mute mobile to ring. Jonathan now hated Stella's mobile phone. They drove into the city centre, which was dark and closed-down-looking. The dereliction of the town and the jettisoning of their intended plans made them wary of one another, as though they were enemy collaborators or conspirators, uncertain of the others' loyalty, wondering who would be the first to crack and expose them all.

'What shall we do now?' Jonathan said.

'Let's find a hotel.' Theresa thought they needed a plan – any plan. 'We might need to stay overnight.'

Jonathan turned the car down towards the promenade road. Sometimes it was still easier not to look too closely, he thought, to pretend that they were all in control of their lives and decisions.

'We need somewhere to stay. We might not hear back from her tonight,' Theresa went on, firmly.

Jonathan managed to stop himself from adding, 'Or ever'. Instead he chose to join in, 'We'll just drive along the sea front and I'll stop when we see somewhere we like.'

'Just the one night,' Theresa said, unable to find a way to disagree. Stella said nothing.

Jonathan didn't see anywhere he liked on the coastal road until they were heading into Thorpe Bay. Theresa pointed out plenty of hotels and bed-and-breakfasts, but Jonathan took one look at them and carried on driving.

'There'll be somewhere better further along,' he said, though none of the places had looked at all bad to either Theresa or Stella. Jonathan remained convinced that the perfect place would turn up next, and he didn't want to miss it. It made him anxious; he didn't want to settle on the first hotel they saw, or the fifth or the seventh, for he knew he'd regret it the next morning. He decided to try and make something of this trip.

'There might be somewhere really nice, and we could miss it,' he told them.

Jonathan finally gave in on the dark stretch of road in Thorpe Bay, pulling into a hotel that he was prepared to consider as 'not too bad at all'. He was desperate for a drink and to get out of the car. They all were. Stella didn't know what force propelled them from the dark car park into the warmly cheerful reception, or what guided them up the stairs, clutching their keys, towards their variously numbered bedrooms. One force – the one thing she could account for – was Jonathan's credit card, which he had, without consultation, handed over to the receptionist. This embarrassed Stella; she hadn't been sure what to say, but knew she couldn't afford a room in this hotel, so she had said nothing, looking to Theresa to deal with the situation.

'Oh,' Theresa said. 'I want to pay for my room. Here's my card too.'

'Sure,' Jonathan said, feeling magnanimous now that he was out of the car and near the hotel bar. 'We can even it up afterwards, Stella, according to our means.'

Beyond the glass

The three of them sat grouped around a small circular table in the otherwise empty hotel bar. The walls of the bar were panelled with fake wood, and a heavy brass light hung above their heads. Someone had tried to capture an old colonial-club feel for the bar, but the heavy tartan carpet, small round tables and small, dark curved-back chairs crowding the room confirmed that they had failed to see this theme through in a convincing fashion. They had trooped up and into their respective bedrooms in a mechanical way, but had nothing to unpack, and the strangeness of the bedrooms, and their situation, had quickly drawn them all to be together again.

The receptionist had briefly appeared behind the brilliantly lit bar to take their order, and then left them alone again, in the silent, stale-aired room.

Jonathan, already on his second whisky, was feeling extravagantly better, and talkative — a kind of rudderless relief.

'My wife and I just lost that touch of love,' he told them, crossing one leg over the other, holding a beer mat in his hand and waving it through the air. 'We couldn't find our way around each other any more. Like we'd lost the map, you know?'

'No,' Stella told him, shaking her head. 'No, I don't know.'

'We couldn't do anything wrong, Stella, to begin with. We were everything to each other, but over time,' Jonathan decided to try it out, 'well, it was as if we just lost touch, but we still lived together, in the same house. We never touched. It's a very lonely feeling.'

'You didn't sleep together?' Stella asked, sipping from her glass, wondering why he was telling them all this.

'No, not literally the touch. She wrote a blog all about me.'

'Did she?' Theresa asked. 'About your marriage?'

Jonathan nodded, looking gloomy and sheepish.

'Bloody hell,' Stella told him, 'I'd bloody kill someone who did that about me.'

'What did it say?' Theresa persisted, leaning forward. 'What was it called?'

'A lot of people commented on it actually – apparently it was quite a successful blog. They all had a lot of opinions.'

'I think I might have read it,' Theresa said, trying to appear calm. '"Washed Up – One Woman Swearing at Her Kitchen Sink."'

'Oh God.' Jonathan sank down in his chair, looking at her. 'Fuck'

'It's very . . . I mean, she's very . . . God! So The Project is all about you.' Theresa stared at him. 'I can't believe she's your wife.'

'She is.'

'Well, it's not that bad,' she said quickly, wanting him to feel better. 'It's only a blog.'

'It is that bad.'

'Yes,' Theresa smiled. 'Yes, it is. You're right. Were you . . . I mean, are you as awful as she says you are?'

'I suppose it was her marriage too. Not just mine,' Jonathan said, staring glumly into his glass.

The two women glanced at him when he said this, and then at each other.

'Is that why you could come with us?' Stella asked, prodding the slice of lemon in her drink.

'We've not actually talked about it. She doesn't know I know.'

'She's in Norfolk,' Theresa said, unable to stop herself. 'She's gone to try and work things out. Once and for all.'

'Why haven't you talked to her about it, you nutter?' Stella flicked her hair off her face. 'What's the blog about?'

'Well,' Theresa wanted to find a way to be polite, despite the gathering hysteria within her, the laughter trying to ease itself into her words. 'It's about The Project. And The Project is that this woman – Washed Up . . .'

'His wife.'

'Right, his wife. She found out that her husband had been . . . um . . .' Theresa paused. It occurred to her that she knew rather a lot about Jonathan, a frightening amount. It was actually rather indecent. She wasn't sure how to continue.

'She *decided*,' Jonathan said with some weight, 'that I'd been unfaithful.'

'Right,' Theresa continued. 'And The Project was all about how she wasn't going to confront him about it, but try and find a way to absorb it. Just carry on.'

'Why?'

Nobody was sure how to answer Stella's question.

'Fuck knows!' Jonathan said.

'I'm rather under the impression,' Theresa ventured tactfully. 'That to begin with she was simply frightened of having to confront the truth, but then the blog took off. The Project took over and she got carried away with that.' She glanced at Jonathan. 'I think, in the nicest way, that she liked the attention.'

'She got the wrong person,' Jonathan said. 'She got my mistress wrong.'

'Your mistress!' Stella snorted, enjoying herself. 'Jesus! Who says that?'

Jonathan reddened. He emptied his glass. He could still sit on a chair and make conversation. What conversation? He looked around the empty room. A large mirror hung on the wall opposite him. He wondered whether the woman from reception would appear again, like magic, or whether they would have to go and fetch her.

'She thought it was this woman I used to work with, and she's put her name on the blog. And now this woman – this ex-colleague – is furious about it. She says I have to tell Tacita to take her name off.'

'Tacita?' Stella sat up straight. 'I know her. She goes to Paint&Sing.'

'Oh, my God!' Theresa put her hand across her mouth. 'I think she might be in my book club. How many Tacitas can there be?'

They absorbed this new, entangled connection in silence for a moment.

'Wow! She was nice at book group,' Theresa said. Then, 'It is a very small town.' The traces and tracks of their lives crossed over, another common thread now hung between them. They were liberated and made more honest by being strangers to one another.

'I thought she seemed sad,' Stella said, staring at Jonathan.

*

'So you're living on your own then?' Stella asked loudly, looking flushed as she sat on a low stool. She had purposefully taken the stool. 'What's it like? How have you managed?'

This made Jonathan laugh, cheered him up.

'I manage fine, thank you, Stella. It's only been a couple of days.'

'I'd hate it. It'd give me the creeps.'

'Have you never lived on your own?' Theresa asked.

'No,' Stella answered blinking, looking defensive. 'Is that weird? My sister, Marie, she's just split from her husband. She wanted to go to Disney World for two weeks. I think it's because she hates the house without him, you know?'

Theresa and Jonathan nod at her – yes, they knew.

'Though I guess,' Stella went on, 'maybe it's weird that I never have. You live on your own. But then again, you were crying when I turned up this afternoon, weren't you?'

Stella looked over the rim of her glass at Theresa. She felt no awkwardness in saying this, she didn't see that it might cause Theresa to feel uncomfortable. Her eyes drifted lazily over Theresa's face and she wondered at the silence that followed her question. Well, honestly, she thought to herself, looking over at Jonathan who was staring at his shoes, she's clearly not all that happy as a person, anyone could see that – nobody who's happy needs to try as hard as she does.

'Shall we eat?' Theresa said suddenly, and loudly. 'I reserved us a table in the restaurant, but I don't know why I bothered. This place is deserted.'

They were escorted across the thick carpet, past all the empty, bare tables and waxy green plants in the restaurant, and into a glass extension attached to the front of the hotel. Outside the windows it was all blackness. Here their table had been laid, with a white tablecloth and an array of glasses.

'We thought you'd like it here.' The waiter shrugged. 'Smaller. Thought you might find it a bit empty back there.'

'I had this boyfriend. He had problems, mental-health problems,' Theresa said; balancing the thick leather menu on her knee. 'It's complicated.'

Jonathan nodded at her; he didn't want for her to have to explain. Not now. Perhaps when the two of them were together, perhaps later in the bar. The thought of being in the bar alone with Theresa later on makes his stomach churn unexpectedly; the thought that he is even thinking of being in the bar alone with Theresa later on makes him queasy. He should really eat. Perhaps he and Theresa might have a nightcap, something warming and comforting, and what would follow after would follow, and it'd probably be nothing. Just as the day has gone, so too would the evening. After Stella has gone to bed — and Stella should be going to bed, he thinks, she looks tired. Huge great dark rings circle her eyes and she keeps yawning and turning her mobile phone on and off.

Jonathan, confused, decided to study the menu instead.

'What kind of problems?' Stella asked, looking across at Theresa.

'He had a kind of breakdown.'

'It's funny, you working in a museum,' Jonathan said quietly, his thoughts still on Theresa, but not on what she was saying. 'I think being in Saffron Walden is a bit like living in a museum.'

'It's not,' Stella said quickly. 'It's not at all. What do you mean?'

'Well,' Jonathan sat back in his chair. 'It's kind of behind glass, isn't it? The whole town. Real, and not quite real. Like a stage set. The edges of their bodies were warmed by each other, and the alcohol. They each considered for a moment what Jonathan had said, feeling their way into the dark, off-stage, private pockets of denial and delusion they carried within themselves.

'What?' Stella said. 'No, it's not. It's just normal, you weirdo.'

'It got very bad,' Theresa found herself telling them as they finished off the second bottle of wine. The clouds had parted, a glossy, deep opening had appeared, and she was going to pour forth. She couldn't help herself. 'He got violent — he didn't mean to. Then he tried to build a scale model of the Battle of Inkerman, and then, well . . . then, oh God, he tried to hurt himself.'

It sounded peculiar, when she said it out loud. She had never said it out loud before. She tried to acquire this knowledge for herself.

'I've never said that out loud before,' she said, taking a large swig of wine. Her head was hurting, and she swayed on her chair.

'The Battle of Inkerman?' Jonathan was having trouble following what she was saying.

'Yes. He's something of a Crimean expert. He lives the research life. That's not much of a life.'

'Right.'

'He was in the hospital, you see. He looked awful. I felt terrible for him, it was awful. And then,' she took another gulp of wine, 'I told him I'd be there for him. That we'd see this through together. But then, I just couldn't bear it. I couldn't do it. So, I left him there.'

'In the hospital?'

'I moved to Walden.'

*

248

The sweet terror of the moment when she realised that she would not be going back into the hospital, or any of the hospitals or clinics Nic might be moved into. She and Nic's father sitting on those ridiculous chairs, stunned, trying to listen to the consultant psychiatrist explaining 'the options'. Sectioning Nic was a possibility; certain criteria would need to be met if he was to be released from this hospital: twenty-four-hour suicide watch, a commitment to ensure that he took all his medication and also met his daily outpatient appointments. 'Extreme vigilance,' he'd said.

Nic's father, in his corduroy trousers, bizarre bow tie and shiny shoes, with his droll, carrying voice, turning to Theresa and saying, 'Rather you than me, darling.' Then he'd winced at himself. 'That was grossly insensitive.' He leant the ridiculous chair back against the wall. 'Sorry,' he'd said, looking defeated and white-faced. 'But all the same.'

They had agreed that he should stay in the hospital for the time being. They'd said it would be the best place for him. Theresa had both believed and not believed this to be true. Weeks passed in a trance. Too uncomfortable to be still, she discovered herself job-hunting, ringing estate agents, putting her flat on the market, on a train for an interview, catching sight of her ghostly replicate face in the window, shrouded in guilt and denial, as the train had pulled into Audley End. Then came the commitment to move, a kind of empty self-fulfilling conviction, swiftly followed by all those giddy, fetching and desperate, warm-hearted enthusiasms, her desire to help others.

'He was a good man. But I didn't want to care for him,' Theresa said, pulling at the line of velvet on her cuff, frowning. 'Oh God, the stories we tell ourselves, you know?'

'He wasn't your responsibility,' Jonathan told her, trying to hide his shock. He'd thought Theresa a manifestly kind person. Then he reached over for safer ground. 'And I don't care how complicated it is – there's no excuse for hitting a woman. I do believe that.'

Theresa stared at him.

'I do, I do believe it,' he went on, pouring each of them another glass of wine, his cheeks flushed.

Jonathan slurred the edges of his words, and some wine slopped onto the tablecloth.

'There are excuses,' Theresa said quietly, sulkily, pushing her chair back from the table.

'Not good ones,' Jonathan insisted. 'No *good* excuses.'

Theresa had ordered fish, and it sat in front of her, swimming in a white wine and mushroom sauce; she pushed at it with her fork.

'I know that,' she said flatly. 'I'm not trying to make any excuses. Just to explain.'

'Bloody hell. I don't know,' Stella said, her mouth full. 'I don't know what I'd do. He doesn't sound all *that*, if I'm honest.'

'Stella!' Jonathan started to laugh.

'What? With this bonkers model, or whatever.'

'Hmm. It was a bit bonkers.' Theresa nodded, grinning at her. 'He was a good man though, really. He just got unwell.'

'Perhaps it wasn't a serious relationship?' Jonathan said, mopping up the wine with his napkin. 'You wouldn't have wanted to tie yourself down, in that case.'

'Yes, it was serious.' Theresa shrugged, and looked from one to the other. 'It was. I was selfish.'

'Who's to say?' Stella said. She laughed. 'My mum says that.'

'Your bloody mum.' Jonathan shook his head.

'My bloody mum.' Stella had an infectious, thrilling laugh. It made them both smile.

'Your bloody mum.' Theresa started to laugh too, and refilled her glass. 'Why are we laughing?'

'Doesn't it feel nice to be out, though, Stella?' Jonathan wanted to labour this point, so he stuck a finger in the air. 'I know it's not under exactly salubrious circumstances, but don't you feel free?'

Stella looked around the glass extension and the barren restaurant behind them. Through the darkness she could imagine the sea on the other side of the road, brooding and choppy. An occasional car went past, but it had mostly been dark and serene outside. If it was summer, she imagined this might be quite a nice place to sit; she guessed that they slid open the doors at the front – perhaps pulled the roof back? There would be other diners then too, sandy and calm from the beach, sitting on their cane chairs, shifting about on the dark-green cushions. Stella wasn't sure that this represented freedom, though.

'I want to find Mum, and then I want to go back home. I feel well pissed, but I don't feel free, no.'

Theresa nodded, but there was a tightness to her face that suggested she didn't believe Stella, or didn't want to believe her.

'So,' Stella said, when the coffee arrived, slumped down in her chair, smiling under her fringe. 'Did you cheat?'

'No,' Jonathan said automatically, his head swimming. 'No. She jumped to the wrong conclusions.'

There was a pause, and the women looked at each other and then back at Jonathan.

'That's well weird,' Stella said, leaning her head on her hand, her elbow wobbling. 'Isn't it? I wonder why she thought it then?'

'Oh, for God's sake,' Jonathan snapped angrily. 'I've had enough of being policed all the time. Yes, yes, I did. Okay?'

A drenched pause fell over the table.

'I wonder why she didn't have it out with you? I'd be all over Zeki if he did that to me.'

'She'll have had her reasons,' Theresa said quietly. 'She probably thought it was the right thing to do. She probably thought it was for the best. I think her intentions were good, but she got – a bit lost, a bit mislaid along the way. I mean, the problem isn't about who we are, it's who we *think* we are – the stories we tell ourselves to make life bearable.'

'It's unbearable,' Jonathan said, tearing up, melodramatic and self-pitying. 'She can't forgive me.' He reached over and put his hand on Stella's. 'You don't know what she's like. I don't see how we can get over this.'

'Have you asked her to forgive you?' Stella asked. 'Why don't you do that? It's not exactly the end of the world, is it?'

Jonathan stared at her, blinked and wiped away a tear.

'Maybe I should call her now?'

'No,' Theresa said, imagining the comments section. 'Not when you're drunk and in a hotel with two strange women.'

'What does it matter whether he's drunk or not? Whether he's here with us or not? Stop thinking like that,' Stella declared, banging the table, and making Theresa and Jonathan jump. 'Just tell the truth. How hard can that be?'

At night

Stella didn't sleep well; she found the bed uncomfortable and foreign, too many pillows, the sheets a little starchy. She wasn't used to drinking, and her skin felt dry and stretched, her throat too dry. She lay quietly, her arms resting by her sides, in the darkness, with her eyes wide open, wondering how long it would take for the alcohol to leave her milk. She stared into the inky darkness, listening to the sounds of the hotel – the clunk of a lift, a couple of doors banging shut, someone outside her window talking in a foreign language; that'd be Polish, she told herself. The mobile was next to the bed.

None of them had had to come to Southend; Stella had made it happen. She had the telephone number. She could have spoken to her mother, with one eye on Jack, whilst holding Mary, with the telly on, from her bed, from her garden, from in the bath to walking down the London Road. From anywhere she'd wanted to. Lying in the strange, warm, clean room, with its soft tartan carpets, she listened to her heart beating; she listened too for the sounds of her own further thoughts, but none came.

It was all silent, unformed and inarticulate. She felt empty spaces were all around her, tricking her, guiding her towards them, crouching in the darkness, entreating her to feel the edges of their emptiness, these pockets of silence and vacancy. As though she was on a leave of absence from her own life. The idea frightened her. Her own life unrepresented, deserted; vanished.

Perhaps this was what her mother had felt. Her mother was alive, and so was she. The vision of that waxy figure lying in the morgue swam into view. How Stella had peered over as the bag was unzipped and had prepared to see the worst, but had seen something yet more terrifying. Not her mother. She who had come to claim her mother was greeted by the face of a woman nobody knew. Her features damaged and unnatural, her skin cold and hard, the eyes still open. Staring from nothing towards nothing. Unwanted. Her mother had just decamped, withdrawn, slipped away from her, from Stella.

She opened and closed her fingers, feeling them spread across the sheets beside her, touching the outer line of her thigh.

And now she had come after her mother, tracked her down. She could feel her own limits. She would like to go now and stand on the seashore, to feel the cold sea on her toes, to watch its darkness, its cloudy, dark muddy waters wash up against her, to throw her head back, to stumble on the pebbles. To take on the experience.

Sea Life

The next morning Stella wasn't in the hotel. Theresa banged on her door and then searched the dining-room, the car park; walked across the road and stood on the beach front, trying to see over the beach huts, trying to see Stella on the grey beach. She did not. The receptionist, when asked, told her that Stella had already gone out.

'She said she was out?' the receptionist said in her sharp, halting English. 'This is true – this is where she goes. She ask for me to tell you.'

Theresa joined Jonathan in the glass extension, where he was tucking into sausages and eggs, looking hungover, his hair messy and boyish at the back. He smiled broadly at her when she came over to join him.

'Stella's gone already. She should have waited. What is she doing?' Theresa said, sitting down. 'What are we supposed to do now?'

She'd tried Stella's mobile, but it was switched off. She left her a terse message, telling her to call back. She wanted to help – this was why she'd come. Stella should have waited, they were here to help and support her. Theresa felt a little sheepish about the night before; she worried that they'd been too reckless, frivolous. She felt shy sitting in front of Jonathan the following morning, looking past his shoulder at the sea, drinking black coffee.

Jonathan suggested they go to the Sea Life centre on the front.

'It'll be fun,' he said, wiping egg from the side of his mouth. 'Let's go to the Sea Life centre.' And there was something about the fixed, jovial way he said this that made Theresa think she couldn't refuse him.

Besides, there was little else to do.

*

Jonathan and Theresa paid their entrance fee and were both given a stamp on their hands, 'So that you can come and go all day.' Theresa felt a little giddy walking down the dark passageway behind Jonathan and his flapping coat.

In the first room, where it was damp on the floor, a tinny version of 'Oh, I Do Like to be Beside the Seaside' was playing rather loudly for their hangovers. Jonathan peered into the first low tank.

'Bass and red mullet,' he said, sounding disappointed.

Theresa walked past him down towards the eel tank, where five eel-ends were poking out of artificial holes in the wall. She thought they were staring at her – they were disgusting, black fingers cut off at the palm. She shivered a little.

'Oh, the girls would love this.' Jonathan appeared next to her, and she could feel his breath on her neck.

'Only if they were interested in eels,' she said, standing very still.

'Children are interested in everything,' he said, smiling at her. 'Really, they are. You know, I think we're the only people in here.'

She looked down at her feet, though she liked the sense of him standing in so close and smiling at her.

'Come on,' he said, suddenly taking her hand and then dropping it again, 'it's the tropical room next.'

The tropical room had been done out as a submarine named HMS *Subtropical*, with more music, and the tanks made to look like portholes. Theresa stood staring at a couple of desultory-looking clownfish.

'Look, a piranha tank,' Jonathan said loudly, and she wondered at this enthusiasm. 'You can go underneath it and put your head inside the tank. Hang on.'

Theresa turned round and saw him half-crouching under the tank, putting his head up inside the glass bowl, the collar of his checked shirt weirdly magnified. She walked over and looked through the tank at him.

'How does it look?'

'Very odd,' she said, laughing. 'What are you doing?'

'Trying to impress you,' he said, looking at her through the water – or that's what she thought he said, but the moment he'd said it, she wasn't sure; he could have said anything, for the bowl seemed to distort his voice a little. A piranha swam in front of his face.

At the seahorse tank, Jonathan said, 'They always look so lonely, don't they? But they're monogamous, I know. Oh God, but look at this: seahorses are dying out. What do they expect us to do about it? I hate all this stuff, all this environmental lobbying – they just want to make us feel guilty.'

'Jonathan!' Theresa laughed. 'It's educational. It is not a conspiracy to make you feel bad. I promise you the world is not specifically geared to make Jonathan Cresswell feel, and appear, guilty.'

They walked past the ray tank, and through an undercover walkway below another deep large tank. Dramatic filmscore music was playing, the water the colour of an ageing bruise. A small shark swam into sight, and was then quickly followed by one or two larger sharks. They swam above their heads and into the tank on the other side.

'It's quite exciting, isn't it?' Theresa said, peering into the green, yellow-lit water. She could feel Jonathan looking at her, and he took a couple of paces closer, bent down and kissed her quickly on the cheek.

'Wanting to kiss it all better,' he said, with a shrug, taking her hand. 'Come on, let's go to the pier next.'

They walked, along the promenade. The wind was high and strong, whistling across the mudflats and through their hair. Theresa looked across the Thames estuary, searching for an oyster-catcher, a grey plover or a turnstone, a curlew.

'They feed off what's in the mud,' she told him. 'Do you think Stella is okay? I worry about her. I worry she's not always all there, you know.'

'I think she's pretty sound.'

Jonathan wanted to catch the train along the pier. He thought it'd be exciting; he thought they could always walk back, if they had to. When they got out of the train he was disorientated by the construction work: the pier was unfinished, and one side seemed to have collapsed into the sea.

'There was a fire,' Theresa told him. 'They're rebuilding it.'

Where the pier had burnt away, only vast seaweedy struts remained, with charred tops erupting out of the sea, looking like lost trees or a devastated arc. The glimpses of sea below the wide planks of the pier made Jonathan feel vertiginous and adrift. An icy wind blew across their faces as they walked to the end of the pier. Theresa looked down at the new, neat wooden planks, looking silvery and soft in the pale sunlight.

'Look.' She pointed to a sign. 'You can sponsor a plank.'

'I'll do that. They can name it after me. A plank from a plank.'

When they got to the far railing, they both leant against it.

'Look,' Jonathan joked, 'look, there's France', pointing out across the muddy waters to a hump of land across the sea.

'Is it called the Isle of Grey or the Isle of Grain?'

'The Isle of Gay Gain, I think,' he said, turning his face to the wind. 'What would you think if your husband had an affair? Would it finish it for you?'

'I really can't answer that,' Theresa said, holding tightly to the balustrade rail, watching her knuckles whiten.

'Or not an affair — not love. Just sex. Would you be able to ignore it, carry on? Or would it eat away at you? Destroy everything? What if you had the affair? I mean, how do the French manage it?' He gestured towards the grey heap of land in front of them.

'I find it almost impossible to imagine. To be honest, I can barely manage one person at a time,' Theresa told him, licking the salt spray off her lips. 'Did you have lots of affairs?'

'Only one. I thought it was love, but it wasn't. It felt separate. Private. I didn't think it through that much, to be honest. I just sort of did it, like a proper middle-aged jerk.' Jonathan was practising the story, preparing for the many times he might need to tell it. 'I forgot all about it — it wasn't important. I wish it hadn't happened.'

'Well, she probably wishes you hadn't done it in the first place.'

'Yes. I got myself in a mess, I didn't know what to do. I couldn't carry on.' Jonathan turned towards Theresa and pulled her overcoat more firmly around her, took her arm and clamped it across her body to hold the coat tight. He turned the collar and lapels up, so that they skimmed the bottom of her ears, and traced a finger across her cheek. 'But we all do things we regret, right? That's okay.

It's what happens afterwards that counts, what we do afterwards. You look beautiful, by the way.'

'I don't regret leaving Nic though. It wasn't a mistake,' Theresa said. 'I just need to accept that I want to do things for me too. When I get back I'm going to write and finish that PhD.'

They stood side by side on the pier, suspended and adrift, out at sea.

'I regret everything. I'm frightened of myself, of what I'm capable of not understanding. I didn't think I was that kind of person,' Jonathan said.

'Jonathan,' Theresa put a companionable hand on his arm. 'I think we might all be that kind of person.'

A distant shore

Stella's body, so accustomed to the rhythm of her baby's habits, had woken her very early in the morning. She pulled on yesterday's clothes and ran her fingers through her hair. Outside the hotel, the street and pavements were empty. Stella crossed the road to go down onto the shore. She found some steps, inching down between the beach huts, her eyes still lidded with sleep and barely remembered dreams.

The beach was heavy with rain and tide; it felt expansive under her feet. She stood and looked out at the swollen grey sea. At the age of seventeen Stella had gone to Frinton with Zeki. It had been exciting for her, but she hadn't wanted to let him know that, in case he thought her unworldly. For Stella, the trip had had a kind of glory to it: the two of them and the sea, eating fish and chips, the grease on their fingers and the silence they'd allowed to hold them. She'd known then that she wanted to marry him, that they would look after one another. She loved how quiet and tender he was with her, his readiness to slip inside her life, curl up there, in the quiet dim light, at the bottom of her mossy green well. Perhaps it wasn't so surprising, or such a betrayal, that he'd borrowed money and not told her about it, for a well has its limits.

Out on the horizon Stella could just see dark vessels, and a crane reaching high up into the sky.

It felt good to be out. She decided to climb the steps back up onto the promenade and walk for a bit. The wind was light, but the morning cold, the sky flat with grey clouds. She pulled her anorak around her more tightly. Was she one of those people that other people hid things from? For her own good. Stella walked on, past a pile of bottles beside a bench and a plastic bag blowing its way down the empty street. She'd grown, day by day, in the same place, had changed and remained unchanged, just like the town. It was unfashionable of her − of course it was, she knew that − to want to keep things small and knowable. The world was large and chaotic, loud and demanding. Everyone wanting more or better, dying to get away, to get on or, in some cases, just to survive. Then again, she thought, chances were that most people's lives were probably like hers, in their own way.

The sea was on her left, and she passed quiet houses and sleeping hotels on her right. As she approached Southend proper, a couple of cafés appeared, their doors still closed, ice-cream signs flapping in the wind. She supposed everyone thought her a bit simple; she'd noticed the way Jonathan and Theresa spoke to her. Stella could see how she was now, but she didn't think she was this way because she didn't know enough. She'd been alone in her sleep last night, alone in her dreams in that cool, quiet room. A car idled past her, and Stella gave the driver a brief smile.

As she came towards the centre the promenade widened to give way to green areas, tiny parks and benches with mean, narrow flower beds. Ahead of her she could see a small fairground, the rides all covered in blue tarpaulin, surrounded by railings and the gate heavily padlocked; and beyond that the windows of a large shopping mall glittered in the morning light. She could see the pier now, scooting out into the sea. Stella headed for a bench beside a sign explaining the local wildlife on offer. She tipped her head back and stared up at the featureless, traceless sky.

She shivered. It was cold, and she'd left her mobile phone back at the hotel. She should be getting back. Standing up, she walked up to the beach wall and, looking down across the wet beach, saw a figure in a brown coat. A figure standing very like her, hands in pockets, feet apart, turned towards the morning light. The shape of the woman made Stella wonder briefly if it was her mother, but on closer inspection she saw it wasn't. This woman had short hair of a deep red-purple colour. The woman swung around in that instant and caught sight of Stella in her pink anorak, high up against the sky, a lone figure behind the coastal wall. The woman stilled, and then tentatively raised an arm, her palm facing outwards.

'Stella.' The woman's voice carried over the space towards her.

She didn't answer the woman's call; she thought it best to keep quiet. The moment was too unpredictable. During the last few weeks, when she had imagined seeing her mother again, she had never imagined it like this – how could she? The woman now making her solid, slow way across the beach towards the steps didn't even look like her mother. Stella watched her for another moment.

Then she too started walking slowly to the right, towards the break in the wall at the top of the steps. She was drawn by memory, the force of old bonds, of bodies that in the universal darkness had mindlessly and helplessly imprinted themselves upon the other. As they moved slowly, in unison – one looking up and the other down

– neither shifted her gaze from the other's face until they met, at either end of the staircase.

'Well, hello,' Sheila Buttle said, putting one hand on the bannister and pulling herself up the step.

And then they were their individual selves again.

*

Stella piled two teaspoons of sugar into her coffee. She made no effort to drink it. She searched the small café, her eyes trailing over the plastic green bucket seats and the shining white Formica tables. There was one couple sitting near the window, their hunched shoulders bathed in an odd light from the neon green posters that were stuck up at the window, advertising the café's competitive rates on bacon-and-egg rolls, and a very old man at the back, sipping a cup of tea and reading a newspaper. She hadn't asked her mother anything yet.

First, she must get used to the hair. Stella struggled with the adjustment. Sheila's hair was now short, quite brutally short, and dyed. Dyed another colour. No longer grey, no longer permed, but a dark, flat red colour. Also earrings. Stella didn't think her mother had ever worn earrings, but there were large, plastic orange discs bouncing against her mother's neck. She found herself staring at her mother's neck, exposed as it was. Had she ever seen her neck before? Stella frowned a little; she did not like this haircut, this hair colour.

The only words they had exchanged were when Sheila Buttle had finally got to the top of the steps.

'Let's get coffee,' she'd said gently, but without self-effacement.

Stella blinked. Her mother, so much now in Stella's gaze, shifted a little on her seat, ran her hand through her hair, played briefly with her earring; this too was a new gesture.

'You're wearing new earrings,' Stella said. 'They're orange.'

'Yes.'

'And you've got new hair,' Stella went on.

'Yes.' Stella thought she could detect the faintest hint of defiance in her mother's voice. 'Nice, isn't it?'

She nodded, but she did not think it was nice. She thought it made her mother look a bit mad, the red-purple colour too heavy; her mother looked like an unusual person in fact, it occurred to Stella now – it made her look a bit unbalanced, as if she didn't know what kind of a person she was, how old she was, to have this aggressive, damson-plum helmet on her head. Stella could not get over the hair.

She glanced around the café. They were both waiting for the other to speak. She saw the waitress behind the counter, writing something down. The waitress had the same hair as her mother! Everyone had the red-purple hair!

'You have the same colour hair as the waitress,' she whispered slowly. 'And the hotel receptionist. Everyone has it here. The Polish receptionist at the hotel is the same.'

'Stop going on about my hair, Stella,' her mother said, looking over at the old man behind her. 'It's rude.'

They sat in silence. Stella drank in this new-look mother, and she began to find it enlivening, amusing. She felt like laughing.

'So. You found me then. You got my message,' Sheila Buttle said eventually, folding her hands in front of her on the table. 'I'm sorry I worried you, Stella. I didn't mean to do that.'

Stella nodded.

'I called your mobile loads of times.'

'I got a new mobile. New number.'

'Well, at least you're using a mobile at last.' Stella smiled tentatively, slipping her hands around the cup of coffee to warm them.

'When I woke up this morning, I was thinking about you. I knew you'd be up early too; we're the same that way, always have been. It made me happy to think of you – and then I was down on the beach, and there you were.'

Sheila opened another sachet of sugar and poured it into her coffee, shaking her head a little.

'It was a lovely thing, Stella. I knew you'd find me.'

'I had to go to the morgue in Harlow yesterday.'

'Oh, love – I know.'

'I had to look at this dead woman.'

'Stella—'

'They thought it was you. How did you know?'

'Someone told me. You must have imagined the worst. I'm so sorry. I didn't think anyone would, not for a minute. Not in that way.'

Sheila looked down, dismayed, more like her old self. Stella swayed on her chair, looking behind the new haircut for the woman she knew. She had always known her mother as a stable person, though she had never formed this notion into anything other than a happy, everyday assumption. Stella knew Sheila was holding something back, something deep and impossible. She imagined that for her mother to do whatever she had done, whatever had happened, meant that Sheila had decided to upend her life and her person. She'd purposefully forced away contentment and the known, had risked everybody's happiness and become unstable. There was a lot to take in.

Stella thought Sheila must know her side of things – she herself was not mysterious. Stella thought herself as plain as light, as clear as shallow water, not just in her appearance, but in her everything, her entire life, lived openly in front of her mother.

'Shall we go somewhere?' Sheila said. 'I could do with some fresh air.'

Give them what they want

Sheila had never been beautiful, but there had always been a vivid-ness to her, and this light came from the very act of creation by which she had learnt to will herself into being.

Her father was a merchant seaman turned door-to-door salesman: well organised, impeccably dressed, with a charming, holy smile. The kind of smile that opened the unlikeliest of doors, persuaded purses to be liberated, casseroles and pot roasts to be shared. He could manufacture the perfect laugh, knew when to be irreverent and when humility or gentle modesty was asked for. He could judge a moment – any moment – to perfection.

'Just give them what they want, girls. Give them what they need.'

Sheila and Joyce sitting on the floor of a strange room, a boarding house or a borrowed flat, beside a one-bar electric heater in their nightdresses, their arms wrapped around their legs, staring up at him, dazzled. He would look down and wink, loosen his tie and puff contentedly on a cigarette. They adored him. He was hand-some, at home in his skin; they adored his dark silk work suit and pressed white shirt, his air of grandeur and certainty, all mixed up with an easy garrulousness and a deep, knowing laugh. He would open his travelling case in front of them, as though he were about to show them the world and was allowing them to share in a particular, very special kind of gift.

'My box of tricks.'

He was a traveller both by nature and profession, and they accepted this condition wholeheartedly. It became second nature to them too. Sheila and Joyce knew how to make friends at any school they attended, for however long; how to chat to the man in the corner shop whose bill had not yet been paid; how to be keen and modest with the landladies.

Everyone thought it strange that he took the girls on the road with him, but he said he couldn't be without them. When they'd been somewhere too long, when their friends' mothers had started to talk or a teacher had begun to prickle at not being able to pin down their history, he would be called in by a head teacher – usually someone younger, more in step with the educational ethos of the 1960s – to enquire about the exact socio-environmental nature of their home life. Then he'd smooth down his hair and drop one leg over the other.

'Oh,' he'd tell her. 'Those girls are my alpha and omega, my day and night, my beginning and end. No question.' And then he'd lean forward and fix her with his very particular look and enquire, 'Is there a problem? Are they misbehaving? Doing badly at school? Causing you any problems?'

And of course Joyce and Sheila never were. They sat in the middle desks, in matching jumpers and skirts, hair tied back by elastic bands, politely armed with open, curious expressions.

'Well, no,' the head teacher would say.

'Then there's no problem,' their father would declare, leaning back in his seat. 'Is there?'

They were bound up in the world of each other, of one another.

The grammar and rules of their lives were made by them – lines drawn to show respectability, to demonstrate normality. They'd give everyone what they wanted, what they needed, in order to protect the flowing, rich, eventful game of themselves. They were used to packing up their things at short notice, driving out of a city early in the morning, leaving behind another set of grey streets smeared with coal dust, temporarily adopted schools and auxiliary friendships. A case of wine rattled in the back of the van, or a pile of books: something taken in part-exchange, something of theirs left behind too. The van was the nearest thing to a permanent home that they knew.

It was Joyce who broke first. When she turned eleven, and Sheila was ten, she got the sense, the idea, that other people's lives were not like her own. She began to want to belong to something bigger than her father and her sister and their van. Once this idea came into her head, she could never chase it out. Discontent grew. She coveted, envied and admired the lives of other children – the girls with a mother and a father, a house on a street and a sense of permanence. She didn't find it fun any more, began to query their decisions. Her rebellions did not, yet, break outside the confines of themselves. She'd turn over in her bed at night and needle Sheila in the bed beside her. 'I'd like a proper kitchen, wouldn't you? With cakes in the oven. I'd like to stay at Greenside Elementary. I want to go up a class. I hate this bed, this room. Janet Moor has a swing in her garden, and she has milk every day after school; her mother says she has to, she says it's good for her bones.'

Sheila lay in the bed beside her, feeling the wind rattling at the windows, and considered their bones.

'We get milk at school,' she said, her heart beating, thumping, in her chest.

And then, with a growing, gnawing sense of injustice, Joyce started talking about their mother. What Sheila and Joyce both knew – had known for as long as they could remember – was that she was alive. She was not dead. She existed. Their father had been very clear on this matter. He would tuck them in at night, folding the sheet across their chests, gently kissing their foreheads. 'Your mother kisses you too,' he'd say, and he'd land another kiss smack on their cheeks, making them laugh. 'She's out there somewhere, thinking about you.'

'I think,' Joyce said, when she was nearly twelve, squiggling about on the sticky plastic van seats, kicking her legs in front of her, 'I think I want to see my mother.'

Their father slowed the van, and slowly wound his window further down. He took the wheel with one hand, allowing his other arm to drape outside, palm open. It was a hot summer day, the fields were full of crops and insects, the air humming and dreamy, and inside the van it was sweet with smoke, sweat and Kia-Ora orange. Sheila sat between the two of them, her eyes fixed on the road ahead.

'Okay,' their father said, nodding. 'Okay, Joyce. If that's what you want.'

'Give them what they want, girls. Give them what they need,' Sheila said quietly.

*

When they met, Sheila knew that her mother was the more nervous. This made sense to her; she, Joyce and their father had themselves. As adults, Joyce and Sheila remembered the meeting quite differently, and would shake their heads at the other, impatient and astonished by the other's faulty recollection.

'She was twenty-nine, didn't look a day over twenty. She was wearing a kaftan, bright purple, bare feet. I thought she was beautiful.'

'She was not. She had on black trousers and a black shirt. Bohemian, chic. She looked her age.'

The one thing they both remembered, and agreed upon, was what she'd said first.

'It was all because,' their mother said, skittish and awash with apology and emotion, hardly able to speak, rocking backwards and forwards on her feet, 'I wanted some space, to discover myself.'

They were sitting on beanbags in a communal high-ceilinged flat in Brighton, the stuffy air suffused with the smell of cheese and damp clothes. Sheila was biting her lip because of the gusts of laughter rising up inside her at the sight of their father, squatting beside her on a beanbag, his trousers rising high up his legs, looking unbalanced and unlike himself, old-fashioned and out of place and as though he might topple over any minute. The smell of incense clung to them.

Sheila had felt no particular connection with her mother, only a little pity – as much as a ten-year-old can muster. Their mother was stumbling over her words, and had a glazed, bewildered look about her, and yet Sheila knew that she wanted to please them, and that struck her as sad. It was warm outside, the sky blank. Sheila's mind turned towards the ice-cream van they'd passed on their way in. Her father looked over at her and winked.

Joyce decided to stay with her mother in Brighton. She said she wanted to stop travelling in that van. Nobody disagreed. Their father was hurt and a little scared, but he hid it well. The mother was thrilled, relieved, she felt forgiven; she wrapped her arms around Joyce and hugged her, breathed down her neck, enveloped Joyce in her perfume, told her that was all she wanted too. She said, '*I feel ready to give myself to you now. I hope you can forgive me. I want your forgiveness.*'

Later, after Sheila had met Roy and agreed to marry and live in Essex with him, Joyce told her that she thought their mother was mad.

'She was barking really, wasn't she? It took me a while to work it out.'

'She was as good to you as she could be.' Sheila was feeding Stella in her highchair, spooning bits of steamed diced carrot into her tiny, willing mouth.

'Yes,' Joyce sighed, thinking of those times. 'I suppose she tried.'

'Can't ask for more than that.'

*

Joyce had imagined that she would find herself, locate herself, in that flat in Brighton with a mother. Life would be steady and constant, humming and rolling to the sounds of a maternal rhythm; her life would be like Janet Moor's because, if she had a mother, it followed that someone would care about her milk intake. Though their father had provided Joyce with a firm idea of what it might mean to be looked after, to be cared for and loved, she now required that from a fixed and permanent female. Joyce, given her upbringing, was able to slip easily into life at the communal flat. She observed the other occupants with a distant interest. Budge, the art student, and Rita, the feminist; and Rita's friend, who didn't have a label, but wide dark, staring eyes and a deep commitment to the power of meditation – these were her mother's chosen companions. It became clear to Joyce when she let herself in from school, eyes bright and the sea air lacing her hair, to be met only by a darkened room, Budge hungover or Rita asleep on her futon, or her own mother lost in her thoughts, that these adults had not yet managed to find the necessary space to 'discover' themselves at all. She would lie in bed at night and listen to them talk, their phrases swirling above her head, mixed up in the blue smoke of their roll-up cigarettes, their noise and silences burning into the night, the questions they asked, the answers they gave. 'Everything is beautiful,' they would conclude. The next morning her mother would hastily ask if Joyce was okay – throat croaky from the late-night talking, nodding like a hungry bird out of fear that Joyce might say that no, everything was not okay – before leaving for the clothes shop where she worked three days a week.

Joyce knew that everything was not beautiful.

She saw that her mother's erratic, pulsing starbursts of love, her wanting to squeeze Joyce's face between her hands and stare, with bewildering intensity, into her eyes, or her shivering anxiety over Joyce's diet and homework, were a far cry from what she'd hoped and longed for.

Joyce had imagined it would be a simple act, the taking up of motherhood. The truth – hazily and patchily arrived at amongst the meditation stools, the dirty pans and the ashes of incense sticks, and her mother's vague affections – dissuaded her thirteen-year-old self from ever thinking to attempt it for herself. She stuck it out for four months, then called her father and Sheila and told them to come and collect her.

'*I wanted some space*,' her mother had said, '*to discover myself*.'

After Joyce returned, the three of them decided to try and settle somewhere. This was for Joyce's benefit – it was a compromise. Sheila, left to her own devices, would have preferred to continue with the limitlessness of possibility that came with the van and the travelling life. The movable feast. She kept this sense of being itinerant, always moving, close to herself, as a memory; always running, motoring inside her head. It never left her. It fed her until she became both restless and sated at once.

Sheila's lack of interest, or connection to her own mother, continued until she became a mother herself. When Marie was born, a fog or a dream lifted inside her head. The sheer act of refusing to know couldn't hold up or hold back when faced with the life force – the fact – of Baby Marie. It began to seep out of the sides of her head, insinuating itself towards her awareness every time Marie's tiny fist clenched and unclenched, every time she felt Marie's warm, heavy, limp sack-of-flour weight against her neck. How could her mother have abandoned them? This was not anger, but a light questioning from deep inside her.

How had she given them up? What had happened to her? How was it possible for her own desires to outstrip the needs of the helpless, frustrated bundle she held in her arms?

These questions, and the silence that followed their asking, gathered in Sheila's head, and after Stella was born – her motherhood condition squared, her love doubled and her life much less her own – she went to find out. She had become her mother, that mother, a mother to two small girls; her love for them was bruising and pulsing and alive. The idea of her own mother bloomed and receded, a tidal experience, against her own life. She had made the effort to become a settled woman, and she would not be destabilised by this, but the yearning to know was impossible to reconcile sensibly; she could not process the amorphous shadow into something as deliberate or clinical as a 'plan' to be discussed, or holiday time to be set aside. Perhaps she didn't expect anyone to understand, or perhaps she didn't want to ask anyone's permission. She put her head down, loved her babies and her husband, put a little money aside each month for over a year; this was not something she could discuss. The hidden rebellious stash of coins grew heavier and larger, until one day she knew she had enough. She'd had enough. She emptied the money into her everyday purse, called Joyce and left the house without her coat.

Sheila knew, from a postcard received the Christmas before, that her mother was living in 'a community' in the Lake District, near Lake Derwent. This much she knew. The year was 1990. She was thirty-six years old. The landlord of the bed-and-breakfast – she'd relished telling the taxi driver to choose somewhere for her to stay – thought he knew the place. They were 'weird', by his thinking, but most local folk thought them decent enough because they 'kept themselves to themselves'.

She certainly does that, Sheila thought, climbing out of the taxi.

The commune lived in a grey stone farmhouse, which sat low and abandoned-looking in a wild spot half an hour's car drive from Keswick. The yard was thick with frozen mud, the windows small, dark and mysterious. Sheila first saw the stiff mud and derelict outbuildings, and then with one hand on the broken gate she pushed it open and stepped into the yard. A painfully bright plastic ride-on bike was parked against the side wall; she had not been expecting children, and she knew she was not expected, either. Her apprehension grew. She reminded herself of Roy, Marie and Stella. Of the life she had built, the order and comfort she had created for them all, a coppery easy light. This trip would change none of that, she told herself – that was safe.

Sheila knocked on the door, but there was no answer. All around her the high sky, the chilly yard and the dramatic hillscape beyond felt and appeared empty. She tried the door, found it was unlocked and gently pushed it open.

The atmosphere inside the house was alarmingly different from the outside. Who knows, after all, what they are expecting until they discover the other?

'I'm baking,' a woman said to her, seemingly unfazed by her appearance in the kitchen doorway. 'Come on in.'

The door opened straight into a low-ceilinged kitchen. It was dark, but not gloomy. A long wooden table ran down the length of the kitchen, a bench beside it. Large fabric drapes hung down from the ceiling, giving the room an enclosed, tent-like feel. Sheila walked under the billowing ceiling and came towards the table. She was at a loss as to what to say. She stared at the woman – was this even her mother?

'Are you Rose?'

'No. I'm Ursula. Rose is out.'

The woman seemed so unbothered by both her appearance and her question that Sheila could think of no way to further the conversation.

The kitchen was dark and warm. Ursula stood at the table with two mixing bowls and a selection of battered tins in front of her, kneading dough on the table. There was a sleepy, yeasty smell in the air, and an anglepoise lamp stood on a nearby stool pooling light amidst the cluttered kitchen. Someone had stuck a child's (the owner of the bicycle's?) bright artwork onto the green-coloured walls; a tray of jam jars sat on the stone floor beneath the window, and piles of thick felted fabric were draped over the chair nearest to her. The chaos was comforting. Sheila watched Ursula pounding the dough on the table. Ursula, she thought, had surprisingly strong arms for such a tiny woman.

'I was looking for Rose,' Sheila said eventually.

'Sit down. We'll have some tea.'

Sheila had good intentions and a purpose, but they were slowly leaving her. She pulled back the chair and perched on the edge of it. Her fingers were freezing. The room smelt of yeast, people and a not-so-long-ago soup.

'I've come up from Essex to see Rose.'

'Are you her daughter?' Ursula asked, without looking up.

'Yes. One of them.'

Ursula nodded, and started to press the dough down into the tins. She was making two loaves of bread. After she had done this, watched wordlessly by Sheila, she put the tins in the oven and filled a vast tin kettle, took down a brown teapot and spooned in loose tea leaves. Sheila watched it all. Ursula wore a flannel shirt and jeans, her grey curling hair tied back in a boisterous ponytail. Sheila sat back a little in the chair, allowing herself to lean against the soft piles of felt that were draped over it. The kitchen was filled with unusual, but not unpleasant smells. There was a rhythm to Ursula's silent movements. Sheila began to take comfort from her ease and peace – nothing needed to be said. Nothing was said. Turning to look out of the window, Sheila could see only the grey sky and bare hills.

'I'm not much good at small talk,' Ursula said eventually, putting two rough cups, without handles, on the table with the teapot. 'Sorry.'

Sheila was surprised to realise that Ursula was nervous. Whilst she had found the silence relaxing, she was surprised to see that perhaps Ursula had been unsettled after all.

'Oh, me neither,' she said quickly, wanting to put Ursula at ease. 'You've been very welcoming.'

'The others are out. They'll be back soon.'

'Rose didn't know I was coming. It was a spur-of-the-moment decision.'

'She does talk about you,' Ursula said, sitting down. 'She'll be pleased – in her way – that you've come to see her. Don't expect too much of her. Have you brought your children?'

'No,' Sheila said. 'I came alone.'

She wanted to ask what Rose's way of being pleased might be, but didn't have the courage. Ursula pulled a pouch of tobacco out of her shirt pocket and bent down to retrieve a dark, battered tin from under her chair. She took out some papers, and a small amount of hash rolled up inside a handkerchief.

Sheila sipped on her tea, and watched Ursula roll and then light the joint. The afternoon sky was darkening with every passing moment.

'There was a bit of a blow-up here, this morning,' Ursula said. 'Words were said. Someone left. It's painful, you know? When that happens?'

'Yes.'

'Rose and Mike have taken him to the train station.' Then, 'I used to work in a solicitor's office in Cardiff. It seems a long time ago now.'

Ursula passed the joint across to Sheila, who surprised herself by taking it.

'What brought you here?'

'Oh, well – life, I suppose. Divorce.'

The smell of rising bread filled the dark kitchen as they smoked. Sheila began to feel the heat and pace of the commune. She sank further back in her chair and grinned at Ursula.

'How many of you live here?'

'They come and go. Only about seven of us are regular. The place fills up in the summer, though.'

'There's a kid who lives here?'

'Yeah, two kids. A family — they're away now. Visiting other family.'

Sheila nodded. She took another drag, feeling the delicious burning heat in her chest.

*

Sheila was asleep when her mother returned, her head lolling against the felt, mouth open and her shoes slipped off; adrift in the empty kitchen in a dark, dreamless space.

Rose *was* pleased to see Sheila, in her way. Her way transpired to be dreamy and aloof, and from afar. Her eyes lit up, on coming across Sheila in the kitchen, and she appeared to relish her presence, but only signalled this by nodding across the room.

Sheila saw a closeness between her and Ursula — she wondered if they were lovers, but did not ask, for the idea made her shy. The only other commune member there that evening was a quiet man called Mike; he was young and ill at ease, surprisingly conservative-looking and a little awed by Sheila's presence. Rose liked to stand close to Sheila or to sit near her during the first evening, but she would not talk to her. Not much. Not in the way Sheila wanted her to.

The next morning Sheila followed Rose out into the yard. She'd awoken, stiff and irritable. She took a blanket from the bed for warmth and stood wrapped, like a baby, staring across the yard at her mother.

Rose was focused on her task. She went into one of the sheds and brought out a large seedling tray covered in a cloth, which she set on the ground. Squatting down beside it, she removed the cloth to reveal hundreds of tiny pieces of stone, clay pottery and glass. She fished through the broken pieces, picking some up to inspect them carefully, rub them clean and then set them down again somewhere else on the tray. She did not look over at Sheila.

'So you know I'm married now, with two girls of my own,' Sheila heard herself say, walking towards her mother. 'This got me thinking about you.'

She looked down at Rose's bowed head, her black and streaked grey hair, and her quick fingers shooting across and through the broken shards and fragments – this massive disorder, which seemed to fascinate her so much. Sheila continued, her stomach beginning to knot inside her.

'I wondered why you'd left us. I mean, *how* you did that.'

Still nothing. To be ignored, again, was impossible and ludicrous. Sheila had not asked anything of her mother, not once, until this moment, when she was asking her this question. She felt herself starting to shake, enraged, on the frozen mud, her breath quick and short, and she pulled the blanket more firmly around her. She felt the madness then. The pieces were jumbled up, jammed in together; there were layers of shard upon shard, some greenish and brown glass, old decorated pots, small red, grey and black stones – there was no reason to them, no order, not even any accounting for their existence or her mother's interest in them. Sheila had not chosen disarray and pieces and chaos, but order and a good home, a careful, managed life. She lunged forward and pushed her mother hard and violently on the shoulders. Rose fell back silently, loosely, too easily, against the hard ground, as though she'd been waiting to collapse. Sheila's hands barely registered, with surprise, how light and bony her mother's shoulders felt, as they bent to scoop up the seedling tray.

Sheila held it in front of her, shook it about, and then above her head for a moment. An animal cry escaped from her and she hurled it with all her strength towards the far wall of the yard. They watched as the tray flew briefly and magically alone and straight, like a magic carpet mysteriously summoned, until it tipped and then the pieces fell behind, in a vast wide arc, discharging its contents, which fell like rain upon the mud. Then the tray hit the far wall with a pleasing crash and fell, splintered, to the ground.

Sheila looked down at her mother, breathless, her arms warm with the effort. 'Oh God!' she said, the blanket slipping from her shoulders. 'I didn't know I was going to do that.'

Rose sat up and surveyed the yard, the scattered pieces of her collection. She shook her head, gently. She looked up at Sheila and smiled, a broad, gappy smile. They both looked across the littered yard for a moment.

'I couldn't,' Rose said slowly to Sheila, as though her life depended upon it. 'I *could* not do it. I'm sorry.'

Sheila squatted down beside her, gently took her arm, to help her to her feet.

'I know,' she whispered. 'I understand. Let's pick all those pieces up again, shall we?'

*

After that morning Sheila and Rose fell into a pattern: they would often work wordlessly with Ursula in the kitchen, or assist Mike with the chickens in the morning. Then Sheila liked to walk out alone into the elements across ground frozen so hard that it hurt her feet. She turned her face up towards the wind, feeling the strength of it in her bones. She liked the returning too, her fingers red-raw from the icy winds, to warm them beside the range.

In the evenings Rose liked to sit next to Sheila at the table. She was a gentle, quiet presence now, no longer nervous around her. They didn't talk much. Sheila kept smoking the dope because she wanted to retain that heavy calm about her, like a cloud.

She was enjoying being this escaped version of herself; she liked waking up on her own, having no responsibilities; she liked the empty afternoons and quiet evenings, the sense of being not quite herself whilst being entirely herself. She had found something of herself with Rose, the lost, unknown part that was inert. There were no answers, no justifications. There was Rose, sucking a cube of sugar, combing her hair, trying her best to get by, to navigate her world, picking through the shards on her seedling tray.

One month later all Sheila wanted was to go home, back to Roy and Stella and Marie, and to resume – pick up – her other life.

So, this is Sheila Buttle

When people do something unexpected or out of character, it can prove, in the end, to be the most personal and truthful act of all.

*

'We were very like you and Marie,' Sheila told Stella, bending down to pick up a pebble from the beach. 'Without the envy. You're like me, and Marie is like Joyce. I can see us in the two of you. So can Joyce. It's uncanny.'

'Did you see much more of your mum?'

Stella wanted to keep this story in her head a little longer.

'Oh, Stella.' Sheila turned to her, her eyes soft and warm. She rubbed the stone between her fingers for a moment, then held it against her cheek, before pressing it into Stella's hand. 'No. Poor woman, she was erratic. Confused. I didn't want her to punish herself.' Sheila looked down at her feet on the shingle. 'I felt sad for her. I'm now the age she was when she died. Perhaps that had something to do with my going off like this.'

Stella and Sheila walked along the promenade in silence, the pebble in Stella's pocket. A chill wind was up, and the sea was breaking into angry waves below the sea wall. It was strange for both of them.

'I suppose, deep down,' Sheila said eventually, linking her arm through Stella's, 'I was always worried that I might be like my mother. Perhaps it's fanciful to say it, but I was used to the open road and, because of that, out of love and fear I made myself stick.'

'Joyce told the police about when you went to the Lake District. I didn't know about it.'

Sheila laughed, stopping on the pavement. 'She never did?'

'She did.'

Sheila considers this for a moment, shaking her head. 'I thought some part of Joyce would understand.'

'I think some part of her did,' Stella told her. 'She didn't seem so bothered, not after a while. I was the one who was bothered. And Marie.'

Stella considered all her mother had told her. She fought within herself to allow the space. Sheila mistook her silence.

'I don't regret a day of it. Of our lives together. Not one minute, that's not what I'm saying – I never have and I never will. Being a mother to you and Marie is the best thing I've ever done. I did . . . this . . . like this, in this way, only because, after Roy died and you and Marie were settled enough, I didn't know how else to stop doing what I was being.'

Stella saw into her mother. She glimpsed the rich, capable, adventurous girl in the van, and the devoted, constant mother she had become without regret, and then the freed, eccentric woman on the moors and the seedling tray. She felt Sheila's widow's house and fabric-conditioned sheets, the routines and familiarities of the town; that one mug, one plate, the dishcloth over the tap, the still air – all this as wordless fragments of imageless light moving within her mother.

'I know,' Stella said.

The memories of Stella's daydreams bulged against her head. She kept walking with her mother, beside the sea wall. Stella glanced over at the circles of orange bouncing against her mother's neck.

'Someone has put up photographs of you, all over town, tied up with orange ribbons.'

'Ah, the thing is,' Sheila looked past Stella's shoulder, embarrassed. 'It's silly to say it – I dare say I'm too old – but I've met someone.'

'Mum!' Stella waved her hair back in the wind, smiling in spite of herself. 'Why didn't you say?'

'Oh, Stella, I could hardly say the half of it. I barely knew myself.' She smiled at Stella. 'His name's Jim. He put up the photographs, and the ribbons. He gave me these earrings too.'

'Why?'

'He was . . . playing.'

The wind rose suddenly, Stella felt it pour through her and rip across the beach, pulling against the sea's onward current. She wanted to stop walking, and so sat down on the cold sea wall, shocked. She felt a creeping wetness through her jeans, but needed something solid beneath her.

'Playing?' she repeated, staring at her strange new mother. '*Playing?*'

Sheila laughed. She looked as she did in the Missing Person photograph, suddenly carefree, young and filled with possibility.

'I know, it was silly. He understood though. He knew that if I needed to go, then I must. Just for a while. So I could break everything up, but that it wouldn't matter, that everything will settle back but differently. He was playing with the ribbons, trying to make light of it. He said the orange cheered up the town no end.'

'He lives in Walden? Not here?'

'Yes. I came here alone.'

'So, you're coming back then?'

'Yes, of course, for the time being. Jim and I talked about moving abroad, but I don't really know if we're serious. The relationship isn't all that serious.'

'You're both *playing*,' Stella said, unable to hide her bitterness.

'Would you mind if I moved somewhere else? I know how much you've wanted me close by but we'd still see each other. I need a change.'

Stella shrugged, and pulled her anorak around her, turned to look at a long-legged bird on the mudflat, the feathers wet and sleek, sticking its beak into the ground.

Stella pressed her hands down on the wall. Perhaps she wasn't ready to hear all of this. Not yet.

'There's something else too. I asked him to get Zeki to price his house for him, I had a feeling Zeki was in some trouble.' Sheila put her hand through her new hair to push it out of her face. 'Jim did some private investigating for me. He says Zeki's trying to rip him off something rotten – he thinks Zeki is in on some racket. Poor kid.'

'You lent him money.'

'Jim was talking to Zeki when you arrived with the kids yesterday. That's how I knew you'd gone to the morgue. That's when I knew this had gone far enough. Zeki's a good man, Stella, but he's struggling. Talk to him. Help him out. You've got to learn to take responsibility, be an adult, because otherwise he's going to end up in all kinds of trouble – and he'll do it all for you.'

'Take some responsibility! Listen to yourself.' Stella turned on her mother. 'That's bloody rich, coming from you.'

There was silence. Sheila waited.

'What you just did,' Stella told her, digging her hands deep within her anorak, turning her head up towards the wind, 'was cruel and thoughtless and selfish.'

Sheila stepped forward and, bending down a little, took Stella, wrapped Stella, folded Stella, held Stella in her arms for a very long time.

*

Stella was no longer young, but it would take many years for her to truly understand her mother's actions. At that time she did not see how her mother's nature had influenced her own. Could not follow the traces and folds of it within her own being. She did not know that when Stella was born, six years after Marie — an unexpected gift — her mother had fallen into a kind of reverie for her. She stroked Stella's skin, cried over her, crooned and rocked her, day and night; had become sensually, impossibly alive to her. Sheila had made a point of conquering dedication and constancy, but with Stella she discovered too a new, pure, deep kind of love. A love that drove her to run to the Lake District for space and peace, forming those gaps and absences inside both of them, and a love that kept her in place for many, many years.

It was a love that Stella had refused to let go of, one she'd clung to, perhaps because all the while she'd sensed in a wordless, intuitive dream her mother's twin desire for freedom. Stella had gripped those invisible strings, until Sheila was compelled to take the most dramatic and severe of actions; until the urge, the desire for herself erupted within her, from a long-ago closed-down space, somewhere exhilarating, irresponsible and unlikely. The place that allowed her to be loved for herself, to dye her hair plum-red and consider the giddy prospect of taking off, one morning, to temporarily, carelessly leave everything behind. One day, Stella would see that Sheila had acted, without thinking, on the inherent powerful truthfulness that comes from not doing the right thing, for once, by someone else.

Later, they would be able to talk more freely to one another about this time. That morning, though, they walked hand-in-hand in silence against the chill wind, back towards the hotel in Thorpe Bay.

'It's surprising, in a way,' Sheila said, as they approached the hotel. 'How you can be two people at once, want two things at once. The way life divides itself.'

When they came into the hotel bar, Theresa and Jonathan were in the far corner looking peaceful, wind-blown and exhausted.

'So,' Jonathan said, with a smile. 'This is the famous Sheila Buttle.'

Home

A small, quiet town sits in a slight valley, encircled by barely-hills and surrounded by the ancient fields of Essex, by acreage of barley, wheat and yellow rapeseed, grasses and vegetables. Above is a large blank sky, white as paper. The air is soft, earthy and easy, when not chilled by the easterly winds and low-slung mists or cut by the marshy tangs of salt carried in on a breeze from far away. It appears as serene, snug and self-contained today as it has always been during a long, yet unruffled, history. Nothing has been broken down; everything is preserved. Restored. Looked after.

Except.

They came in past the airfields of Duxford and approached the town from one of the slight hills around it. Windmill Hill swooped down towards Saffron Walden, lined on one side by a high red wall and on the other by silent fields. The three of them were quiet in the car, miles away, knowing that their speech had limits. They were as quiet as the town, as quiet and as wilfully ordinary. Nearing the bottom of the hill, the car slowed as the road narrowed beside a vulnerable, yellow, low-slung Tudor cottage. The facts were the same but everything had changed. The currents around them, fading and flowing, were real now. They were not for dreams of rescue or escape, not for conservation of how life had been or should be. Each had been frightened, wordlessly so, like the permanent clenching of a fist, a heartbeat, hanging on. They breathed deeply, felt themselves spread into light and space. The town was the same but everything had changed.

RACHEL HEATH

The Finest Type of English Womanhood

'Heath combines imaginative, fast-paced storytelling with an unerring sense of
period, place and mood ... an exceptionally well-written, suspenseful novel'
GUARDIAN

It is 1946, and seventeen-year-old Laura Trelling is stagnating in
her dilapidated Sussex family home, while her eccentric parents
slip further into isolation. A chance encounter with Paul Lovell
offers her the opportunity to alter the course of her destiny –
and to embark on a new life in South Africa.

Many miles north, sixteen-year-old Gay Gibson is desperate to
escape Birkenhead. When the girls' paths cross in Johannesburg,
Laura is exposed to Gay's wild life of parties and inappropriate
liaisons. Each in her own world, but thrown together, the girls find
their lives inextricably entangled, with fatal consequences ...

'Excellent on the atmosphere of post-war Britain and the lure of South Africa ...
compellingly told, reminiscent of early Doris Lessing ... the twists keep the
reader glued to the novel'
INDEPENDENT

'The writing is strong and when the girls' paths become entwined it is
thrillingly macabre'
DAILY TELEGRAPH